DEMONS M...

LOST TALES FROM ESOWON COLLECTION

ANTOINE BANDELE
MATTHEW CHATMAN
CALLAN BROWN

BANDELE
— BOOKS —

Interior Design: Vellum
Publisher: Bandele Books
Editors: Fiona McLaren, Callan Brown, Josiah Davis
Cover Artist: Sutthiwat Dekachamphu
Cartographer: Maria Gandolfo | RenflowerGrapx
Character Art: Vivian A. Friedel

Paperback, First Edition | May 6, 2020

ISBN: 978-0-9998483-6-4

CONTENTS

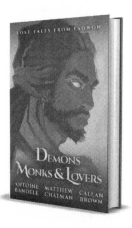

Demon's, Monks, and Lovers is a collection from the *Lost Tales from Esowon*, a series of standalone stories expanding on the world and story presented in *Tales from Esowon: The Kishi*.

For suggested reading order visit
antoinebandele.com/esowon-timeline

If you enjoy this story and are interested in the rest of its world, you can join the *Tales from Esowon* e-mail alerts list, where you'll get free content, notifications for new book releases, exclusive updates, and behind-the-page content.
Visit antoinebandele.com/stay-in-touch

LAST OF MY KIND

Lost Tales from Esowon

ANTOINE BANDELE

PRONUNCIATION GUIDE

Characters
Ki·sa·ma - kē'sä'mä
O·ba - Ō'bä
Pem·ba - pem'bä
N·ko·si - en'kō'sē
San·je - sän'jā
U·zo·ma - ü'zō'mä
Ye·mi - yeə'mē

Terms & Titles
A·ba·ra - ä'bä'rä
A·ya - ī'yä
Ba·ba - bä'bä
Du·la·gi·a·la - dü'lä'gē'a'lä
Ki·shi - kē'shē
U·ga·ra - ü'gä'rä

Locations
Ba·jok - ba'jōk
Da·ji - dä'jē
E·so·won - e'sō'wän
Gue·la - gwe'lä
Jun·ga - jün'gä
Ny·o·ka - nē'yō'kä

Southern Reaches of
THE GOLAH EMPIRE
(FORMERLY)

LEOPARD'S GORGE

THE BLACK ROCKS

Uzoma's Homestead

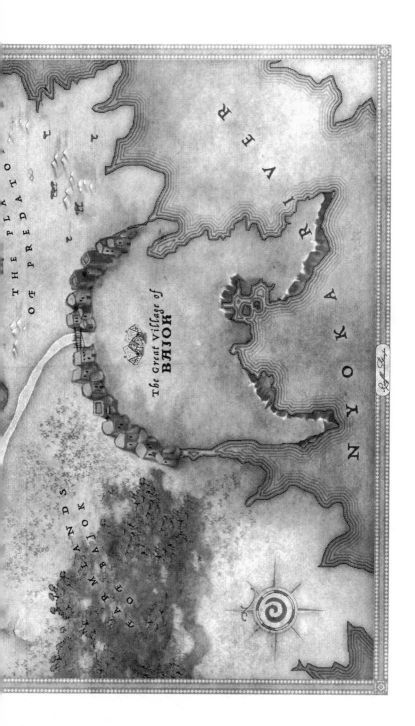

"You heard the story of this place, I'm sure," Yemi said. "About the heroes of Bajok: Chief Oba and the Great and Mighty Uzoma. The Bajoki say they killed the kishi, forced them back into the rocks. But that wasn't true. They didn't kill me."

— EXCERPT FROM *THE KISHI*

ONE

BLACKNESS SHROUDS EVERYTHING. THAT DARK WHERE you can't even see your own hand in front of your face. I'd use my second head—it's got better eyes for the shadows— but Baba tells me it's too dangerous. We've got to hide from the humans.

"Stay close, Yemi. We're almost there," Baba tells me, his deep voice reverberating against the cold, narrow walls.

I reach out my arm so I won't trip and fall. My hand's waving stupidly in front of me until it catches against jagged rock, splitting open.

"Ow," I groan, sucking at my bloodied knuckle.

Baba's weight turns to me. "I said stay close. We don't got the time."

He snatches my hand, squeezing hard. It hurts but I don't whine about it. Baba hates when I do that, especially since the war started.

I hate the war, can't wait for it to be over once we kill that human Uzoma.

Uzoma.

Bajok's savior.

The Great and Mighty.

The *Kishi* Killer.

Baba says Uzoma and his other human warriors always caught our clan off guard. That's why we're running now as the other of our kishi warriors fight him and his comrades off. Our home, The Black Rocks as the humans called it, is our last defense.

We'll see how strong Uzoma is in a straight-up fight. No human has a chance within the confusing collection of cliffs and crags. And within the stone towers lies our secret cave homes with their endless mazes. I'm a kishi and I can barely see in here myself, tripping over rocks and crevices like some cub — not the most intimidating sight for the humans.

"Can't I use the hyena for a little while?" I ask. "I don't have to use the eyes, just the nose —"

"No, you keep it hidden, like I said."

"It's so hard hiding it. And how am I supposed to fight without —"

"We aren't fighting."

I stop walking but Baba pulls me like I'm no bigger than a child. I keep telling him I'm not one, but he never wants to hear it. Four more years and I'll be a man grown.

What does he mean we're not going to fight? Does he think I'm not strong enough, that my powers have not yet fully matured? "I can fight good, Baba. Those humans are weak."

He ignores me, just keeps on walking like I didn't say a word. I'll show him who's weak. If the humans catch up, I'll rip the first one's head off. He'll see.

There's a snarl at the back of my head. My locs part, brushing against my ears as a snout sniffs the chilled air. My hyena, my second head, must want to know what all the fuss is about.

As its snout presses into the cool air I can smell what he smells.

A faint stink of human sweat lingers at the mouth of the cave. It seems like one of the humans is stupid enough to chase us through the dark caves. That's a mistake. The humans might be safe out in the open with their spears and their arrows, but here in the tight web of boulders and stones, they're at a disadvantage. This one must be keen to die.

My second face stirs, blinking black eyes. Now I see what my hyena sees. The cave slews in zigs and zags, its walls like wax crawling down a candlestick.

I sense the human's approach. It's like the feeling you get when you know someone is watching you or when you know someone is lying. The "knowing" is the best way I can describe it, though Baba says it's our *a'bara* at work.

As we turn down a corridor pocketed with light from above, I push my knowing back down the cavern. But I don't sense what I expect. Whoever is following us in the cave has no issue traversing the uneven paths. They're sure-footed and gaining fast, and I sense no fear from them. No, worse than that; I sense only complete confidence.

Only one warrior could be so bold.

"Baba, there's a human—"

Baba turns quicker than I've ever seen him move. Before I can even blink at his motion through the sliver of light, I'm struck across the face and flying through the air, my body about to crash into the cave wall.

I call on my second body, transforming half of it into the strong hide of a hyena. My back fills with thick, spotted fur, its muscles growing larger, as strong as a beast's. It takes most of the blunt punishment as I smack against cold stone, though the edges of my human ribs bruise in the process.

As I come down, my animal instinct takes over, landing on all fours as a good kishi should. My human head cracks back, revealing the full snout of a growling hyena. Chest convulsing, I look for the one who attacked us, but there's no one in the cavernous room but me and Baba. It takes me another second to realize it was my father who knocked me back.

I turn my hyena snout to the still air and try to sniff out the one who pursued us, but the scent is gone. Was I wrong to think we were being chased? Were my nerves getting the better of me? My hyena tells me we still aren't safe, but he's been wrong so many times before in this war. For now, I tell him to hush.

Before I can catch a breath or relax my arched back, Baba pounces on me in his kishi form, a dark mass of fur and fangs. I turn on my spine, showing him my human side —a sign of submission.

"What did I tell you?" his human face grunts from behind his animal head. His hyena breath is hot against my face.

"You said to hide but—"

"No buts. You will die if you do not hide."

I've never seen his hyena eyes so serious before, almost human. But I don't understand. Uzoma might have been on our tail. Whether I was wrong or not, how would hiding my hyena be any help? I have enough sense not to talk back again though—his fangs are bigger than my fingers. So I nod, relaxing my tense muscles.

"Good," Baba says, retracting his hyena maw from my neck. "Now, hide your face like I told you to."

I hate when I have to hide my head. It's wrong, like a part of me is cut off. I do as he says, but not without frowning first.

"Breathe deep," he tells me as I struggle to concentrate.

The hyena doesn't want to go back inside. I don't blame him. Scrunching up my brow, I force him down like the nasty vegetables the elders make us eat. He crunches into my skull, biting at my locs as though that'll save him. I try to reassure him, tell him in my mind that he'll come back out—when the time is right.

He doesn't believe me.

"Settle down, son. Settle down." Baba touches my arm, filling me with a mystical warmth, like nothing in the world could go wrong. My hyena head feels it too as he's lulled into my human head. It's one of the abilities all kishi have. The talent, the a'bara, to soothe another's emotions. "*You* control the hyena. He does not control you."

Baba lifts his hand from my arm and the pleasant sensation goes away—and with it, my control over the hyena. My head snaps from side to side again of its own accord, thrashing against sharp rock that brings fresh cuts to my brow and cheeks. The hyena thinks I'm weak. It's time that he learns I'm not.

I bite down on my tongue; pain always helps me focus. My flailing passes into shaking, then into a mild shiver as I tame my second head. Another moment and I have my hyena back under my command—and back inside my head.

Baba places both hands on my shoulders. "Don't worry. I sensed him too. But I left a few surprises for him. It'll take time before he finds us here."

So I wasn't wrong. Uzoma *was* chasing us. Then why was Baba being so calm about everything? My eyes dart from left to right, trying to put everything together in my head. There has to be a reason we are hiding back here, but what?

Baba watches me with a bright expression. Through the shadows it looks like he's smiling. But that has to be my imagination.

I haven't seen him smile since this all started.

Unlike most kishi, Baba's head is shaved bare. The rest of us have to use long hair or headwraps to cover our hyenas. The elders said he's the only one who can hide his.

13

If they weren't killed by the humans all those moons ago, they would know I was the second.

Baba says hiding our heads should be something all kishi should know how to do. We do it all the time with the fur on our backs, it's just a matter of extending that mystical veil to our heads. It's easy for him to say. He's the strongest kishi in our clan. Learning to hide my own hyena indefinitely has been a lifelong challenge I've yet to achieve.

"Listen to me careful," Baba says. "This isn't practice anymore. What I tell you to do, you do. Understood?"

I dip my head low. "Yes, Baba."

He points behind me, deep into the cave. I didn't even see it at first. A set of rocks look as though they've fallen into each other, and at the bottom is a small gap, a perfect fit for someone like me. I know what Baba wants me to do, but I don't want to do it.

I shake my head hard, locs whipping across my face in a dance of protest. Baba doesn't care. Without a word, he points his large finger into the little gap.

Jaw clenched, eyes narrowed, and pride wounded, I get on my hands and feet and crawl into the wide crevice. Gravel scrapes against my knees as I slide through. I'm not even small enough to fit! How could Baba force me to just watch?

I must be putting on a mean face because Baba is chuckling like he always does when I do. It's the first time in weeks I've heard his laugh, that familiar blend of a human jape and a hyena's cackle.

"If we get out of this, remind me to teach you how to look tough," he says.

I don't give him the satisfaction of a response, scrunching my face into a scowl. He keeps to laughing.

"Don't hold to that hate, Yemi," he says, finally ending his last chuckle. "It's good fuel, but it burns hot and quick like a fire not tended to correctly."

I frown, digging farther into the hiding place. If he wants me in here, I'll do it right and proper.

Baba sticks his hand into the hole and flicks me on the forehead. "What's our greatest strength as kishi?"

I perk up. "Our hides when we turn. Not even *Ugara's* Spear can pierce it!"

Baba puts his head down and sighs. "No, son. It's our gift, our a'bara to touch others' states of mind and to hide our own." I roll my eyes like always. I'll take a giant maw over *thoughts* and *feelings* any day.

"Tell me, what am I feeling right now?" Baba asks.

I repress a groan. I never know what his mood is. He's too good. But when I reach out to sense what's inside him, I'm met with a warm sensation, like when the sun hits the back of your neck real nice.

I chew on the word before I say, "Joy."

Baba purses his lips like he does when he gets to thinking. "I suppose that's right."

"How can you be happy? We lost. Everyone's dead. Elder Lanje, Elder Fuma, Kinsasha, Bundu—"

"But you're still alive." He flicks me on the forehead again. "That's what matters."

I go quiet, thinking hard on what he says.

"Promise me you'll stay in here no matter what happens," Baba says.

I don't like his tone, so I say, "Even if you need help?"

"*Especially* if I need help. Understood?"

"Yes, Baba." I keep my fingers crossed behind my back. I'm no craven. If my father needs an extra maw, I sure as hell will help him instead of hiding away like a grass mouse.

"I love you, Yemi," Baba says.

I don't respond. Though I can count on one hand the number of times he's said the words, I still don't like it when he does.

"I'm supposed to be quiet," I finally say.

He gives me a dark grin. "That you are."

Baba lifts to his full height, his head nearly brushing against the top of the cavern. The farther he moves from my hiding spot, the less I can see his figure. There's a hole near the top where the sun shines through, but I can only see when he passes it. Looks like he's smelling the wall for something. I have half a mind to do some sniffing myself, but I keep my hyena head hidden.

After he's done nosing around the cave, he sits with his knees to the ground, hands on his thighs, and palms facing up. I can't see good, but it looks like his stomach is twisting into itself as he breathes deep. Then he lets out an exhale and his stomach goes out like a round hill.

He does this for what feels like forever. After a few moments I imitate his strange exercise, just to see if it'll put a stop to my nerves.

It doesn't.

When I smelled the cave before it seemed like Uzoma, or whoever was behind us, was close. Perhaps the traps Baba said he laid did slow them down after all. Maybe they even killed the human who gave chase.

I start to breathe a little easier, and then my hopes are dashed.

At the edge of the cave, just past where Baba sits, Uzoma, the humans' savior, is standing tall.

I can barely make him out though. A sliver of light from the cave's hole shines across his short hair, one of his golden eyes, and down his broad chin.

I've only seen him once: when our pack was driven from the plains. From afar he looked large, but now, only a few paces from where I hide, he looks like a giant.

"So you figured out the breathing techniques of the Junga, then?" Uzoma asks, his voice baritone, mild instead of intimidating as I expect.

"No, the Dambe people," Baba corrects him.

Uzoma sucks his teeth. "I never got that far north. Glad to see it's working for you. I can't even see impression lines on your head. How did you do it?"

"You didn't come here for a lesson in meditation."

"Right you are." Uzoma outstretches his hand. The light glints off the tip of his short half-spear.

Baba stands up in one fluid motion, nearly matching Uzoma's height but missing by a finger's length. My heart smacks into my chest so fast I can feel it in my throat. Baba's the strongest man I've ever known, the strongest kishi among our pack. There isn't another of us who can challenge my father. And besides, what could a single human do, even one as "great" and "mighty" as Uzoma?

Cracking his neck back, Baba transforms into his kishi form, his human legs twist back into hind legs, and his hands contort into paws. His bare back is no more, now covered in a coat of black with ash-brown spots, and the back of his head is no longer smooth skin but the face of a hyena.

Uzoma's in real trouble now.

"Your home, your move." Uzoma nods, I think.

Baba pounces for Uzoma and I lose all sense of the fight. The room fills with the grunts and groans of a merciless scrap. Sometimes Uzoma's spear catches light. A sigh of relief parts my lips every time I see it's free of my father's blood.

Thuds come next, deep impacts against skin and cave walls. Each blow pounds against my skin as though I'm in the fight myself, competing with the beating of my heart. I can only hope it's Baba that's doling out the damage. It takes everything I have to hold still, but my body wants to leap out, to join the fight.

A shriek pierces the noise of grunts and groans. Human or hyena? I can't tell.

It sounds like, I hope, Baba pinning Uzoma to the

ground. Perhaps he's bit his leg down, maybe an arm. I squint, trying my best to see in the dark. But I can only make out the impressions of fur. Does that mean Baba is on top, finishing Uzoma off?

The spear crosses the cave's light again, stabbing down. It lands, making contact with skin, but it does nothing.

Uzoma, you fool! Nothing can break a kishi's hide.

The stabbing slows as life drains from its strikes. I'm breathless, adrenaline pumping through my veins. Was that my hyena head shifting through my hair?

The slashes halt. There's no more movement, no more sounds, except for a trickle of dripping water farther down the cave.

Baba did it. He killed the Great and Mighty Uzoma. And it only took a couple moments. I'm about to lift myself up but forget I'm pinned by the tight walls. I stop trying to free myself when I see a figure lift itself into the light. The sight of it keeps me locked in place.

The figure wasn't Baba. It was Uzoma.

But I *saw* Uzoma stabbing with his spear. He was trying to kill my father when he was already down. My head throbs as I try to figure out what happened.

Uzoma drops to his knee. The sound of metal scraping against rock rings out as he retrieves what can only be his short spear. When he rises again, I catch sight of the back of his head. It's not at all what I'm expecting; it's not at all what it *should* be.

Horror takes me whole, empties me out with naked fear.

Uzoma is a kishi.

It doesn't make sense. He was the one who followed us through the cave. I smelled a human scent, not a kishi one.

I have to remind myself that Uzoma is different. What had he said to Baba about someone named Junga—or was it Daji? Perhaps they learned how to hide themselves from whoever those people were.

Uzoma was not in kishi form when he pursued us. Even when Baba or I hide our kishi, the smell of them goes away with it. There was no way I could have known.

That still didn't explain why Uzoma was being attacked with his own spear, unless that meant... it wasn't Uzoma who was trying to strike Baba. Somewhere in the fight, my father must've taken control of the spear, but it didn't work.

I turn my gaze to Baba at Uzoma's feet. A streak of blood stretches out from his body, glistening in the lines of light within the cave.

Reaching out with my feelings, I try to call to him, to his a'bara. He can't be dead. He just can't. No one has ever defeated him, not even the strongest in our clan.

But as the seconds stretch, there's nothing I can do but believe what is in front of my eyes.

Baba isn't getting up.

I turn dark eyes to Uzoma, and I refuse to let the tears fall. It's all starting to make sense now. No human could do what he had achieved. They said he could take on two kishi at once, even three. That only made sense if he had supernatural abilities, which apparently he did. And if was a kishi himself, those feats weren't so impressive. It was worse. It meant Uzoma was a traitor.

Did the humans know? Were they using him as some sort of pet? No, a human could never control a kishi; they're too weak. Uzoma must have been playing them, using them as allies against our clans.

Where naked fear dominates the pit of my stomach, it's quickly replaced by raw anger. I'll kill Uzoma for what he did to our kind, to my father.

Uzoma's hyena head sniffs the cave walls. Can he smell me? Sense me? That's why Baba told me to stay calm. He must have known about Uzoma's true form. How long had he known, and why keep it from me?

I slow the heavy breathing in my nose, ceasing its loud

exhale against the ground. As brave as I felt a moment ago, the weight of Uzoma's presence and the lethality of that hyena maw locks my heart down to a full stop. Reality shatters my youthful pride. If I don't get a grip, he'll find me. And kill me. We kishi can sense each other's emotions, and in such a small cavern, Uzoma would find me with no issue.

I tell myself to be calm like Baba, to hide my emotional scent. But how can I when he's lying there dead?

Fear of failure creeps through my body, funneling to the back of my head. If I can't hide myself, I'll have to fight.

Uzoma turns his head to my hidden hole. In the glint of light, his fangs glow bright, bared wide. And under their sharp tips a low growl rumbles. As I let the hyena out from the back of my head, the grunt from Uzoma's own stops, whipping away from the dark hole where I hide.

I clench my fists against the cold ground, bracing for the first attack.

But it never comes.

Is this a trick? It has to be. He's just baiting me to come out, to look for where he's gone. The moment I do that he'll jump on me and snap my neck. *Nice try, bastard. I'm not falling for it.*

Then I hear pounding feet echoing down the cave walls. Too locked into each other's smell, neither of us had sensed the approaching humans. Uzoma drops down from the top of the cavern—hiding like I thought he was—just as the first human approaches.

"Uzoma," a strong voice says. The other footsteps stop. I can't tell how many, possibly four or five pairs. Too many for me to take on alone, even without Uzoma among their ranks.

"War Chief Oba," Uzoma replies as the fur on the back of his legs regresses into human skin. A lump wells up in my throat. Only Baba could hide his hyena—at least, that's what the elders told me. How much had he lied? He said he wanted me to pass on the ability.

"You should have waited, Uzoma," the first voice says. I guess this one is Oba. I've seen him before. Wherever Uzoma went, he was not far behind. "We took care of the rest outside the cavern."

"How'd you do it?" another man asks. His voice sounds low, as though he's examining my father. A fire kindles in my throat as I imagine human hands rubbing their stink on Baba.

"I was lucky," Uzoma grunts.

"That wound at your side could become infected," Oba says. My mouth parts. So Baba was able to injure Uzoma, at least. "Let's get you back to the village. Have the shaman look at you."

"What about him?" the second voice asks.

Uzoma shuffles to Baba's body. It's faint but I see him drag his spear across what looks like my father's neck. A shriek of iron and sinew cuts against Baba's skin. And the horrific music never seems to stop.

Slice. Slop. Slice. Crunch. Slice. Ooze.

Each beat a stab to my heart. It takes everything I have to hold the bile at the back of my throat. *Oh, Dulagi'ala…* I try desperately not to be sick as Baba's head finally separates from his shoulders, ending the melodic misery.

My hyena head starts to growl. I clamp its snout shut with my hands.

"Let the rest of him rot," Uzoma decides. It sounds like he's the first to leave, the others following close behind. One warrior says something about Uzoma being the fiercest man he's ever known, but I'm not listening anymore. For the first time I see the whole of Baba's mangled body, his arms twisted back at slanted angles.

I DON'T MOVE FOR AN HOUR, TOO AFRAID UZOMA IS STILL baiting me. I sense nothing, don't smell anything either, but I'm terrified all the same.

Baba would be ashamed to see me now, holding myself tight like a cub that needs its mother. I grew up without a mother. I'm tougher than this. But the tightness in my chest just won't go away.

It's not just that I'm alone. It's that I'm completely stripped, bare to the world and its dangers without my father. A few moons ago, nothing could hurt me, certainly not kill me or my clan. And there were few things that scared me. Fear and I were acquaintances before, a healthy relationship, but when the humans attacked us, we soon became fast friends. With Baba dead and gone, I'd say I know fear as intimately as I do my own kin. Now I shudder at every echo through the cave.

It must be another hour before I make my first move, shifting rocks under my weight. Each scrape too loud for my ears adds another half-hour to my waiting.

It feels like a moon cycle has passed when I poke my head into the chilly cavern space. Light no longer shines through the hole near the top, and cool night air clams my skin.

I use my hands to look for Baba. His hyena back is the first thing I touch, soft and comforting. My hand runs up his back until I find the gash at his neck, jagged and unsettling. There isn't anything else after that, except a trail of blood on cold rock. I try to move him but his body is locked up like it's made of stone.

"Baba…" My voice cracks. I know calling to him is useless. Death is nothing new to me. Baba and I had feasted on many women together. It's our nature. But cracking voices, tears, and sadness were for the weakling humans, not for kishi.

Baba taught me we are above the crippling emotions of sympathy, that we are experts of empathy. The word he used was "empath." I never understood the difference between the two until now, in the face of my anguish. How could I be the master of sentiment when I am controlled by them?

I tell myself this, but it doesn't quite settle. We are half-human, after all, and this is different. This is my father. Dead. Motionless. Little more than meat now. No more lessons about our kind, races along the plains, or nightly hunts against villages.

Vomit sits at the top of my throat as my second head lets out a low cry. I didn't even notice he was back, his ears curled down against my locs. Patting the back of my head, I don't even try to hide him anymore.

My body cracks and contorts, my back twisting to the ground and my belly to the top of the cave, fully changed into kishi form. My hyena nuzzles the fur on Baba's back, then bites at it as though playing.

It dawns on me that he doesn't realize Baba is gone. In the past, before the war, Father's own hyena always liked to play when he let it out. If only we could go back to that time before the humans uncovered us.

Something wet drips down my cheek and into my hyena's maw. When I realize it's a tear, I pinch my cheeks into my eyes hard, forcing the rest to stay put, though they do their best to crest my eyelids.

My hyena whimpers softly, still nuzzling. Soon his cries turn to soft howls that echo down the long cavern. It's a faint growl, one that translates to "wake up," but it still makes me nervous. What if one of the humans is standing guard outside?

I slam my head into the hard stone, hyena head first. "He's gone," I tell it, short and harsh. "He's gone."

But my hyena keeps biting at Baba's paws, trying to force him to play. Can't he see that Father doesn't even have a head anymore? Doesn't he understand? In light of his weakness, I find strength. One of us has to act like the kishi we are.

"We know who did this. We know what we have to do."

TWO

I PUSH MYSELF TO MY FEET, THOUGH MY KNEES ARE shaky—from fear or soreness, I can't tell. Bucking up, I rip back control of my kishi form, breathing in new air. Instantly, all my senses heighten; primary among them is the smell of rain approaching from somewhere outside.

The "knowing" within me says the sun will soon rise. On all fours, I bound against rock and stone until I reach the mouth of the cave, where the hard ground turns to soft earth.

At the cave's edge there's trails of blood leading to a set of headless bodies. Baba's men. The last of our clan. I can only hope they took some of the humans down with them.

I don't stop to count the dead as I cross the rocky threshold, letting the howling wind against my ears blow away all fear.

You'll never catch me, Uzoma.

But deep down I know better. If Uzoma wanted to give chase, he'd catch up to me with ease, bite down around my neck, and rip my head clean from my shoulders. Each thought of the Great and Mighty sends a shiver down my spine. Blurs of gray and black fly by as a terrible thought shoots through my whole body.

Before Baba and the others found the cave, we hadn't seen any other kishi for days as we were driven back deeper and deeper into The Black Rocks. Now that Father's gone, am I the last of my clan?

The weight of the thought doesn't hit me as I thought it would. The fear of being mauled at any moment helps with that, I guess. Which is good. Right now, I just need to survive.

I sink my paws deeper into the earth, driving the worry even further back. I run until there are no more craggy passages to run through, until the stretch of rock walls opens to the cold and misty plain.

I turn around to survey what was once our home. The humans had come to fear the collection of towering black rocks, like giant stubby fingers crawling out of the earth to bring it back down. Now it was no more than a hollow piece of land, a broken mountain scarred by filthy humans.

My hyena howls, his voice carrying across the massive plains. I use his eyes to see an expanse of brown and green ahead of us, bruised-colored skies calling in the rainy season. Had the fighting really lasted throughout the harvest?

I think I can make out a pair of giraffe heads on the horizon as they pick at the trees. With nowhere to go, I turn my nose up in the morning air. And with a few sniffs, I catch a familiar scent to the east where the sun crests the horizon. I follow it, keeping to the high brush to avoid the eyes of other predators, animal and human alike.

The dawn casts long shadows on the plains. When the clouds are gray, that's when the lions and other hyenas do most of their hunting—or so Baba always said.

I think back to Uzoma. How would I ever catch him off guard? The humans, and that giant mud wall protecting

Bajok, always surround him. I definitely can't do it while parched or with an empty stomach.

As the sun rises behind a sheet of gray, I find myself smacking my lips. My mouth is as dry as desert sands. There has to be a watering hole close. Another hour in this direction and I would be well into the territory of the Guela people. If I remember correctly, there should be a place to quench my thirst nearby. The scent I've caught is in the same direction, anyway.

It's midday when I find the watering hole and, with it, a trio of bare-chested boys. Each has long hair, locs like mine. And, judging by the length, they are all different ages. The boy with hair down his back, the oldest, holds what looks like nuts in his hands, which the boy with the shortest hair picks at, eating them ravenously as though they're the only thing he's had in ages. The third boy with hair draped just past his shoulders—and a double-chin hanging beneath his mouth—keeps watch. He's not doing a very good job. I'm able to sneak up on them.

I rise from the brush, introducing myself with open palms. My movements must've been too sudden because the fat one's first reaction is to turn tail and run. In an instant, he's changed into full kishi form, galloping atop the water like it's as solid as sand.

So they're kishi too. I'm not alone after all.

The other boys turn. The oldest sucks his teeth, then snaps his fingers at the other. "Pemba, ain't nothin' but a boy. Get back over here."

The one called Pemba turns mid-lake, sniffing with his hyena snout.

"Some lookout he is," the youngest one says through a mouthful of cashews.

"You should know better," Pemba shouts back in what sounds like a Guela accent. "If someone runs, you don't question it. You just get to goin' too."

27

It was a fair point were he talking about gazelle and zebra, not kishi.

The oldest boy looks me up and down. "You N'kosi's son, ain't you?" He dusts nut shavings from his hands, standing at his full height. Our hair is about the same length —mine is probably a finger shorter—but he's a head taller than me. He may recognize me, but I don't know him. Many kishi clans fought each other before we banded against Uzoma and the other humans. He may have been a rival. My father was the best of the best, so we have—had —a lot of those.

I glance down at the boy's posture. Baba always said to watch for the enemy's legs. It's often the first tell in a fight. Without thinking, I'm already leaning one foot back, ready for an attack. My face must be fixed with a mean stare because the boy flashes an exaggerated smile of ivory white.

"Relax, brother," he intones. "We're all friends here. Name's Sanje." He holds open hands to his side as I had, the gesture of the Bajoki people, which means he doesn't have a dagger to stick me with, at least.

I swallow hard before saying, "I'm called Yemi."

The other boys introduce themselves. The youngest is the kid-brother of Sanje. His name is Kisama. When the big one called Pemba returns, shaking water from his hyena coat, he introduces himself with a lumpy hug.

"I'm a hugger!" He wraps me closer in his wet embrace. "Good to see we ain't the only ones alive." The boy is all smiles—his mouth and his chins.

After he lets me go, I dunk my hand into the water and shove it down my dry throat. The water's as cold as ice, frozen by the cool air—the rainy season is on us, all right— but I drink it down all the same. It tastes like iron though. I nearly spit it out when I realize dry blood covers my hand. Baba's blood.

"All right, can we go already?" Kisama asks, nose

turned to the gray sky. "We need to get out of here. Them humans can't be far behind."

"No, they're not following us," I say as I get done drinking. "I've been walking for hours and I haven't seen them."

Pemba shakes his head. "That's how it always be, ain't it? They always finding us when we don't expect it."

"Trust me," I say, washing my hands of the blood. "They think they've won."

A brief silence cuts through the group, the obvious question hanging in the air until...

"They *think*?" Sanje mutters with disbelief, crossing his arms. "How'd you figure that? I mean, you're alone. We're alone. We ain't seen nobody from our clan in days."

Pemba lifts a hand to his mouth. "Oh, shit. They done killed N'Kosi too, didn't they?"

I bend low to wash the red from my palms. My silence is answer enough.

Kisama tugs at his brother's loincloth. "Come on, Sanje, we got to get out of here."

"You heading to the jungle too?" Sanje asks after I get done washing.

I shake my head. "Just gettin' away from the village to rest up. But I'm going back. Got to find a way to kill Uzoma."

A hush whistles against the cool breeze. It doesn't last long. A burst of shrill laughter, only uttered from a mix of human and hyena, rings across the plain. All the boys grab at their sides in guffaws. Sanje holds himself up on his knees. Kisama follows suit, imitating his older brother. Pemba embraces his middle as though to hold in his chuckles at the stomach. I'm the only one not laughing. I don't even crack a smile, my mouth a thin line.

Pemba catches my expression through his red-faced laughter and stops suddenly. "Oh shit, I think he's serious."

He looks to Sanje with concern. My thin line turns to a full scowl.

Sanje stops his laughing too, throwing his locs over his head, his brow etched with a deep crease. "Uzoma can't be killed, brother. Our best bet's to move on to the Kunda jungles. No humans go there."

"And there's more boys like us meeting there," Kisama adds.

"I still say we oughta run with the hyena in the far plains," Pemba says. "We'd be gods to them."

Sanje sighs, pinching the bridge of his nose. Somehow it seems Pemba has made this request several times before. "They'd never accept half-breeds. They more as like to attack us than follow us."

"The jungles are better," Kisama echoes.

I can't believe the words coming from their mouths. And I thought I was the coward. These boys want to run away like pride means nothing to them. I suck my teeth and flick my hand in the air with disgust. Turning on my heel, I head back into the brush—I've had my fill of water—but Sanje grabs me by my arm. His grip is stronger than I expected.

"Where you going?" he asks.

"Back to Bajok. The fight isn't over." I rip my hand from his grip but fall flat on my ass.

Sanje and the others stand over me, all humor gone from their faces. Sanje shakes his head solemnly. "It's over for us."

"Well, it ain't over for me." I spit into the dirt.

Pemba gulps, glancing back at the other boys before saying, "You ain't told us about your father. What happened? Uzoma did him in too, didn't he?"

There's a knot in my throat blocking me from speaking. Flashes of Baba's fight spring to mind. His lifeless body under my hand throbs to my touch.

"He ain't got to say nothing," Sanje says darkly. "N'Kosi's dead. Just like everyone else stupid enough to fight."

So the boys are all alone, like me. My eyes turn to slits. "How could you not want payback? Your fathers would be ashamed. Let's go back into the village tonight and kill the one responsible."

"It's not that easy," Sanje says. "I've seen Uzoma fight. More times than I would've like to. He ain't like them other humans. We wouldn't even last a minute."

Does Sanje know who Uzoma truly is? No, he couldn't. He said "like other humans." Should I tell them? If I did, Pemba would probably start running again. And Kisama doesn't look any more ready for a fight. The little boy still has baby fat in his cheeks.

No, I won't tell them.

If they think Uzoma is just a human, then all the better. But if shaming them wouldn't work, maybe simple logic would. Going back to the village alone would be suicide for me, but with three other kishi at my side and a good plan, something might just work.

"There's more of us than there are of him," I finally say.

Pemba shrugs. "So what?"

"Let me finish." I stand back up. "I'm not saying we challenge Uzoma to Ugara's Dance or anything like that. You're right, Sanje; we wouldn't last. But if we walk into the village as children, no one would think twice before we rip out Uzoma's throat in his sleep. Easy. We'll be in and out before anyone knows. We can sense him and he won't be able to sense us."

Or at least I hope he won't sense us. He won't sense me, at least. But didn't Baba say something about protective magics in the village? Something about our hyena heads being hidden, repressed by shaman magic? That could work to our favor as well. Like I said, I can make use of three more bodies with me. One way or another, I'll see Uzoma dead.

"But what about all them guards?" Kisama asks with his small voice.

I turn to him and put a hand to his shoulder, sending tender waves through him like Baba did for me in the cave. "If we're going at night, they won't see us. Humans don't see right in the dark."

"Neither will we if we can't change," Sanje reminds me. "There's supposed to be some protection on Bajok, right?"

Damn. I hoped they hadn't known.

Pemba nods in agreement. "And how we gonna rip his throat when we can't change?"

"It doesn't matter," I say. "It might even be better that way. We'll use daggers instead of our teeth."

Kisama and Pemba look almost convinced, but Sanje has a deep frown.

"It *might* work, Sanje," Pemba says.

"We'll just look like kids, like he says," Kisama adds. "If we caught, we can outrun any human."

"That's if we get out of that village in time," Sanje says slowly.

"Right," Kisama says. "No problem."

We all turn our heads to Sanje, who's crossing his arms and tapping his foot. "Fine, but you're going in front. And if I catch a whiff of anything off—"

"I'm sure Pemba will be the first one to run." I smile for the first time.

THREE

DARK CLOUDS LOOM HIGH OVER BAJOK AS WE ALL HIDE behind a cut of rocks. I can make out a half dozen warrior-guards atop the village wall, faces lit by torches. There's only two at the wooden gate.

"How we gonna get past all them?" Kisama asks with slumped shoulders.

I turn to the group, each face betraying fear. Crouched nearest to me, even Sanje looks uneasy, avoiding my eye contact as I tell them what they have to do. He fixes his attention on the village walls as though Uzoma himself will come bursting out. Pemba brings up the rear, hanging back a few strides.

"Are you listening to me?" I ask them, snapping my finger. The sound echoes off the rock and shakes them from their tense stupor. Sanje mouths, *What in the gods' names?* I ignore him. It was time to get serious. "It's easy. We'll use our kishi forms to climb up the wall. It's tall, but not that tall."

I glance over my shoulder once more to measure the height. From the ground up, the walls couldn't be over twenty paces high, twenty-five at most. So long as we have enough momentum going up, even with the shaman's magic tearing our kishi forms away, forcing us into a human form once we get to the top, we should get over it safely.

I twist back to the boys again. Even in the dark, I can see a pool of sweat coming down around Pemba's eyes. "Listen, it'll be fine. Just run as fast as you can up the wall and go for the edge. You'll be forced to change the higher you climb, maybe even as soon as you touch the wall. But just keep going and you'll reach the top."

"Lot of *you's* in all that," Sanje says, his voice stilted. It looks like he's fighting back a gulp.

"I'm going too, obviously," I say.

"What about them guards though?" Pemba takes a step back, eyes drifting up and down the wall as though he's measuring the distance himself. The harder and longer he stares, the more he seems to cower.

I look back to the warriors. Any human on watch is prone to mistakes, especially now when they all think the war is over. I had been watching them. The only ones we have to worry about are the guards at the gate. Their gazes never wander from their post. Those must be their elite. Makes sense, having them near the only entryway. The only *usual* entryway.

But the ones perched on the walls are slow in their scan of the outskirts, especially the ones nearest the far right, where the farmlands begin. That's where we'll climb over.

"We just have to wait until two of the guards leave a blind spot. It shouldn't take more than a few seconds to climb. And in the dark we'll have the advantage," I say.

"Sound like you have it all figured out," Sanje says. "You'll be going first, I take it."

I whip my head to him. "What?"

"Ain't nothing changed. I told you if something feels off, you're the one who's going first."

I bite down on my retort. He's right; that was the deal. I only figured he'd want to go first because he's the leader of his small group. That'll be the last time I underestimate his cowardice. Muscles or no, the boy is more craven than a meerkat. Leaders lead.

"Watch me close," I tell them. "We'll only get one shot at this."

For a moment, I consider the idea of them leaving me. If I scale the wall—and if I make it seem difficult—there's nothing stopping the others from simply abandoning me to fend for myself. If I were as prideless as these cubs, it's what I'd do.

Taking a deep breath, I shift to my full kishi form, paws digging into the earth.

Simple, then. I've just got to make this look easy.

I tilt my hyena head to the wall. Suddenly, the twenty paces up look more like a hundred.

Baba's voice echoes in my head. What had he always said about my fear? If I want to conquer it, I shouldn't sit in the brush and think about it. I have it face it head on.

My hyena eyes drift between the guards, waiting for the right moment. The second their attention is drawn away, I bound forward with silent paws, one of the many benefits of being a kishi: light feet.

I hit the bottom of the wall hard, and as I expected, the protective magics run through my body, fur regressing to skin, hyena snout retracting into my head.

I won't make it the whole way in kishi form.

Halfway up the wall, I twist my body into a half-circle, bringing my human front forward. I press the ball of my foot—which has already transformed—into the thick of the mud wall and push up. With both hands, I grab the edge and heave myself over.

Flawless.

But there's still one issue. The moment the guards turn

35

back, they'll see me standing there on their battlements. And it doesn't help that each section of the inner wall is lit by a torch.

"Holy shit." Pemba's voice rings out from the rocks. The guards hear him too.

"What was that?" the one on the right says, looking over his parapet and into the dark. My heart thumps against my chest. Either the guards go looking for the others or they turn around and see me. Neither was a good outcome. At least now they weren't focused on the wall top. I just need a distraction.

"You heard that too, right?" the guard to the left asks. "Could just be the wind. The rainy season's a coming."

I look down into the village—more a town, if you ask me. Most of their huts, if you could call them that, are almost as high as their barrier.

Looks like I've climbed over the wall nearest to their market. Below me is a set of barrels and baskets filled with beans, eggs, and millet—wait, millet!

"It's your turn to check," says the first guard.

The second sighs deep. Instead of making a move down, he says, "Who's there?" The lazy option. Obviously, he gets no response.

The first guard chuckles. "Nice try. Get your careless ass down there."

"Fine, fine," the second guard relents.

I twist my head from left to right like a ground squirrel. If the guard goes down there, he'll scare the boys away, leaving me alone. There has to be something I could use— there! Just what I need. A few paces from me, one torch sits alight along the parapet. I quickly pull it from its sconce and throw it into the millet. The fire starts small but soon lances through the twine of the other baskets.

I push my back against the inner wall, away from the

blood orange glow below. The guards' attention is pulled inward.

"What the hell happened?" one of them asks. Too scared to move my head, I can't tell which. If they look even a few paces to one side, they'll find me. Sweat beads on my forehead. If it's from the rising heat or my nerves, gods know.

"Don't just stand there," one of them calls out. "The chief will have our heads. Put it out."

Both of the guards jump into the market, trying their best to smother the fire with heavy clothes from one of the market stalls. But the fire is already too strong, reaching baskets full of cow dung. I cover my nose instinctively from the stink of burning shit.

This is my chance.

I lift my head over the wall, facing the others, and cup my hands around my mouth. "Now, now, now! Go!"

But no one comes running from the dark border.

So they did leave me, just like I said they would.

A furious heat curdles through my neck and into my head. It may be what I expected, but it still hurts. How am I going to kill Uzoma without help? How could any kishi? We all tried, and we all failed. Maybe it's best if I run away too. The guards will be too busy to see me...

No. I have to finish things now or never.

Just as I clench my fist in anger, Sanje pelts from the cut of dark rocks and climbs up the wall just as I had. He slips near the top but I help him the rest of the way.

"Way to think on your feet, brother," he says, out of breath. I return his compliment with a regretful nod. Maybe he isn't so gutless.

I turn my head back to the rocks just as Kisama starts his run. He makes it four paces from the top, missing the edge, but Sanje and I are there to pull him the rest of the way up.

The glow of red-orange dies down within the market.

One of the warrior-guards seems to have found water in one of the clay pots. The moment they douse the fire, they'll turn their attention back to their post—and to us. We need to work fast.

Nervous sweat dews my palms. I wipe it across my loincloth. We need all the leverage we have to pull up Pemba.

Each of us looks over the wall once more as Pemba pushes forward. What he lacks in speed he makes up for in strength, his kishi form more robust than pudgy, as I thought it'd be. But he's barely three-quarters of the way up before he loses momentum. He tries to twist like I did but it doesn't help.

"Grab my legs," I tell them without thinking. Rushing forward, I jump over the wall and reach for Pemba's arms, hoping to feel the others' holds around my ankles. My stomach goes empty as free fall takes me. My hands clamp around Pemba's wrists, locking down hard. Just as I feel myself falling, there's a tug at my calves. Thank the gods, the village only represses our forms and not our strength with it.

Put those muscles to good use, Sanje.

But Pemba is too heavy. I haven't been holding his wrist for more than a second and he's already slipping, his wrist damper than a freshly caught trout.

"Pemba, you really… need to lay off… the second servings of beans," Kisama says from behind, his voice strained. I realize now that I'm being held by two pairs of hands, and they seem to be slipping as well. There isn't much time; the guards will have the fire out soon, and if they catch us like this, it'll just be embarrassing.

There's nothing we can do though. Do we really need Pemba? He'll just slow us down in the end. If I just let him slip, Sanje and Kisama should be enough for what I have planned.

Sorry, Pemba.

As I loosen my grip, Sanje and Kisama seemed to find a second wind, pulling me—and Pemba—up and over the parapet.

We all fall with a great thud on the platform, each of us more tired than the last. But it's Pemba's sweat that drenches us the most.

"No time to rest, Pemba," Sanje says. "We've got to get off this wall."

Sanje pushes him into the market, where the large boy splashes into a pool of beans. We follow suit, one bean splash after the other. Each of us pulls Pemba from the large basket and into a dark corner of the market.

Finally, the guards put the fire out.

"You didn't put the torch into the sconce right, did you?" one of them asks.

"It wasn't me. Someone's trying to distract us, you fool. We've got to tell the others."

We hear their footsteps trail away before lifting our heads again.

Pemba lets out the greatest sigh I've ever heard, as though it came straight from the endless bowels of his gut. "Thank you, Yemi. Thought I was a goner."

"Yeah, good lookout," Sanje agrees. He's eyeing me with a respect I've not seen from him until now. I wasn't really thinking of saving Pemba like that. I just couldn't have him missing his jump, was all.

I'm not used to being thanked; it always makes me... uncomfortable. I never know how to respond, so I don't. "We don't have much time. Uzoma's spot is at the village center. We can make it there before they warn the others. Just follow me."

I lead them through the stretch of rounded huts, bouncing my weight on the balls of my feet, light and quiet. All but the warrior-guards seem to be asleep. Save for those few making their rounds through the alleys of the huts. There's no one to stop us.

But just as we round the corner to Uzoma's hut, a woman's voice comes from behind. "You children know better than to be out this late."

My body goes stiffer than stone.

FOUR

We turn to the woman's voice with a start, eyes wide. The woman closest to us—the speaker, I assume—has a long neck, wide nose, and a scarf wrapped around her head. At her side is a shorter woman carrying a basket of grain on her head. They must've been late coming in from their harvest.

Their eyes are kind at first, but once they see our locs, their friendly smiles turn to frowns. The shorter of the two is already taking steps away from us, and I lift open palms to my side instinctively, showing them the Bajoki greeting.

I can almost hear Sanje's thoughts in my head, his chide remark of "I told you so." I don't dare make eye contact with him though. We can't afford to take our gazes away from the women.

I sense stark fear rolling off the other boys. And where the women's moods were at first amicable, their expressions are swiftly turning hostile.

As the short woman opens her mouth to scream, I reach out with my power, a'bara rotating my eyes in a hypnotic trance. Whether or not it will work, Dulagi'ala knows.

Baba was the one who had bewitched the women we

encountered through the years. He never got the chance to train me. But I don't have any other choice.

I cut the woman's scream short. It splits into a half-shriek. A new wave of panic cycles off the boys. Was her yell loud enough to wake the other villagers? Did I stop her in time? For now, I have her and her friend in my hold. They look like little more than dolls now, placid faces and dead eyes. Now that I've the chance for a better look at them, they seem to have the same wide noses, though the shorter of the two's neck is thick-set while the other's is long. Perhaps they're sisters.

"We were just heading home," I say, letting my kishi voice take hold.

But it's not working right. Granted, the women aren't screaming their heads off as they should be, which is good, but they don't look pleased either. Baba had told me before that my a'bara powers wouldn't work well on grown women, not until I'm grown too. The attraction's just not there, he said. But I can't let this ruin our plans. Not when we're so close.

"We can use them," Sanje whispers in my ear. "Uzoma's hut will be guarded."

I turn my head back to the women, straining against their resistance. Baba's voice rings clear in my head. *"What's our greatest strength as kishi?"*

It's not just about our strong hides, not about our maws. This is what he meant. I hear my own voice like a whisper. It sounds childish now, indignant. *"Our hides when we turn. Not even Ugara's Spear can pierce it!"*

"No, son. It's our gift, our a'bara to touch others' states of mind and to hide our own."

I push out my a'bara once more, letting it ensnare them, wrap them in a floral aroma. I might not be a man grown yet, but boys have their own power.

"Please, sister." Instead of casting off an aura of attraction, I aim for a tone of innocence. "Can you help us?"

The women twitch in their stone-like postures. Deep down they know what I'm doing is unnatural but they can't resist my call. Their scowls and pointed brows ease into gentler expressions, their eyes softening to a mother's gaze.

A short moment passes and the women drop their baskets to the side, the grain rolling in the dirt. I have them now. Fresh confidence burns through my veins at the familiar rush of power and dominance. I'd normally take a moment to savor the sensation, but I know my limits well enough to know this won't hold for long. The shorter of the two seems particularly strong.

"We need Uzoma," I tell them. "We need his help. Can you take us to him?"

"Of course, little one." The taller one tilts her head, though it looks more like she's nodding off, bucking against sleep. The short woman does not respond, neck tensing. I might not be able to force her to speak for me, but I can keep her mouth shut, at least. So long as I funnel my focus on the other, we should be fine.

I push my a'bara out again, forcing the women into a hurried pace toward Uzoma's hut. I keep a straight face in front of the others. They're scared enough as it is; I can't let them know how hard this is for me.

When we catch sight of Uzoma's large home—guarded by two towering warriors that look more gorilla than human—I direct the women to work their own charm.

"This kid's amazing," I hear Pemba say from behind. I don't stop to take in the praise, waving a hand to another hut where we can hide as the women walk ahead.

The pair trade smiles with the warrior-guards, who look them up and down. Even without my influence, the men are already interested. Despite their intrigue, sweat beads on the top of my brow. This'll have to be fast. I can't hold out much longer.

"Come spend a few minutes by the river with us," the taller woman says.

I try to get the shorter of the two to add another flirtatious remark, but she does not heed me. Instead of smiling or flitting those rosy eyes like women do, she looks like she's smelled a bad fart.

"What's wrong with her?" One of the guards asks.

The taller woman steps in front, ignoring the guard's question. "Uzoma's a big boy. He can handle himself." She puts a finger on one warrior's broad chest.

The man removes the woman's finger. "Uzoma would kill us if we left our post."

The tall woman frowns as though discouraged by the man. I push against her resistance, try to get her to say something nice again, but she won't respond.

That's it; I've spent all the a'bara I can muster. Maybe I could get them to smile but I can't make them speak for me. I've never used the ability for more than a few minutes and never with two at once. It's hard enough with just the shorter woman straining against me, let alone the two of them.

As my control on them slips, the women's eyes go from seductive to strained. The shorter of the two clutches her temples.

"Something wrong?" the other warrior asks. He grabs her just before she falls. There's nothing I can do as they're freed from my influence.

There's an itch on my nose. I rub it and blood comes away on my fingers. My head spikes with needling pain. We need to run fast. They'll out us the first chance they get.

"It's just been a long day," the shorter woman says. But how? She should have been turning to where we hid, throwing a finger in our direction.

44

"Could you help me get her to the river?" The tall woman's voice is sultry again, but I have nothing to do with it.

What is this? My influence was gone. Why is she still playing the role of the coy maiden?

I jerk my head to the others. Sanje's eyes twist within themselves as he holds out a hand, the others mirroring his gesture. I turn back to the women. They walk off with the warriors, clearing our way to Uzoma's hut.

"Thank you," I say.

Sanje grabs my shoulder, holding it tight beneath his grasp. "Ask for our help next time, brother. And it's you I should be thanking."

"For what?" I ask through labored breaths.

"For reminding me we are beasts to be feared." Sanje's voice is dark, and I swear I see a fire deep in his eyes. He turns to the others. "Let's go kill us a legend."

Pemba and Kisama nod, smirks on their faces, their bodies tensed for the kill.

These are more like the kishi I'd want to fight alongside with, the kind my father rallied to his side. A loyal and able pack.

Did I underestimate their potential? For a moment I consider reframing the plan, but it's too late. We're here and there's no turning back. If they're worth their weight in salt, they'll come out of this alive. Otherwise, it's survival of the fittest.

I turn my head to Uzoma's hut. Now that we're here, I don't feel so bold. My mind keeps pulling itself back to the cave. Maybe it wouldn't be such a bad idea to retreat to the jungles, meet up with the other boys they mentioned, at least for now, at least until we're old enough when we could truly challenge Uzoma with our own army.

I shake the thought from my head as soon as it seeps in. If a coward like Sanje is ready to fight, I should be too.

Suddenly, Sanje speaks up. "Kisama, stay out here and keep watch."

The little boy frowns deeply. I wonder if that's how I looked when I protested Baba's decision in the cave. "I can do it, Sanje. I want to help."

Sanje puts a gentle hand to his brother's shoulder but I don't feel his a'bara soothing his him. He must know his words will be enough. He knows his brother will trust him. "You are helping. If them warriors come back, we gonna need a signal."

"Don't worry, little man," Pemba pats him on the back. "I'll get a stab in for you." Pemba pulls out his wooden stake from his loincloth.

"It'll only take a minute," I add. A lookout is a good idea, and for some reason, I don't want to see the little boy hurt.

It takes a moment, but Kisama agrees, crossing his arms and wearing a scowl I know all too well.

I turn my attention back to the hut. Uzoma is likely sleeping. But I wonder if he could sense the tricks we were playing on the women. No, if he did, he'd be outside his hut, looking for us already. How strong is a kishi in sleep, I wonder? Will he wake as soon as we enter his domain? Will our wooden stakes even be strong enough to pierce his skin?

The others still do not understand who the Great and Mighty truly is. Their fearlessness stems from the idea that, after all, Uzoma is only human. If only that were the truth. Perhaps then the fluttering in my stomach would go away. I try to keep reminding myself that Uzoma is powerless in this village too, but it doesn't help much.

I step forward toward the hut, pulling at the straw door that covers the threshold into the home. Inside, it's dark and deep, like the mouth of a cave ready to swallow us whole. I feel the nervous energy from the others, but it's no longer the fear I've felt from them all night. Now it's the anticipation of the hunt.

Get yourself together, Yemi. Even they're ready.

Cool air from within brings bumps to my skin. I stifle a shiver as my eyes adjust to the darkened room. It's a simple home, divided into two areas, a small place for a fire and pot and another for bedding.

Flickering embers smolder under the pot and from its depths spews an awful smell of iron mixed with urine. I don't think it's *actually* urine, obviously. If I'm placing the smell right, it's a medicinal potion and a strong one at that. The boys smell it too, covering their noses and mouths with their hands.

Breathing through my mouth, I turn my attention to the bed, where a lump rises and falls deeply under a set of animal skins. I can't stop my heart from pounding as I pull out my wooden stake. I hear the subtle brush of wood against loincloth from behind; Sanje must be mirroring my movement.

This is it. We will kill Uzoma and avenge Baba and all the others this traitor has killed.

My lips part as I lift my stake high above my head. Tension rushes my hand as I pull the animal skins from the lump in one tug, like plucking a thorn from the skin.

But underneath is a small woman with full lips and tiny eyes. Who is she? Did we enter the wrong hut?

At first, silence stuns the woman, but quickly her eyes go as wide as the moons. Before she screams her eyes drop into a dewy gaze like the women from before. But I did nothing to influence her. Must have been Sanje saving my ass again.

I turn to the boys and my heart stops. It's not Sanje who's holding the woman.

At the mouth of the hut looms a dark, broad figure, a familiar cackle echoing from the shadow. Before I can shout

47

a warning, the figure grabs the back of Pemba's neck with a crunch. I think I hear the stout boy say "get off of me" before his neck snaps and he drops limply to the floor.

I try to transform but the village's magic still holds my hyena in its mystical chains. Yet Uzoma, somehow, blocks our path in his full kishi form. How has he changed when we cannot? Is he truly so powerful to negate the shaman's magic? There's no shortage of surprises with this two-timer. And he has us right where he wants us.

There is only one way in and one way out.

I've led us straight into a trap.

But that's what I wanted, wasn't it? The boys were supposed to act as a distraction. Pemba was always going to be a sacrifice. But I was hoping he'd be more useful than a quick kill. I do my best not to move my eyes to his slump body in the dirt.

Sanje is the first to spring an attack, stabbing out with his stake. Uzoma bats it away like the boy had attacked him with a feather and the stake goes bouncing off the wall.

I jump forward, slashing at Uzoma's leg, but before my strike is even halfway to its target, I'm met with the heel of Uzoma's foot to my face. I fly back hard against the wall with a deafening thud, blood spurting from my mouth.

Sanje is at it again, coming at Uzoma with his fists. The boy has heart—I'll give him that. He even seems to keep up with the older man. How? Not even Baba could match him. It looks as though Uzoma is pulling his punches and his hyena head is slow to bite. Is he toying with us?

For an instant I see Uzoma's snarl twist into a wince. No, he's not playing with us; it's the wound at his side. The one Baba inflicted. The man must be hurting badly. My mind flickers to the urine-smelling potion. He must have still been healing. Maybe we still have a chance.

I lift to my feet again, coming in with my stake raised high. Before I can bring the sharp wood down, I'm slapped away once more, straight back into the wall. It and I are becoming fast friends.

Sanje keeps at it but he isn't doing any damage. Uzoma's mostly grabbing at him but Sanje slips out of reach each time.

I've never seen a kishi fight like Uzoma does. Half-human and a half-hyena. At one moment he's using his hyena maw to snap and bite, and in the next he's transformed, using human fists like the fighting-men. Was this what Baba had to deal with? An entirely new form of dual kishi and human fighting?

With all that thrown at Sanje, none of this feels right. Even if the kid was the best young fighter we kishi had, and I know he isn't, Uzoma's injury shouldn't be hindering him to where he's *actually* struggling.

A jolt from the bed draws my attention. The woman seems to be half-flailing against the covers of the skins. That's it. Uzoma's still controlling her, his attention split. And not just that. He's protecting her, fighting defensively.

I can use that.

I grab my stake again, but this time, instead of attacking Uzoma, I go for the woman.

"Let us go or... I'll kill her." My voice shakes more than I expect.

Uzoma smacks Sanje across the jaw, forcing him into the wall. I can't see the man's face, but I expect his eyes are shooting fire. In an instant, he's on top of me, clutching at my neck, hyena paw transformed into human hand. I'm utterly useless, squirming against his hold, kicking and flailing to no avail.

I failed. Baba would be ashamed to see me now as I flounder around like a trout out of the water.

So I stop. I won't die like this, scared and desperate. Darkness curls around my vision as Uzoma's grip crunches the muscles in my neck. Only another second and...

"Run!" Sanje shouts as he throws the hot pot onto Uzoma's wound.

The man lets out a howl, dropping me to the ground. Sanje pulls at my arm and drags me out of the hut. I'm too dizzy to keep pace with him.

"We have to go back," I mutter to him, but he keeps dragging me away. I don't have the strength to fight him as he tugs me through the night.

"What happened? Where's Pemba?" I hear Kisama's voice, though I can't see him right through my bleary vision.

"Not now." Sanje shoots a cold look down at me. Through my spotted vision, I see what look like tears welling in his eyes. He's doing a good job of holding them in as he spits out a snarl of frustration. "We have to run."

FIVE

WE NEVER LOOK BACK AS WE RUSH ALONG THE NYOKA River. Blood cakes my paws and hind legs. I try to forget that it's Pemba's. It's not lost on me that the blood could have easily been mine, with my mangled body on the floor of Uzoma's hut and the others running away.

The moons peek through sheets of black and gray clouds as if they fear the raging storm that finally approaches. Beetle-sized rain drops pound against our backs, leaving welts on delicate human skin, and a terrible wind howls in my ears.

At least it's washing away the blood.

The faster we run, the more the deluge seems to pour, our paws sinking into pools of mud. With each footfall we fall deeper into the earth, disrupting our purchase with it. I try my best not to slip as Sanje and Kisama pull ahead.

None of us dare to stop until fatigue forces us into the muck, our backs too heavy to carry us any farther. Leagues of farmland surround us, filled with tall green plants I don't know the name of.

I see the jaws of hyena everywhere, their fangs stretched across the teeth of the leaves or their heads jutting out from our imprints left in the mud. It's my mind playing tricks on me, I know, but knowing doesn't help. And the images of hyena aren't just in the sprouts or the dirt, but in the storm clouds above and the streaks of lightning that flash across the dark sky. They're everywhere. Each wailing gust sounds like a hyena's cackle to my ears. I need to get a grip on myself. No one was chasing us when we ran from the village, and we're impossible to track in this storm.

But how could we fail so badly? How had Uzoma known we were coming? None of us were in kishi form—though we were influencing those women. Was that the giveaway? Or can he sense us no matter what form we take? Even if we could switch to kishi form, we wouldn't be a challenge for him, injury or not. But there had to be some way to bring him down.

A straight attack will never work. He'll always know we're coming. We'll have to play the long game, like wood and marbles with Baba. Though I often won at the beginning of that game, he always came back to beat me in the later rounds.

"It's all about positioning," he would say.

No matter how long it takes, I have to find a way, whether it's a week, a moon, or five harvests from now. Somehow, I need to set him up, let everyone in the village know who he truly is. And to do that, I have to be one of them, earn the humans' trust the same way Uzoma did.

"Did you see what he did to Pemba?" Sanje says, still catching his breath. "Snapped his neck like it was nothing."

How could they be thinking about Pemba? We needed to figure out a way to get back there and not end up like him.

Kisama's cheeks stream with wetness. It looks like rain at first, but then it's obvious that the streaks are tears.

"Buck up, Kisama," I say, taking on the tone Baba did

whenever I cried. "You're not a cub anymore. Stop that crying."

Sanje lifts on his elbows, his voice has an edge of warning. "Watch who you're talking to, brother."

"There's no time for this." I snap back. "We're at war. Don't you get it? We need to think about how we're going to get back into the village. We just have to be smarter about —"

"*Back* to the village?" Sanje snarls. I can't see his face but his tone tells me it's fixed with disgust and bewilderment. "Pemba's dead. Our *friend* is dead. If my little brother wants to cry, then he should."

Kisama buries his face in the mud, hiding his tears, probably from me.

Sanje rubs his brother's bare back, encouraging the tears. I fight back a grimace at his needless coddling. Were it my father I'd get a much different response, one that resulted in welts and bruises.

Another moment of nursing and Sanje turns to me, his voice low and dark. "So Uzoma's a kishi too?"

"Seems that way," I say slowly. The change in the boy's tune has me nervous.

For what feels like several minutes, Sanje is staring at me in the dark and my chest fills with that sensation we kishi use to influence others. What is he trying to pry? Does he think he's strong enough to get the truth from me? After a moment the sensation spills away, but Sanje keeps to staring.

"And you knew?" he finally asks. I can only guess at the ugly look he's giving me. My first instinct is to lie, but something halts the falsehood at the tip of my tongue.

Sanje tilts his head to the side as though searching my eyes through the shadows. "You set us up..." A streak of lightning brightens across his face, and with it, a realization flashes across his eyes suddenly, the honey hue of his irises flaring like a flame. His voice is barely above a whisper. "That your plan this whole time?"

"We can still kill him," I shout defiantly, ignoring his question. "We just need to go about it a different way, is all."

Another streak of lightning dances across the dark clouds, revealing another face of contempt from Sanje. Kisama stops his crying, lifting his head from the mud to listen to our conversation. My heart beats strong against my chest. The truth would come out one way or the other.

"You didn't care shit about us, did you?" Sanje's voice sounds almost like a man grown. "You don't care that Pemba got slaughtered at all, *do you*?" Each accusation was meant to hit deep but somehow it all feels so hollow.

"Of course I did…" I stammer, but the words ring false even to my own ears. I'm glad it was him and not me. That's the truth. I barely knew the boy. Besides, he was the last one in; he should have had our backs. If he would've just done his job right, we wouldn't have been trapped like that and he might still be alive. "I didn't know Uzoma could change in the village."

"So you admit it," Kisama says. His small voice next to his brother's booming one does more to me than anything else. For the briefest of moments, there's something like remorse in my heart. I drive it out straight away. These boys are weak and they want me weak as well. I'm not letting that happen.

Sanje stands tall, a grand silhouette across the lightning-struck sky, reminding me he has height and weight to his advantage. Does he mean to fight me?

I start to lift myself from the mud when little Kisama speaks. "Come on, Sanje." His head darts from him to me. "If we leave now, we can be to the jungles in two weeks, like Baba said. The other boys might not have gone in yet."

"No, I'm not done with this one yet." Sanje takes a step

toward me. I stand up quickly, tensing my muscles. Sanje doesn't have his palms out and open anymore.

"Listen to me," I say, jabbing a finger with each word. "I was wrong to attack tonight. I'll admit that much. But we can still kill him. I want him dead more than anything else. You know that."

"No more of your words." Sanje stalks closer. He's just waiting for the right time to pounce.

I back away. There has to be a way for him to see reason. "Look at our wounds." I throw out my arms to him. "We can use them to our advantage. The villagers will think *we* were the ones attacked by kishi."

"What about the women who saw us?" Kisama asks.

I bite at my lip as Sanje backs me down in the mud. "We can deal with them. We just have to—"

Sanje scowl halts me. There's murder in his eyes. "Do you ever stop talking?"

I try to throw out my kishi influence. "Sanje, you're not thinking here. You're just afraid, is all."

"It's you who's in your fear. The hell you need us for? To die like Pemba?"

"Of course not." I push on my a'bara some more. Sanje halts in his stomp.

Did it work?

The older boy's mouth goes flat, almost slack. The surrounding sound seems to go dead quiet. Even the thunder has subsided. "I know damn well you're not trying to *soothe* me."

"I…" is all I say before Sanje leaps into the air, tearing into kishi form. I shift in the same instant, and we meet in midair in a clash of paw-strikes and snapping bites, our howls and grunts muted by the thunderclaps that play audience, an applause to each strike and push.

Neither of us is at our best but we give it our all. I snap at his heels and he snaps at my neck, each fighting for balance in the mud. Then suddenly, I trip and Sanje's fangs are in my shoulder. I twist away, and flesh rips with it.

How had I tripped? I made sure not to fall in any of the pools of muck.

Before I can see what disrupted my balance, I'm on my back again. This time Sanje's biting at my side. I throw my fist into his ears, using Uzoma's dual fighting methods, until Sanje lets go.

Bounding away, I look to the ground again. It's uneven and lumpy, sure, but there's nothing I could have tripped on, so what happened?

There's a rustling of plants to my right. From the stalks comes a tiny paw sweeping at my legs. I jump over it just in time. It's Kisama. I hadn't been stumbling over my own feet, but his. The little shit was playing dirty.

My hyena head gives a low growl and I pounce into the brush. My bite catches nothing but thorns and sap. I turn just in time to find both brothers lunging for me with their maws, Kisama on my leg and Sanje back on my shoulder. I struggle against their weight but it's no use; they have me pinned. I've lost. Once my body goes limp they pull away, hovering over me like the hyenas they are.

I don't got the strength to retreat. I'm not even sure I can stand at all.

"My Baba says we don't kill our own," Sanje finally says. Though exhaustion—and a bit of anger—undercuts his voice, he sounds oddly sincere. Still weak, even in victory.

I know I've lost but I can't help opening my mouth again. "That's because your father was weak. It's why he's dead."

Sanje jumps on me again, his hyena head over my neck. "I *could* kill you." He turns to his little brother, who looks anxious. "But I know you gonna go to that village. And you gonna get yourself killed anyway."

"You're a fool, then," I spit. "I'd kill you if I were in your position."

Sanje draws his head closer to my neck. I'm ready for the final bite, but instead, I'm met with his soft pitch. "I'm not you, Yemi. This war might have brought the worst from you, but I know what truly matters now. A lone kishi is weak. The pack, together, is strong. We coulda won this war if we knew that, if we wasn't fighting each other as much as we should have been fighting them. One day, I hope you get that."

He lifts himself from my body, letting me breathe freely again. I try not to gasp for the air I sorely need. I may have lost but I don't dare look defeated.

"Let's go, Kisama." Sanje gestures to his brother, who I now see has a bloody maw. "We need to be far away before day breaks. If Yemi goes back like he says he will, he could buy us some time."

Kisama follows him without protest, blood dripping into the dirt from his mouth. It's only a short moment before they disappear into the crops.

I look down at my leg where Kisama took his bite. It's a bloody mess but not too deep. The little boy hadn't committed to the bite.

I drag myself awkwardly to the river to wash my wounds. My calves tense once the water touches the open cuts. Clenching my jaw, I dip my body in further.

As I lie here wincing in the water, I consider Sanje's words. They were sweet sentiments for a fairytale, but far from practical. Our kind is a violent one, held together by the will of our strongest brothers, not the weakness of a herd.

Sanje is right about one thing, however. Though I'm alone, wounded, and without allies, I'll still go back to the village. But not yet. I'm not ready. I need to learn how to control the hyena if I'm ever going to gain the villagers' trust. There had to be a way to hide it for more than an hour. Uzoma must've been hiding his for years. I just don't know how I'll do it without the others' help.

I drift off undecided, tucked away between a row of plants, falling to a deep and troubled sleep.

SIX

I WAKE WITH MY NOSE IN THE DIRT AND SOMEONE'S fingers in my hair. Rolling onto my back, I kick out instinctively, eyes still blurry from sleep.

"Get off of me!" I shout at the figure above.

"You one of them kishi who attacked last night?" comes a deep, guttural voice.

My heart quickens. I should have walked farther before giving in to my fatigue. My legs are still sprawled against the river's edge, one foot slumped over the bank. How long had the man been going through my hair? Without thought, I hide my hyena head, sinking it back into the recesses of my hair.

"I'm not no... whatever you just said," I say as I slap the man's hands from my head. He's silhouetted against the morning sun painted by rolling clouds though I make out his set of broad shoulders. Was he one of Uzoma's warrior-guards from last night?

A string full of what looks like hyena fangs drapes his neck. Many of the Bajoki warriors wore them as prizes. This man must have killed six kishi if my count is right. He doesn't have a weapon with him though. That's good. I

59

just need to create some distance between us, then I can make a break for it. But my aching muscles argue otherwise. They feel as sore as they ever have, every cut and wound forcing my body into the dried mud with the weights of bagged rice.

"Then what's this?" He overpowers me, turning my face into the dirt. He digs his hands back into my hair but finds nothing. At first, his hands work slowly, likely nervous of reaching into a wild dog's maw, but when he doesn't find what he's looking for he starts pulling at my locs angrily.

"Ah, stop!" I cry in pain. "I told you I'm not one of them."

"Why your hair not cut?" he asks when he finally releases my head.

"I didn't know it needed to be." I shuffle away from the man. I can see him full in the light now. His muscles seem to have muscles, and his jaw is as wide as the Nyoka. Scars cross his torso and arms, most of them cuts, others, bites.

At least some of my brothers fought well.

"What are you doing out here?" the man asks, looking me up and down. I don't think it's appropriate to ask for his name so I just call him Muscles.

I try to lift myself to my feet but my body will not have it. I need to come up with a story quickly. I had a plan yesterday, right? Right.

"I was attacked by a beast," I finally get out. The story sells better if I don't know the name. The less I "know" the less I have to lie. "It bit me all over. Looked like a wild dog, but it was huge!"

Muscles raises an eyebrow at me. "Where you from?"

"Guela," I lie.

"You're a long way from home…" The warrior trails, his tone a question.

"We was attacked by them beasts like I said…" I don't know why I'm talking like Sanje, but I am. It sounds like how one of the Guela should speak. That's what he and Kisama sounded like to me, at least. "They got my Baba. He died so I could escape." Not entirely a lie.

Muscles pushes his meaty hand into his chin, his forehead curled in thought. "You're coming with me. It ain't safe out here alone."

I scoot away in the dirt, fighting with my tender wounds. "I don't know you."

"Don't matter. You'll still come." He scoops me up without effort, slinging me over his shoulder. My mud-caked body flakes over his back. I think on making a fuss. Maybe I should pound his chest? But if I'm really supposed to play the role of some scared human child, I should embrace the kind and open arms of a stranger. But with my extra weight, it'll take at least two hours to return to the village.

I've never suppressed my head for so long.

"As soon as we get back, you need to get that hair cut," he says as we pass along a farm of bean plants.

I protest, adding Kisama's whining tone. "But Baba says that'll kill the ancestors that live in my hair."

"Tradition don't matter anymore."

As we approach the great village, it looks even more foreboding than before. The boys and I didn't take the main path to Bajok, instead keeping off-trail. But as the village walls grow nearer, stakes dot the horizon line, each topped with small specks.

Oh, Dulagi'ala. Those dots are heads!

It's not until we're a few paces away that I can smell them, rancid and ripe. Flies buzz around sunken cheeks and graying skin. As we pass each stake, the warrior shoos away vulture after vulture. But the moment the birds know we're out of reach they return to continue their feast, battling over tongues and eyeballs.

The foul stench fills my nose and crawls straight down into my stomach. If I had eaten anything in the past day, it would've come up on the warrior's back.

Thankfully, most of the heads had decayed. I don't know if I could control myself if I had recognized one of the heads. If I had seen him...

My heart races as a snout curls through my locs. My hyena strains to see his brothers, letting out a small cry.

Muscles stops in his tracks. He lowers his back and looks through the brush next to us. "What was that?"

I convulse, forcing my hyena back into my head. "I ain't heard nothing."

It's a long moment before the warrior rises from his crouched position. His hand hovers next to his waist, grabbing at nothing. Had he lost his weapon in the storm? Eventually he walks forward again, this time at a slower pace, taking his time to listen for every squawk and trill across the plains.

Every agonizing second this warrior takes to get to the village, the harder it is for me to suppress my hyena. He wants so bad to see his brothers again, to play with them as he did with Baba's corpse.

Just get to the damned village, I want to tell the large man. I hate that I have to rely on the magic's protection to save me. But it's the only way I'll survive. Another moment and there's nothing I can do to stop it. Maybe if I only let him out for a little while. Just for a little relief. I'd only need to stop his crying. I still have my hair, after all, at least until we get to the village's gates.

Just as I let my hyena breathe new air, my eyes settle on the next kishi head raised on a stake.

It's Pemba's.

His face hasn't rotted yet — that might have been better.

Had it rotted it wouldn't be able to stare straight at me with those wide and petrified eyes of his. A small pang of guilt cuts through me. I turn away, biting at my lip to repress the cry and howl that wants to escape from the back of my head.

That was a mistake. Pemba's face is nothing compared to the head mounted across from his.

Empty, gaping sockets pierce straight to my heart, and my head swims. The eyes are lost to the vultures still circling above. An impossible expression etches the face, something between shock and pain sunken into itself like a caving candle. It's too much, but I can't look away.

Baba...

I hadn't seen his face when he died. I wish I never had. Tears stream down my face. For once, I just can't help but let them fall. Each drop rolls down the warrior's back, like a river cutting through a deep valley.

Muscles turns to me. "Sorry you had to see all this. It's for *them*. Not for you."

This time it's my hyena that seems to console me as it nuzzles my hair. Every tear that drops gives way to another and another until I'm sobbing.

"What's that you got there?" another man's voice yells from across the path.

"Found this little one out in the farmlands." Muscles drops me gently to the ground as though he doesn't want to disturb my weeping. I still can't stand, so I slump to one side in the dirt, my tears pocketing the earth with mud.

Through my watery vision, the second warrior-guard tilts his head down at me, a big gap between the teeth in his wide mouth. "What's wrong with him?" he asks.

"Says he's from Guela," Muscles says. "Kishi got to his family."

Snot dots my nostrils as the warrior-guards let me cry, giving me space to heave and cough. I've never cried like

63

this before. I've wept and whined, but my father would never have allowed sobbing. It's like I've built a fountain of tears over the years and they're all flowing free.

Funny, I thought the act would make me feel weak, hollow, useless. But as I let out my last shuddering sob, I don't feel worse—I feel better, the way you feel after you throw up a bad meal. And what remains is a clarity I never thought I could achieve. My body is free of that crushing weight, the chains around my heart, the lock I feared would break open. I feel lighter.

I touch the back of my head, rubbing my hand as the wet snout licks my palm. Slowly, my hyena head recedes into my skin once more, with no outcry or lashes at my hair. I don't even have to bite down on my tongue for the pain, the source of what I thought was my greatest power over my hyena.

"*What is our greatest strength as kishi?*" Baba's voice says to me again.

Empathy, I reply.

I hadn't mastered control over him because I lacked the truth of that one word. Empathy was not a one-way path. It was a split, fissured thing as diverse as the colors of the rainbow and as branching as the bough of a tree.

I couldn't hold my hyena down because I did not truly understand him. How could I when all I showed it was anger and resentment? I played at odds to him when I should have listened, felt, accepted, ebbing and flowing in concert with him like the tracks of my tears.

It's why I couldn't hold the women for long as well. I was dominating their will with my own. I should have been guiding them, not forcing them. To bind them fully would take knowing their hearts better than any could in one night alone.

That's what it meant to be a kishi, not our strong hides or our fangs, but our intimate knowledge of the soul and what feeds it, whether through pain, fear, joy, or even sadness.

Suddenly there's a hand on my shoulder. I turn to see Muscles looking down on me with somber eyes. I didn't even need my a'bara to bring this one's guard down. My own emotion, my true sorrow, was already working plenty.

"I know it's rough, but we've won this thing," he says.

No, you haven't.

I gaze up at the village wall. This close, without my kishi form, it looks even taller than before and it feels like every warrior, with their sharp spears and trained bows at the ready, is looking straight down at me.

"So is the boy one of them or not?" the man with the tooth gap says.

"I thought so at first," Muscles says. "But I didn't see any snout."

Tooth Gap sucks his teeth. "He's got them golden eyes though, don't he?"

"So does Uzoma. And so does your cousin, and they ain't kishi."

Tooth Gap flaps a dismissive hand. "Yeah, yeah, but he's a cheetah-shifter, ain't he?" The man tilts his head down at me. "You some shifter too?"

I shake my head, but I think of another lie. "My... mother was one though."

"There." Muscles says as though that resolved it. "Can I borrow that?" He points to the dagger at the guard's side.

"Have at it," Tooth Gap says, handing over his weapon.

I realize that I can have them cut my hair inside the village. "Why aren't we going inside?"

Muscles frowns. "It has to be done here." He cuts my first loc. "We've got protection against them kishi." He cuts a second. "Even if we cut their hair inside, their hyena head don't show." I swallow hard, trying not to look at all the faces I recognize on the stakes. Especially not his. My third loc is cut when I feel a familiar cracking at the back of my head.

What's going on? I thought I had my second head under control.

"You found another one out there?" comes a gravelly voice from the other side of the gate. When I see the familiar face through the slits of the log gate, I understand why my hyena's blood is running hot.

Uzoma stands tall, his eyes pushing past the warrior-guards and straight at me. Why's he here? Has he sensed me as he had before?

The men stand up straight, chests out in honor of their village's hero. Lucky me, another cut and Muscles would have seen a wet snout cresting from my skin.

"We're not sure, War Chief," Muscles says. "I was just cutting his hair now."

My hyena urges to push out of my head and attack. I tell it to settle down before it gets us both killed.

Uzoma lifts a finger and throws it left and right. "Now, now, I'm not War Chief. You know that."

"Of course. My mistake, Uzoma." Muscles stands as still as a stone.

"Open the gate," Uzoma commands. Tooth Gap pushes the gate open without a second thought, his lax smile wiped for a warrior's gaze, his movement succinct.

A nervous heat climbs my spine, rising to the edge of panic as Uzoma walks through. His eyes never leave mine, nor mine his. It's probably better if I stop staring. I knew I'd have to meet him again at some point. Now is not the time to lose my nerve like some whimpering pup. A low growl echoes through my mind. I don't dare lift my hands to stop it; it'd just give me away.

Quiet!

"I'll take over from here," Uzoma says suddenly, holding his hand out to Muscles. The warrior-guard doesn't spare even a second before handing his dagger to the larger man. To think I had thought him large before. He looked like a child compared to Uzoma. Each time I had seen the traitor it was in the dark or from afar. Now, full in the light of day, it made all the sense in the world that he could defeat Baba and the rest. I'm not sure how anyone could defeat him.

Uzoma drops to one knee, gritting his teeth. A collection of *dawa* root covers the wound at his side, held together by twine. It takes him a breath of a second to cut three of my locs.

"Where are you from, boy?" His question sounds more like a demand.

"Guela," I say as three more locs drop into the dirt. My throat goes dry. I've stopped my hyena from growing past a tuft of hair, but any more and Uzoma will see. I can't blame my second head for his bloodlust. I feel it too. The traitor's only a finger's length from us. It would only take a second. One quick bite at this neck and...

No. He's baiting me like he's been baiting all of us this whole time. That's what he wants me to do. He wants me to reveal myself.

"Guela, you say." He continues cutting at my hair, already finished with the left side and moving to the right. "So the rest of those *filthy beasts* are cowering to the north then." He puts a nasty emphasis on "filthy beasts." I won't react. It will not work; I won't let it. I've just got to keep this damned snout under my hair.

As Uzoma starts to cut at the front of my hair, he looks at me again. I have enough sense now to look away. But for a moment he sits there, examining me as though daring me to look back.

"Do I know you, boy?"

My breath quickens. Uzoma isn't even attempting to hide that he's trying to influence me. How would I resist him without him knowing?

"My family says I look like my mother." It's not a lie. Baba always said I had her face and his eyes.

Uzoma purses his lips. A chill crawls down my body. He doesn't believe me, does he? He keeps trying to force his influence into my mind, prying at my truth as though gutting a fish. I have to make him believe he's ensnared me, that he's in control. How do I do that while hiding my vengeful hyena at the same time?

"Your eyes have been filled with nothing but malice since I arrived, boy," he finally says as he lops off five more locs. "Why do you make such eyes at me?"

I settle my expression, letting my pain be my foundation. My words come cold and true. "You killed my father."

Uzoma stops his cutting, a new light shining in his honeyed eyes. "Did I now?"

"You didn't even care," I spit in a fury.

"How'd you figure that, boy?" The dagger in his hand glints against the morning sun. I can almost hear its call, its sharp tongue ready to taste my neck.

I measure my words carefully before I speak, looking Uzoma dead in the eye. "You and your warriors care only for Bajok. You let my father die when the demons attacked."

"Oh," Uzoma says, letting out a small sigh. "Yes, I've been telling our War Chief we should have continued our sweep to the north."

The strain in my neck finally subsides. The snout retracts into smooth skin once more.

"I'll never forgive you for what you did," I growl. "You brought this war on us. We never asked for it."

Uzoma looks back to the warrior-guards. Neither of them dares to look at him or me, no semblance of agreement crossing their faces. The others on the walls have lowered their spears and bows, awaiting Uzoma's response.

"You are right..." he tells me, looking for a name.

68

I reply defiantly. "Yemi."

"Yemi," he repeats. "I can do better. I *will* do better." He turns to his comrades once more. "On *Àyá's* next forest moon, we will help our brothers and sisters of the former Golah. This I promise you all." He turns to me. "And to you, young one."

The energy among the warriors calms. A feeling of achievement rolls through me. I've accomplished all this with nothing but my words and eyes. No need for my a'bara at all.

It only takes another moment for Uzoma to finish off the rest of my hair, all of it scattered in the dirt like a nest of serpents. I run my hand over my head; it's the first time I've felt the coarse stubble of short hairs along my dome. The air against my bare skin feels oddly satisfying.

"All right then." Muscles approaches us. "Let's get the boy to the medicine man. Them wounds will only get worse."

"Yes, yes, let him see the shaman." Uzoma waves for the warrior to take me away.

Just as Muscles lifts me, a trill splits the morning sky. In the distance, an osprey glides from the blue, straight down to the village gates. But it couldn't be any ordinary osprey; it's flight path's too direct. This has to be a shifter.

A few strides away from us, the hawk transforms into a young woman—no, a girl—only a few years older than me. Her hair looks almost like a nest, sticking out at odd angles, and her head swivels in an endless twitch.

"They found them! Out by leopard's gorge," she says quickly, her voice pitched high. "Two boys with the heads of hyenas."

I swallow hard. She could only mean Sanje and Kisama.

SEVEN

I INSIST THAT I BE TAKEN TO THE VILLAGE SHAMAN, playing up the pain in my wounds. If Sanje and Kisama see me, they'll rat me out, no question. Muscles agrees that I should be taken in. My hair was already cut, after all. But Tooth Gap comes ambling about, his wry smile returning as he gives me a sidelong glance.

"How many of them boys did you say attacked last night?" he asks Uzoma.

The Kishi Killer rubs his bare chin with the flat of his dagger in thought. "There were three."

"Three, he says." Tooth Gap looks between me and the two small dots approaching over the farmland horizon. What looks like four warrior-guards surround the tiny, faint figures in the distance.

I almost shout a retort that if there are two boys coming and three attacked, the third couldn't be me when Pemba's head hung dead on the stake. But Yemi from Guela wouldn't know any of that. All he knows is that he was attacked by two beasts, beasts who have plagued his humble village. In fact, his face shouldn't be shocked at all.

If anything, Yemi from Guela should enjoy seeing whoever it was who attacked him.

The change on my face comes too late for Tooth Gap though. His eyes bore into me. He must know I have something to hide.

"We'll call the medicine man once everything's figured out," he says. "A few more minutes ain't gonna make a difference."

I bite the inside of my cheek. I want so bad to say his reasoning doesn't work. Hadn't Uzoma or Muscles realized his count was off? But the pair of them seem more intrigued with my reaction than Tooth Gap's words. And Muscles can't stop looking at the back of my head. With all their eyes on me, there's nothing I can do but put on the right mask and hope they don't start pointing fingers.

I dig my nails into my hands to stop their fidgeting as we watch the group change from indistinct hazes to the detailed figures of people. Sanje and Kisama are dragged by large men who lead them by ropes. Fifty paces away and I can see their hair is half cut, mostly at the back, where their hyena heads snap at the air.

I look up to Muscles at my side, trying my best to put on the voice of a frightened boy. "Them the boys who attacked me, ain't they?" I can't help but think I sound like Kisama.

Muscles turns his eyes down to mine. He gives me a half-shrug. "They could be."

"Why ain't they dead?" I ask, moving behind Muscles' tree-trunk leg. To him, it may look as though I'm afraid of them, but it's really a way for me to hide my face from the boys. Perhaps they won't recognize me right away with my head shaved clean like this.

"That's a good question," he says to me, then turns to Uzoma. "I thought we was ordered to kill them on sight."

Uzoma doesn't turn to answer. Maybe he's too preoccupied trying to identify the boys himself. But he answers offhandedly after a short while. "Yes, that's true. But I ordered the others to bring them in alive. I've some questions for the cubs."

It's only another moment before the boys are brought before our small group. I look back up the village wall. The spearmen and archers stand firm again, their weapons trained on the pair of kishi boys.

I'm only a few paces from Uzoma and the others. If anything goes wrong, I could make a run for it through the bean plants just next to the village wall. Uzoma wouldn't risk turning in front of so many humans and I'd be fast enough to get across the Nyoka. A twitch in my muscles reminds me that won't happen. Without proper care, I won't be doing any running. I need to settle my nerves. I've gotten out of two close calls today already. What's one more?

I step from behind Muscles' leg to see Sanje and Kisama. Sanje is bleeding from the mouth, lip swollen like he's been stung by a bee. Kisama's got a big welt over his eye, like a piece of *fufu* is stuck under his skin. Their chins slump against their chests. They avoid the eye contact I'm sure Uzoma is penetrating them with. Or perhaps they're averting their eyes from the heads on the stakes. Had they seen Pemba already?

Part of me wants to smile at their misfortune. It serves them right to attack me and leave me alone out in the middle of nowhere. Yet the feeling of retribution never comes. Had it not been for Sanje's words or Kisama's tears, I might have been dead already, uncovered as a kishi who couldn't hide his head. I owe them... something, don't I? I drive out the thought as soon as it comes. I didn't come all this way to sacrifice myself for them.

Uzoma leans down to the boys, dropping his head to

their downcast faces. He holds his dagger in a loose and casual grip, as though baiting the boys to go for it like he had with me. "I don't want to spend too much time with questions, so I'll make it quick. Are there more of you out there?" The man bobs his head from boy to boy, his voice almost too matter-of-fact, callous. "If you do not tell me, I'll stake you alive, simple as that."

Sanje's face is fixed with stone. I'm not sure he's even moved since he was thrown to the ground. Even his hyena head has stopped its biting. Uzoma isn't going to get anything out of him.

Kisama, on the other hand, is the opposite of his brother. His chest convulses, heaving up and down like a cheetah after a chase with a gazelle.

"Hey." Uzoma slaps Kisama across the face, releasing tears held back from the boy. "You don't have any right to cry right now. You attacked me. You better own to that —"

"I... I never... attacked you..." Kisama stammers, each word harder to get out than the last.

Uzoma slaps him again. "Don't lie to me, beast."

"I ain't..." Kisama cries, nursing his reddening eye with his bound hands.

Kisama's pleas tug at my heart as an uncomfortable knot expands in my throat. The little boy doesn't deserve this. But better him than me, right? Somehow the thought doesn't make me feel any better.

"There was..." Kisama utters.

"What? There was what?" Uzoma bellows.

"Another boy..."

Fear slices through me. He is going to betray me. So they had seen me, hadn't they? My previous sorrow for them falls away instantly. I can play that game too.

"They attacked me!" I point from behind Muscles' leg. "Them boys attacked me last night."

Sanje and Kisama look up to me in unison, their mouths

agape. A new light sparks in their golden eyes as they recognize me. So they hadn't seen me. Kisama was talking about Pemba. I swallow hard at my mistake, but I have to own up to it.

In an instant, their miserable faces turn hot with anger as they shout down my accusation. I scream back all the same and we enter a battle of who can raise their voices higher than the others. The warriors hold them back as they try to come at me.

"Silence!" Uzoma's booming voice cuts through our argument, making our voices sound like thin cries next to his growl, the kind you feel in your chest, like a lion's roar. Once we've all shut our mouths, he continues. "I'll listen to what each of you has to say. But if anyone of you talks out of turn, I'll kill you straight away, got it?"

Our silence is all the answer he needs.

"You can't believe them, Uzoma," Muscles says. "We cut the boy's hair. He ain't no kishi."

Tooth Gap grabs at my shoulder, making me grimace. "What about these bites? He ain't no kishi now, but come Àyá's next…"

That's not how it works, you fool.

Just as I catch myself from saying the thought out loud, Uzoma twists on his heel and faces the warrior-guards. "Who told you that crap? The beasts don't turn humans through bites. You know that, Awa." So that's Tooth Gap's name. "Were it true, you and the others would have turned moons ago."

"That's 'cause we got fixed up right away," he's quick to say. "This boy's had his wounds for hours —"

Uzoma's glare halts whatever Tooth Gap's about to say. When he's satisfied with the warrior's silence, he turns to me. "Let's hear from you first. What's your telling of it?"

My gaze shifts from Uzoma to the boys. Fury and

betrayal fill their eyes, Sanje with his scowl and Kisama with his doe eyes.

"It happened like I said," I start. "I was running from Guela when they saw me. They attacked me next to the river."

"And why didn't they kill you, then?" Tooth Gap asks. Muscles seems to be pondering the same thing. The other warriors holding the boys await my response with bated breaths. I swear I see a shadow of a smirk on Sanje's bloody lips. He knows I don't have a good response to the question.

I bite at my lip before I come up with my story. Part of me wants to say, *I don't know. Why don't you ask them?* But that's the wrong play here. I can't give them control of the story. So instead I say, "I think I caught them off guard. They wasn't interested in me. Looked like they was running away from something. When I fought back, they just kept to running. I heard them talking about some name…" I act like I've forgotten.

"What? What name?" Muscles asks down to me.

"The little one was crying about a boy named Pemba—"

"You heard all of this while they was attacking you?" Tooth Gap asks, unconvinced.

Uzoma puts up a hand. "Let him finish."

"They said something about meeting other kishi at some jungle," I say, feigning as though I'm looking for my words. Kisama's lips twitch like he wants to say something. Venom fills Sanje's eyes. It's the last marble I have to play in this game. If the humans are going to trust me, I have to give them something besides my story. It might take a while for them to prove it, but if Sanje and the others are telling the truth, the humans will find more kishi to the north like they said yesterday.

"Kunda?" Muscles asks. His head shifts to Uzoma. "You see, they're gathering again."

Uzoma considers my words as Kisama shouts, "He's a lie! He's hiding a hyena behind his—"

A bright light, like a shooting star in the day, streaks across Kisama's neck. It takes me a moment to realize Uzoma's just slashed him with his dagger.

A thin red line parts Kisama's throat. Then a flood of crimson comes trickling down. The tiny boy grabs at his neck with his bound hands but it's no use as the blood spills through his fingers freely, like a wine-colored waterfall through rocks.

Sanje's scream echoes across the plain as he kicks at Uzoma. He misses, pulled back by the two warriors holding him with the rope. It doesn't matter to Sanje. He keeps to thrashing, his rage unbottled. He's howling but his words don't make sense, like he's speaking in a different tongue, one mixed with the bark of his hyena.

My mouth parts in shock as I watch Kisama wither on the ground, life draining from his little body. Even the warriors are stunned in their speechless faces.

"Shut that one up," Uzoma orders, pointing to Sanje. The warriors take more rope and wrap both of Sanje's mouths, human and hyena alike.

No one else dares to speak as Kisama gurgles for his last breaths and Sanje cries through his gag.

I can hear my heart in my ears, pounding like rolling thunder. It had all happened to so fast. Kisama was talking at one moment and then… the blood. So much blood. Uzoma wasn't playing games with any of us. I'd have to choose my next words carefully or I'd be next.

Once Kisama stops moving, Muscles is the first to break the silence. "Like I said, Uzoma… you checked the boy. He's clean."

Uzoma's eyes bore into me again. He and I both know that a hyena head can be hidden. But he doesn't know that

I can do what he can. Is that what his deep expression is considering now? A cold sweat sprouts from the back of my neck. The man stares at me for what feels like an eternity when he finally says, almost too cheerfully, "Well, don't stop. You were telling us your story."

It takes me a few starts, but I tell him the rest—though the remainder is all true. I tell him I was left by the river, found by Muscles, and brought to the village, where Uzoma found me. My voice quivers as I speak. The pit in my stomach feels like it has no bottom. My eyes never leave Kisama's as I finish my story. I don't dare look at Sanje. I can only imagine the curse his eyes have for me.

"Show me the back of that one's head," Uzoma commands. The warriors twist Sanje around to show his hyena, who is already chewing through the rope. Uzoma looks to me. "Boy. Yemi, this is the one who attacked you, right?"

I finally turn my gaze to Sanje. To my surprise, his eyes don't have any malice. The fire that was there before has seemed to cool like he knows how this will all end for him.

"Yes," I reply.

"Did you find any more of them out north?" Uzoma asks one of the warriors.

"We did," the warrior closest to Sanje says. "Right next to the southern edges of Kunda. All of them cubs. We didn't go after them because you said—"

Uzoma lifts his hand once more. "We'll deal with that at another time, as I've told everyone else."

"So what's that mean?" Tooth Gap crosses his arms.

"It means our boy Yemi here is telling the truth as far as we can tell," Uzoma says. "Nnedi, can I ask you to take another trip north for us?"

I almost forget that the shifter had bared witness to everything. She gives Uzoma a quick nod and flies off back into the blue sky. It looks like more storm clouds are coming in the distance.

Tooth Gap goes to Kisama's side, putting a hand to his chest, I guess to make sure he's gone. Once the warrior-guard's satisfied with his examination, he raises his head to Uzoma. "But there were three boys who attacked you, you said."

He points between Kisama and Sanje, and then he settles his eyes on me.

"I know what you're suggesting, Awa," Uzoma says. "And you're right. There were three who attacked me last night. The one at your feet now. This one here who's roped up and…" Uzoma points to Pemba's head on its stake.

Tooth Gap takes in a deep sigh and snaps his fingers. "Right. I forgot about that one." Shoulders slumped, he turns his attention to me. "Sorry, kid. I'll go get that shaman for you." He lifts himself and goes to open the gate to the village. Once he closes it behind him, Uzoma approaches me with the dagger in his hand. The hilt is pointed towards me.

"Before I let you in," he says, "I'd be rude not to let you take your revenge." His wide smile makes me uncomfortable. I look between his eyes, the dagger, and Sanje. I shudder to think what he's asking of me. I can't kill Sanje. Not after what's happened to his brother.

Like always, it seems, this is another test of Uzoma's.

My hand quivering, I take the blade from Uzoma's. How hard would it be for me to turn the dagger and run Uzoma through with it? I could just lift it and slash it across his neck like he did with Kisama. But that would be impossible if I couldn't stop the trembling in my fingers. The traitor would know what I'll try to do even before I make the move. With a slow pivot, I turn the blade to Sanje. I just can't seem to get my feet to move over to him.

What am I so afraid of? This is what I wanted, isn't it?

This is what had to happen. I couldn't just let Sanje walk around telling everyone my secret. By now he must understand that I can hide my hyena. And if he lets that be known, then Uzoma would have my head on a stake next to his.

Despite the reasoning, it doesn't help my shaking hand or my stiff legs.

"Don't be afraid of him, boy," Uzoma says. "He won't hurt you anymore."

I breathe in deep through my nose as I take a slow shuffle to Sanje, who's fallen in the dirt. As I stand over him, his eyes seem hollow, like he's in another place, far from here. I flinch when his gaze suddenly shifts to me.

Though the boy doesn't say a word, his stare says so much. Maybe in a different scenario, a different time, we could have been partners, worked together. If only I wasn't so foolish and selfish. None of them had to die.

But nothing can be done for it now. It's either him or both of us.

As we stare at each other for the last time, I consider the whole of the situation. I alone am responsible for these boys' deaths. And I didn't lift a finger for any but one. I curl my head over my shoulder and look to Uzoma. He gives me an encouraging nod, his brow furrowed.

That's what I'd have to do with Uzoma. Earn his trust, wait for the right opportunity, and strike, using others to do it for me as a sort of shield between him and me.

I might not be able to work with Sanje or the others, but I could rebuild again in the shadows. It will take time, but eventually I'll have a loyal clan of kishi who can help me take hold of Bajok and bring Uzoma down. But for now...

I swipe the dagger across Sanje's throat. Like his brother, he gurgles, reaches for his neck, and fights for life until no more life flows through him.

Thank you, Sanje. I'll never forget what you showed me.

Uzoma takes the dagger from my trembling fingers and wipes it on Sanje's loincloth.

"You did well, Yemi," he says. I look up to him, into his confident smirk, his despicable golden eyes.

Little does he know, he'll get what's coming to him.

Yemi

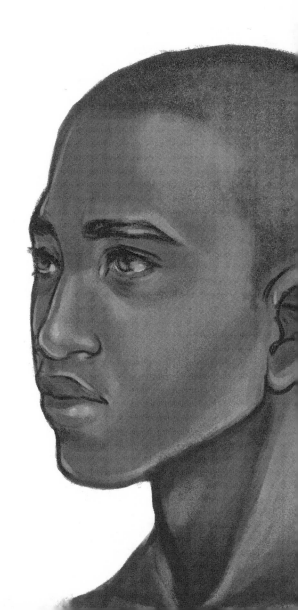

A NOTE FROM THE AUTHOR

Thank you for reading my debut novella. There were many characters in *The Kishi* that I didn't get to explore, one of them being Yemi.

Writing him in the final chapters of *The Kishi*, after his reveal, was a lot of fun so I wanted to dig deeper into his childhood and see how he survived the war with the humans.

If you enjoyed *Last of My Kind*, please leave a review on your favorite retailer or social media.

A SERVANT'S WORK

Lost Tales from Esowon

MATTHEW CHATMAN

BANDELE
— BOOKS —

PRONUNCIATION GUIDE

Characters
    A·man·a - ə'mä'nä
    A·vi·shal - a'vē'shȯl
    La·ta - lä'tä
    Ma·na·li - Mä'nä'lē
    She·khar - shä'kär
    Ten·da·ji - ten'dä'jē
    Vi·vek - vē'vek

Terms & Titles
    A·ya - ī'yä
    M·kahr·a·la - m'kär'ä'lä
    Pel·le·pe - pel'le'pä

Locations
    A·be·rash - ä'bä'räsh
    E·so·won - e'sō'wän
    Jun·ga - jün'gä
    Zy·e·ta - zī'ye'tä

SOUTHERN
E'SHIYA

SUMMIT OF
Junga Mountains

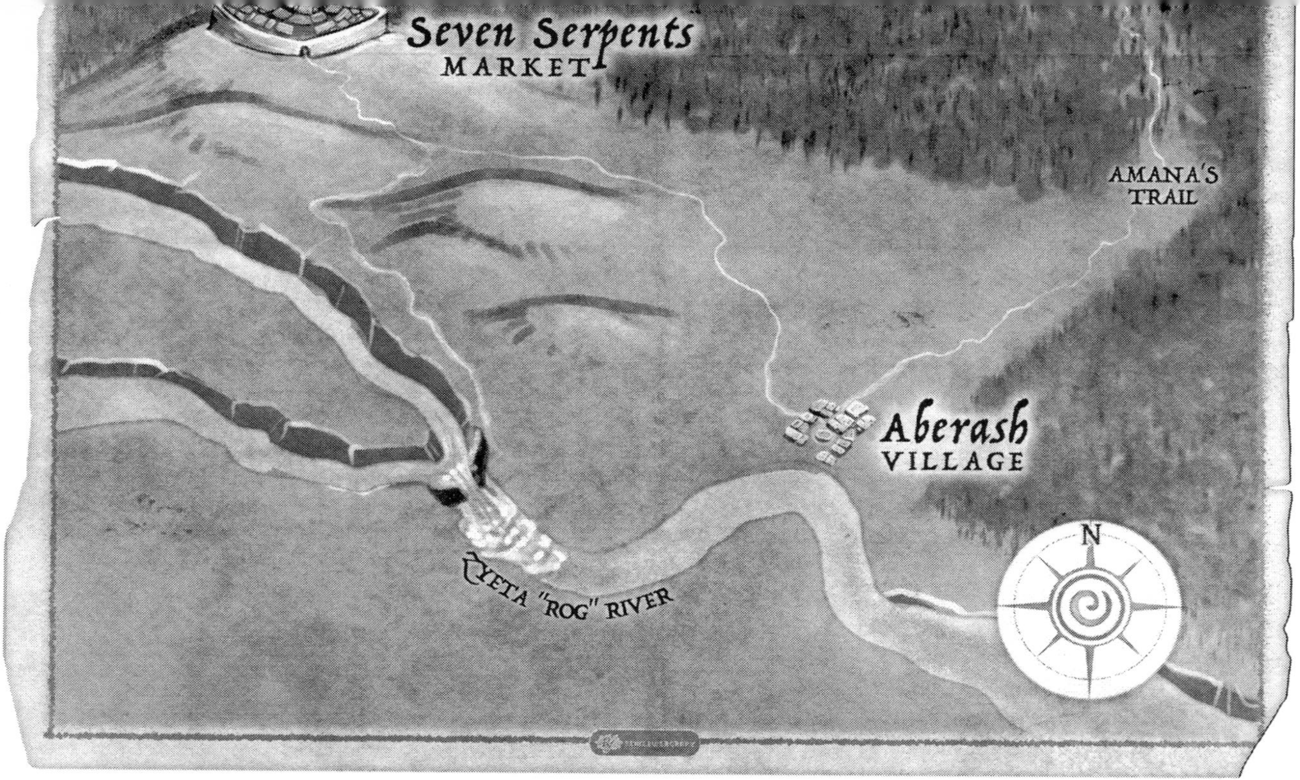
Seven Serpents
MARKET
AMANA'S
TRAIL
Aberash
VILLAGE
N
YETA "ROG" RIVER

"One day, I came across a trader from the east, a Junga monk, who spoke about enlightenment and heightened senses and all that. So I disguised myself as a devotee, spent the better part of a year apprenticed to him until the day I was kicked out. One of the monks told me that my intentions were not genuine — which was true. I followed the code, said all the words, but there was a darkness in me they could sense, an eagerness. I only sought enlightenment for my own betterment, not to get closer to the Supreme One."

— EXCERPT FROM *THE KISHI*

PROLOGUE

To climb a mountain is to be reborn. The act changes all men. No matter where he comes from, or where he's going, no other trial requires more from the wanderer. And no other journey may offer more in return.

But some gifts can never be taken. Some can only be shared. If he is lucky, upon reaching the summit, an extraordinary sense of pride takes hold and a strange and intoxicating power surges through the climber.

If he has suffered injury along the way, then he has emerged stronger. If he has reached the finish without tribulation, then he has outwitted, or else, asserted his will over nature. He may have arrived sure-footed, straight-backed, and proud, or broken and bent, hunched over, and crawling on dusted knees. No matter the case, he has earned the right to laugh in the wicked face of fate, and to weep in the warm grasp of destiny's hand.

The mountain cannot bend and will never bow. Yet the mountain will honor the climber all the same. It has surrendered its secrets and offered up keys to gated mysteries the wanderer could never have imagined from the base. A tired and aching heart shall ease to tap to the beat of triumphant fanfare. Haggard lungs cease to draw ragged breaths, and cool, clean, soothing air brings forth a new, sweet sensation. For the first time since the start of his journey, the wanderer no longer needs to cling desperately to life. He is finally able to embrace it.

The dose of perspective completes the act of transformation that began at the ascension. Only from the peak can he see the valley beneath in all its splendor. The wanderer feasts famished eyes on the world around him... and the past behind.

From his vantage point, everything, even himself, seems smaller and more widely spread, and yet somehow grander than before. Food is more satisfying here. Water tastes sweeter.

For a fleeting moment, the man stands as conqueror, lover, son, and heir to all the mountain surveys. He, like the ancient rocky mound he stands on, has risen above all. Together they are masters of the past and stewards of the present, champion and witness. As one, the pair turns their gaze to the unknowable and infinitely possible future.

How has the climb changed him? Where will his journey take him from here? If he is lucky, he will descend from the summit safely, with face forward, and walk all other roads in good fortune. When he feels uncertain—and he will if he is wise—he will remember the clarity cast in the pure light of every summit's sunrise. When glimpsed from the peak, such a wondrous sight can impart an arid life with renewed meaning. When summoned from behind lowered eyelids, the mere memory can serve as much a guiding light to a lost soul, as a star to a weary wanderer, traversing the darkest sea.

But Junga is not a mountain like any other.

Luck alone is not enough to ferry even the most fortunate through her trials, her summit's dawn brought with it neither wisdom nor clarity.

Junga is no friend to the lost.

ONE

AMANA WAS HARD AT WORK. CROUCHED DOWN ON HIS knees, he scrubbed the floor of the enormous outcropping that served as a courtyard and meditation ground for the elders during the day. He had been here for what felt like an eternity, but the dark sky above meant only a few hours could have passed.

Barefoot and naked from the waist up, Amana shivered against the chill of the night air, which burned his lungs as he breathed. The skin of his hands, feet, and knees stung against the harsh ground. He was alone, and apart from the bucket and cart of tools at his side, the circular courtyard was empty.

Five spiraling paths of cobbled stone paved the walkways between five carved entrances etched into the mountain on the north end, and a labyrinthine garden to the south. Each cave led to a different level within, each dedicated to a different area of study.

It was not necessary to enter the courtyard to traverse from one level to the next, but it was the favored route. The monks regarded crossing its convoluted walkways as symbolic of adhering to the trying Paths of Boism themselves. Constructed atop a flat expanse of rocky cliff, the outer courtyard was a place of quiet peace. Save for the sounds of the many crashing waterfalls, far off in the distance, the only noises to be heard were Amana's ragged breathing and the scraping and sopping of his brush.

Long strands of twisted hair swished as he rocked back and forth. The rhythmic sound of the brush filled his ears, and he had grown groggy. He grunted and scrubbed harder, working himself to a savage pace, but time, in its perverse way, seemed to slow.

How long have I been here now? Amana wondered as he dunked the brush in the bucket. *How much longer will I have to be?*

He was too angry to sleep and too weary to focus on what he was doing when awake. Every now and then he shook his head or gnashed his teeth to fight off fatigue as the tedium of his task set in. A dismal hour of brushing later, the fight had only grown harder. Aching joints and pain in his shoulders and lower back left his limbs feeling heavy and his movements awkward.

By the time another hour had passed, he had begun to entertain the notion he might be on the wrong end of a losing battle. He came to a sudden stop as boredom gave way to true exhaustion, and his languid gaze fell upon the few strands of hair hanging motionless and limp before him.

That's how long I've been here… he thought, as he stared at the length of his stray locs.

WHEN HE HAD FIRST COME HERE NEARLY A YEAR AGO, HE had sworn to uphold the tenets of Boism. The Mountain Monks wore their hair in locs, which supposedly granted them power from the Old Gods. Amana had seen little evidence that the style did anything more than express the monks' lack of vanity. Even so, he had adopted the style himself upon being accepted into their order. Now his own locs were so long he'd dragged a few tips through the soapy water pooled on the stone floor as he worked.

He looked up at the perpetually cloudy sky above and thought back to the life he led before he'd come here. Even that first day had felt like the end of a long and arduous journey.

At that time, he didn't know much more about the fabled "Mountain Monks" than anyone else. He'd heard tell of their legendary self-discipline. He knew they were rumored to possess extraordinary abilities, yet for pious reasons, refrained from using such powers in their dealings throughout the world. He'd grown up hearing tales from travelers and adventurers who'd claimed to have visited the hallowed rocky terrain the monks called home. They had described it as being majestic as it was mysterious, and the tales called to mind the same images for all of Amana's generation.

Great jutting spires of granite and graceful towers of alabaster sprung from the ground like white plants in a golden garden encircled by pillars of marble, and ziggurats of limestone. Oases of lush flora dotted the otherwise arid landscape and here and there blindingly white waterfalls adorned the sheer cliffs feeding tributary rivers that had formed the ancient, craggy canyons below.

Most curious of all though, it was said that the summit of the tallest of the Junga mountains was shrouded in a perpetual cloudy haze. Nobody he had ever met, nor heard of in either story or song, had ever claimed to have seen the top. To hear it from the revered elders themselves, all things were clear when viewed from the peak.

Before meeting the monks, he wasn't so sure he believed in all the tales surrounding them, but the grandeur of their stronghold had more than lived up to his expectations. By the time his private pilgrimage had brought him to the base of Mount Junga, he felt he'd be willing to do anything to be welcomed into their ranks.

That fateful evening, he had approached a hooded figure kneeling on a stone dais a few meters beyond a jewel-encrusted archway. The moonstones flecked the black stone of the arch with sparkling light that contrasted gently against the sheen of the dark marble. The man looked impossibly old and his solidly black eyes sparkled with brilliant blue-white light from the stones above. Amana prostrated himself before the old one, hands turned upward, head bowed.

"I am Amana," he had declared, his voice low and deferential. "I hope to apprentice myself to the monks to achieve enlightenment. What would you ask of me?"

For a long moment the man merely stared. Just when Amana was on the verge of repeating himself, the old man turned and walked into the dark gloom. He motioned to Amana and together they meandered through the mountainous passageway to the great temple above. Eventually, Amana would admit to himself that he'd never have been able to reach the temple on his own. He didn't think of himself as a weak person. On the contrary, his career as a pirate had required great skill in combat and a knack for manipulation and quick thinking. Beyond that, his innate mystical talent to see briefly into the future gave him an edge over most people. But his short-sight was less than optimized for the task of climbing Mount Junga.

The moment he'd set foot to the cliff-lined pass all those moons ago, he felt his perception had been dimmed in some way, like the Junga range itself, peaks and valleys, characterized his memory of the journey. His vision had become cloudy and his hearing less acute than it had been before. Though in fine health, he'd felt as though he was suffering from a terrible head cold. His sinuses seemed congested, and his bleary eyes and plugged ears made the mere act of walking difficult. At that time he had simply thought it the result of climbing to such high a peak, but by the second evening, he'd come to accept that some unknown element was at play.

Something about this place just wasn't right. That night had been too dark to be natural, and the light of the following day too harsh to believe. On the third morning they had descended into a rugged canyon scar, and at various times he felt overwhelmed by the constant buzzing noise of swarming insects—though he never saw any. At others, the land seemed so quiet that his footsteps echoed, the only sound for leagues around even as his guide kept no more than ten steps ahead.

When it all became too confusing, he had demanded an explanation from the guide, only to find his own voice inaudible. He'd tried screaming a second time, only to experience the same effect. It was like shouting to be heard above the high winds and crashing rain of a nonexistent storm.

The higher they climbed, the less Amana could see before him. Unable to see past his nose due to the ever-present, opaque mist that surrounded them both, and unaccustomed to the eerie quiet of the night, he found himself easily disoriented.

Four days into the long trek, he lost a great deal of his strength. He was provided with no food and drank only what little water he came across in the wild. As he sat resting one day, he realized that he could no longer safely turn back even if he wanted to.

Not only was he sure to lose his way in the unnatural Junga mists, he didn't think he'd have the strength to complete the journey. At that point he had been wholly in the hands of his guide, who never spoke to him throughout the entire journey and only stopped on those few occasions when Amana insisted upon rest.

Finally, on the fifth morning of their climb, Amana had been rewarded with his first vision of the great temple. The massive structure had been built so as to appear as an extension of the tallest Junga mountain. Parts of it seemed to run underground through subterranean trails, or deep into painstakingly carved corridors that ran directly into the mountain itself. Large patches of the wall were covered by natural rock formations and overgrown vines. True to the stories he'd heard as a child, the mountain's peak and even the temple's uppermost level were hidden by an obtrusive layer of fog.

After signaling him to stop, his guide had proceeded on his own up a wide stairway leading to a small antechamber into the ornate temple, leaving Amana at the steps outside.

Weak with hunger and parched with thirst, he'd desperately wanted to collapse then and there, but his instinct had told him to remain standing for the first moment the monks laid eyes on him. Four monks descended from the temple above. The first, his guide, proceeded down the steps at the same steady pace he'd carried throughout the climb, and he walked straight past Amana without a glance in his direction —seemingly returning to his vigil at the mountain's base. The three remaining figures stood motionless at the top of the steps for a long moment. Eventually, Amana assumed they were waiting for him to approach them. So he did.

"Masters," he called in a voice weak with thirst and exhaustion. "My name is Amana. I have journeyed far to apprentice myself to you."

The youngest, tallest, and broadest of the three spoke first. He took a step forward and in a voice as deep and calm as the sea itself he asked, "Tell me, Amana. What is it that you seek?"

"I seek enlightenment," Amana cried with as much emotion as he could summon. He wanted the power the monks had, a power that would allow him to achieve vengeance. "Recently, my life seems to have lost all meaning. I've come in search of a new one. Teach me your ways."

He had rehearsed the words several times in his head during his ascent. He could only hope his words sounded genuine enough.

The tall man considered him for a moment. He cast a sidelong glance to the others who both stepped forward to join him. "I am Vivek," he said before motioning to his companions. "And these are my fellows Shekhar and Lata."

Amana bowed slightly to each as Vivek continued. "There is no founder of our way, and no single teaching. Truth can only be known through M'Kahr'ala's balance."

Lightheaded and starving, Amana swayed slightly on his feet. "Tell me... please, what must I do to achieve balance?"

Shekhar, the thinner hunch-backed monk to the right, spoke with a hoarse voice, little more than a whisper. "What do you know of M'Kahr'ala?"

Amana did not believe he knew the name. He had heard many superstitious tales throughout his travels with sailors and adventurers. There were so many old gods ... hundreds. But something whispered at the back of his mind.

"The god of balance... the god of scales," he murmured.

"Clear your mind," Shekhar said quietly. "Open your heart. You must learn to walk in step with M'Kahr'ala, as we do."

The monk who stood in the middle, a short woman far older than the others, looked Amana up and down before bringing her gentle eyes to rest on his own.

She was barefoot like her fellows and wore loose fitting robes accompanied by shawls of purple and white. Her back was strong and her posture straight. She wore no jewelry but carried a staff taller than she was, which she held in a firm grip but did not seem to actually need. Amana wondered if it was one of the magical staves of legend. He had thought they were all relegated to mystic soldiers in the great armies, not to a lone monk on an isolated mountain peak. Amana couldn't tear his eyes away from it. They were quite valuable in the Sapphire Isles.

The woman's grizzled mane of matted gray hair must have been at least twice as long as she was tall and it lay splayed haphazardly on the ground behind her. Her toothless mouth opened, and a thin reedy voice said, "You have come this far along the Junga trail. Though paths before you will not always be clear, as you must already know. But take heed—you must never give in to despair. As each day is obscured by the dark of night, night must yield to the light of day. All things are clear from the peak of Mount Junga. To stand there, M'Kahr'ala must stand beside you."

"I will do whatever you ask of me." Amana kneeled before them and bowed his head. Anything that would give him their elusive power. "I am at your command."

"We issue no commands here," Vivek proclaimed in a stern voice.

Lata followed him with her softer rasp. "Remember, there are many paths to truth. Do as you are asked and we shall guide you on the path we follow."

AMANA'S EYES BURNED AS BEADS OF SWEAT TRICKLED down his brow. He blinked through the stinging as his thoughts returned to the present. Standing, he started down the courtyard paths as the pain in his joints subsided. Anger and frustration were getting the better of him. He needed to move through this.

As he walked, he thought about how much time he'd wasted over the last year, and his footfalls grew heavier, his mind sagging with weariness. He ceased his pacing at the center of the paths and sank to the floor in a meditative position. No matter what he looked at, and no matter how he tried to forget, scattered memories of the past year danced before him.

Fine then. If I can't stop thinking about it, then let's think about it... he closed his eyes and he cast his thoughts back to the beginning, sinking into the source of his frustration.

TWO

AFTER HIS FIRST MEETING WITH THE MONKS, AMANA HAD been permitted to eat, drink, and bathe. He was shown to a small room where he collapsed onto a simple cot. He couldn't say how long he slept there. Perhaps a day. Perhaps a week.

When he finally woke, he listened to his new instructors speak at length about what he must do to conform to life in the temple. Amana took up their traditional style of dress of simple robes. He had agreed to abstain from stealing and other wrongdoings. He had given up his belongings—that much had all been easy enough. But untethering himself from worldly concerns, as the monks professed to do, meant more than merely surrendering possessions. To join their ranks, Amana had also taken up a vow of celibacy, albeit with a distinct lack of enthusiasm. He had no intention of going back on his word if only because he couldn't see any reason why he should... not now that his wife Asha was gone.

And so his work began.

In the beginning he'd agreed to do only as he was told. He had no problem submitting himself before the wisdom of the elders if it meant learning from them. But for those first few weeks they asked him to simply sweep the halls surrounding the monastery's inner sanctum at the lowest level. So as not to be disruptive, all work that took place in the corridors throughout every tier of the temple had to be performed in silence. Those initial days had seemed to snail by at a mercilessly slow pace.

Amana was then tasked with assisting in the dipping of candles in the cellars. Tutored at first by Vivek, he was left to continue the job without the monk's assistance after a few hours. The monk continued to survey his handiwork every now and then throughout the following days.

After that point he had been permitted to work alongside an even younger apprentice named Avishal, with whom he'd been allowed to converse as they worked. Soft-spoken and friendly, Avishal was thin and carried out his duties with a quiet enthusiasm. After a few days of working together, Amana found that Avishal had been with the monks for several years, but for some strange reason, the young man had never ascended to the floors above. Avishal had never learned of the greater mysteries the monks had to teach, nor did he profess any desire to.

When pressed about how this had come to pass, Avishal's answer was always the same. "I came from a land torn by war. I came here hoping to find my place in the world, and I succeeded."

Stories like these were fairly common among the other apprentices with whom Amana had grown familiar with. Few of the monks spoke with him, though as far as he could tell, they didn't seem to speak amongst themselves very often either—not openly at any rate.

Amana wasn't sure what had curbed the ambitions of so many of his cohorts. Perhaps they were just too easily satisfied. Shelter, a hot meal, dignified labor—these were enough for some.

Then there were those who had come in search of a new beginning. Many like himself had been the victims of old traumas, and perhaps even a few were guilty of dealing out undue trauma to others. These were people hoping to forget what the past had brought to them, or to be forgiven for that which they carried within. And there were those like Avishal who had come from nothing, hoping to discover themselves. Amana stood apart from them all. He knew who he was, and he wasn't running away from his past. He was here to take hold of his future.

Amana hadn't been able to see how making candles would lead him to a greater understanding of his innate powers, and so he thought the monks must have had some other reason for instructing him to mold the waxy sticks. Frankly, he hadn't even seen what it might have to do with their own professed beliefs or codes of behavior. He supposed it was a job that needed doing, and the monks probably felt that such menial tasks belonged to those at the lowest level of study. Amana, still eager to please at that early stage of his apprenticeship, had simply shrugged it off and gotten on with it.

He tried to think of the work as its own reward, and felt somehow, even without calling upon his gift of short-sight, that great things would come to him if he stayed on the path the monks had set before him. The task required a certain measure of patience and skill, and so he'd performed without complaint.

A moon later, after ascending to the second floor within the mountain, he began to work in the kitchens. This exercise had, in a way, seemed even less instructive to him than the first, but he'd been excited to have reached the next level so quickly. Looking back on it now, it was easily his favorite period of service. The tasks of the day varied widely, and the busy hours made the days roll by quickly. At times he wondered where the monks came by their stores of food. He supposed the monks grew their own fruits and vegetables, but the rest remained a mystery.

After several weeks he'd reached the third level within the mountain where closets full of cleaning utensils flanked his new living space. For three miserable moons he'd polished furniture and windows all throughout the temple and the cavernous mountain halls.

He performed these tasks well, sometimes under the watchful eye of an elder, though just as often on his own, carrying on without complaint. But where grit and determination had once gleamed in his dark eyes, now a deep-seeded and smoking rage smoldered behind them.

One morning, as Amana sat cleaning while Vivek observed from behind, he had allowed his anger to boil over for the first time since arriving at Mount Junga. As he stared at his own image in the copper pot he'd been polishing, he'd had time to reflect on how he had felt bored, confused, and even wasted since being welcomed into the temple. Until reaching this level, however, he could at the least say he had never felt insulted.

Trying to ignore Vivek's presence was like trying not to notice a foul smell in the air. Although both had been cordial enough since they had met, there was always a certain rigidity to their interactions. Amana couldn't say precisely why, but of the three elders who had greeted him when he had first arrived at the monastery, Vivek was the only one he disliked.

Though Amana had never spoken openly of this to anybody, he had the distinct impression the feeling was mutual. There was little Vivek did not see. His roving eyes took in the full measure of everything and everyone he saw —a teacher's gaze. Amana made a point of keeping his back to the monk to avoid it.

"You have something you'd like to discuss, apprentice," Vivek said without making it a question. "You think this task beneath you," he continued before Amana had time to summon a proper retort.

"No, not exactly," Amana said resentfully. "It's just… pointless."

Vivek raised an eyebrow. "You think so?"

"Well." Amana considered his words as though giving great thought to the matter. "You can't make something shine without tarnishing something else."

How's that for a little Junga wisdom? he thought to himself.

"Do you value your cleaning rags so highly?" Vivek asked coolly.

Amana snorted quietly at the stupidity of the question. He quickened the pace of his polishing, trying once more to put Vivek's presence out of his mind. As if in direct response, the monk continued talking, straining Amana's patience even further.

"Have I ever told you about Uzoma?" Vivek inquired.

Amana rolled his eyes as he went about his work. *Not another fable.* "You've mentioned a failed apprentice before. The Lost One I think you called him."

"Uzoma was talented when he came to us, just as you are," Vivek said, gazing out of the room's lone window. "But he was also brash, willful, and worst of all, impatient. Again, like you."

Amana took a moment to examine his handiwork before answering. "I'm not sure you intended it, but that's the closest you've come to paying me a compliment."

"Perhaps you think I'm out to get you. That I want to see you fail," Vivek suggested thoughtfully. "This is not so."

Amana said nothing, but the scowl he wore intensified. The monk's words did nothing to ease the sense of doubt he hadn't realized until now he'd been feeling.

"Uzoma showed great promise," Vivek said, taking a few paces forward. Amana still refused to face the monk directly, but the older man's voice grew louder as he moved closer. "He had extraordinary powers of his own. I knew from our first meeting he had the potential to stand as one of the greatest among us—given time. Before apprenticing himself here, at Mount Junga, he even saved my life," Vivek finished solemnly.

"What happened to him? Where is he now?" Amana asked, more to fill the silence than anything else. He didn't truly care about the answer. All he wanted was for Vivek to go away.

Vivek sighed heavily. "The road to truth a winding and treacherous path. Some of us lose our way. One must be strong and righteous. Uzoma had strength in abundance, but strength alone is not enough. Our paths are paved by self-assurance and discipline. Not certainty and arrogance. Uzoma outgrew us. We were wasting his time. He had better things to do."

In spite of himself, Amana couldn't suppress a feeling of sympathy for the Lost One now that he knew firsthand how the monks went about teaching.

"You still seem troubled, apprentice," Vivek remarked, his voice calm and matter-of-fact. "May I ask why?"

"If you have to ask, then you probably wouldn't understand," Amana said without facing him. In the vase's reflection he saw Vivek brush a small fleck of dust from a cabinet.

"Perhaps I'm less interested in what I can see than I am in what you have to say," Vivek countered, his voice still maddeningly calm.

"And what if I haven't got anything to say?" Amana asked, almost turning in his frustration but catching himself at the last second.

"But you already have."

Amana swung around to glare at the monk, only to find the corridor empty.

For several hours he thought his outburst might have

gone too far, and that the monks would ask him to leave. But nothing out of the ordinary happened over the next hours, and so he'd returned to business as usual the following day.

Several weeks of buffing and shining later and he'd been escorted by Shekhar to the fourth level within the mountain. There he had pushed carts of books and delivered scrolled messages all around this floor and that, the chambers of which were otherwise reserved for monks who had mastered their studies.

Masters greeted him at the beginning of each day and thanked him at the end, but never conducted business in front of him, nor offered anything in the way of conversation or tutelage. When they required privacy for meetings, they dismissed him from their presence, and he would instead tend to the hearths that warmed the communal hall, send orders to the kitchens below, or replace burned candles throughout the many meditation rooms.

While on a candle run to the cellars one day he'd said, "ah well," to Avishal, who looked as though he hadn't moved since Amana left him in the cellars. "At least now I get to play with fire every once in a while. Adds a touch of danger. Yeah, *kijana*?"

Avishal didn't respond like always, continuing his own work in silence. Amana thought using the more casual island slang would stir the young man, but it did nothing for him at all.

As he prepared a cart loaded with logs shortly before the next morning's dawn, he rounded a corner only to run into Shekhar, who was accompanied by Vivek. Without a word, the younger monk had taken hold of the cart and continued up the hall while Shekhar led Amana to the fifth level.

As they walked, Amana reined in the impatience he felt and asked the old master what he had in store for him today. Steeling himself for whatever dreary chore was in store for him, he glanced sideways to catch Shekhar's eye as they climbed another set of stairs together.

"Today," Shekhar said quietly, a knowing glint in his eye. "We are going to play with fire."

Mouth agape, and paralyzed by shock and regret, Amana stopped dead in his tracks, though Shekhar continued forward. After a moment or two, Amana simply shook his head and smiled in nervous disbelief as he jogged to catch up. His euphoria was almost palpable. They had accepted him to the upper echelon of the temple. Finally, he was going to learn the mystic arts from a master. Finally, he would take a step closer to achieving the power he truly desired.

THREE

"BREWING TEA IS A DELICATE ART," SHEKHAR SAID AN hour later to a sour-faced Amana. The younger man stoked a small fire beneath the kettle between them.

A fresh wave of disappointment had sapped Amana of the vitality he'd felt during their long walk to Shekhar's room on the fifth floor of the temple. Familiar frustrations were bubbling back up to the surface of his temper—ever strained these days.

Really. You should have expected something like this. It's your own fault for getting your hopes up.

Shekhar crumbled what looked like a small white pebble into a green jug filled with water. He stirred without offering an explanation for his actions before lifting the lid of the teapot to peak at the simmering contents.

"The flames are too high," Shekhar said gently. He pulled a small pouch from inside his sleeves and sprinkled dried, red-orange leaves into the pot. They glowed like the flyaway embers of a campfire.

Shekhar went into the process of steeping the tea away from direct heat. Once that step was complete, they would then drain the liquid from the pot, leaving only the dregs, at which point the pot would be filled again with cool, clean water and returned to the fire.

Lost in a kind of stupor, Amana was paying more attention to the ugly furnishings around them than he was to Shekhar. He rearranged a bit of kindling as the two knelt on the purple mats of Shekhar's chamber. Shadows cast from the flames danced in a flicker over garish green carpeting and pale orange walls. As the old monk went on, Amana honed in on the sounds of chirping birds. Their song carried through an open diamond-shaped window. The small patch of clear blue sky he glimpsed far off in the distance was the nearest source of beauty.

Shekhar shuffled off to a corner of the room. Amana had his back to him as he poked at the embers, but he heard the clinking of porcelain and the heavy *thunk* of wood as Shekhar rummaged through a cabinet in the corner behind him. When the elder returned he was carrying a large tray bearing two empty cups, a bowl of water and a large black basin covered by a fine mesh strainer.

Amana watched as Shekhar took another small white pebble from the jar he had pulled from an inner pocket of his robes. Shekhar held the stone between his thumb and forefinger and examined it for a moment before dropping it into a mortar and crushing it with a pestle. He added the powder to the bowl of water which he swirled gently with his hand until the—whatever it was—dissolved. He dipped his fingers into the water and coated the backs of his hands and knuckles before motioning for Amana to do the same.

Shekhar poured a cup of tea for each of them. "Have you ever heard of the *pel'lepe* plant, Amana?"

Amana thought back to rumors he'd heard during his former life, dredging up memories of tales passed around by pirates and tradesmen. "Fairly inexpensive, prized for its brilliant orange blossoms," he said as he accepted the cup. "I've heard it called the Forest's Fire. I've never heard of it being used in preparing tea before though... It's not an especially rare plant is it? Or is this some sort of secret recipe?"

"The pel'lepe leaf is easily acquired," Shekhar admitted. "But the skill to brew tea with it is not, poisonous as it is."

Hoping he had misheard what Shekhar had said, Amana said nothing and simply stared at the old man, as though imploring him to start making sense.

"What is it that we do here?" Shekhar asked suddenly as he clasped his hands together.

Amana blinked in confusion at the sudden change of subject. He felt unsure how to answer. Even after all these moons, he had no earthly idea what the masters did behind closed doors. A part of him wanted to scream as much in the elder's wrinkled face. Was he about to be chastised for not having caught on to some hidden meaning the monks were able to divine in the dusting of shelves? Or perhaps he was about to be presented with a charming anecdote concerning the quiet dignity of the emptying of chamber pots. Maybe another tale of a lost student...

With a considerable effort he quelled the impulse to rage at the elder monk. As unfair as he thought it was to be tested with these probing questions after having been taught nothing, he felt certain the elder would expect a proper answer. Even an incorrect guess would probably be taken as Amana having invested some thought into the matter. He didn't want the monks to think of him as a quitter who had just thrown his hands up in frustration. He very nearly had, of course, but that didn't mean he wanted to be thought of that way. So he appraised the old man as he took his own steaming cup of tea in hand and said what he assumed the elder wanted to hear.

"We toil here in an effort to master ourselves," Amana said evenly.

"Why?" asked the elder in a bald voice.

Amana went on, speaking with more confidence than he truly felt. "To achieve control over the body and mind."

"Why?"

"Great discipline is required to study the Five Paths."

"And why do we study the Five Paths?"

"To achieve enlightenment... to have M'Kahr'ala return us to True Balance," Amana stated without any real conviction. Privately, he thought the platitudes had sounded nice enough as he'd said them, but a part of him regretted just how hollow the recitation had felt. The words tasted soulless on his tongue, and it had taken effort not to spit them out. He had been quoting the monks themselves, but had discovered neither falsehood nor truth in their mantras throughout his time in the temple.

Shekhar fixed Amana with a challenging look which gave him the distinct impression the elder knew exactly what was going on in the younger man's mind. Amana felt his chest tighten uncomfortably, but he fought to restrain any additional physical clues that might hint at his defensive mood.

"What is True Balance?" Shekhar asked patiently, his voice as soft as his face was hard.

Amana shook his head slightly. He had expected the question, but something about the way the monk had asked it disarmed him. The mounting anger and stress he felt waned, and he looked back to the window as though hoping to find the answer floating in the sky above.

After a long moment he said, "I've come here in search of True Balance... I'm afraid I can't say what it is exactly. I've never felt it before."

"If true, this poses an interesting question for you." Shekhar paused for an instant before saying, "If you don't know how to recognize balance, how will you know once you've found it? More than that, if you don't know what it is, how do you know it is what you want?"

Frustrated by this stupid game, Amana glared at Shekhar and allowed a long moment of silence to pass between them. Wanting to simply stop this inane conversation, he ignored the question and asked one of his own.

"Could you not have brewed this tea without me?" he demanded, his voice deeper and more aggressive than it had been before.

Shekhar raised an incredulous and incredibly bushy eyebrow as he spoke. "Of course I could have."

"Is it necessary for me to drink the pel'lepe to achieve enlightenment... or to know True Balance?" Amana asked brusquely.

"No, I don't suppose it is."

Emboldened, Amana went on. "Well, if you don't need my help making tea, and I don't need to drink it, then why am I here?"

Shekhar closed his eyes, drained his cup and set it on the ground before answering. "I don't believe I've ever encountered a cup of tea that I *needed* to drink. But I can say with certainty I've never encountered a cup of tea that I *regretted* drinking." His half-lidded dark eyes found Amana's fierce brown ones. "Can you say the same?"

Amana attempted to hold his gaze as he sipped his own tea, but as soon as he took his first swallow, the effort grew suddenly taxing, and he felt his eyes begin to droop. His head felt too heavy and began to loll, rolling to either side of his neck.

He slumped forward a little, his shoulders slouched, and his mind went dull. He struggled to stay lucid, but he didn't think he could. He tried looking to the window again. He strained for the sounds of the singing birds, but their song grew distant and faint, replaced by a rush of blood flowing through his veins and the beat of his own heart pounding in his ears. He tried yelling for help, but his voice died away in his throat. He had killed it. He didn't need help—no—he didn't want it. This was amazing! This was fantastic!

The world seemed to fall away from him, and for a moment that might have been an eternity, time seemed to stand still. Tastes he enjoyed danced across his tongue. A pleasant tingling sensation tickled his fingers and licked at his toes. Aromas he'd half forgotten filled his nose, and memories he'd thought dead and gone resurfaced. The smell of fresh bread baking from his childhood brought a smile to his face only to be replaced by something else.

It took a long moment for him to identify what it was, but when he did, his smile drooped momentarily and emerged wider and grander than before.

It was perfume.

The lingering scent of perfume trapped in Asha's hair. The delicate laughter of his daughter Sanaa telling a joke. A feeling of sublime contentment stole over him and he felt for a moment as he had years ago... when times were good... before he had lost Asha and Sanaa... before they had been taken from him.

He inhaled deeply to take in the scent again. It was a spicy sweetness he had often smelled before sleeping at night, and while waking in the morning, sometimes before even opening his eyes. Now, he opened eyes he didn't remember closing. As quickly as it had come, the sensation washed away. Awestruck, he stared from the cup in his hand to the monk sitting across from him. Nearly overcome with emotion, he took a moment to center himself.

"What..." he began in a stammering voice. "What is this stuff?"

Shekhar surveyed him with a strange look on his face. It struck Amana as a bizarre combination of satisfaction and pity, and he wasn't sure what to make of it. He raised his cup to take a second drink. Before the cup had reached his lips, however, the old monk bounded forward and with improbable strength and speed caught Amana's arm in a binding grapple.

Shekhar jammed his left thumb into Amana's wrist. His hand pinned between the elder's thumb and fingers, Amana's grip was forced to slacken, and with a twist of Shekhar's other hand, he freed the cup from Amana's limp grasp. Surprised by the unexpected action, the younger man kept his seat as the elder vaulted away from him.

For an instant, flowing robes, beaded necklaces and twisted hair seemed to fill the tiny room. Coming to a momentum defying, yet graceful halt, Shekhar resumed his stooped position on the mat opposite Amana. The entire exercise had taken no more than a few seconds from start to finish, and despite the blinding speed with which the elder had moved, he'd spilled not a drop of the pel'lepe.

"Why did you do that?" Amana asked. "I was only —"

"The pel'lepe leaf requires great care to handle properly," Shekhar interrupted in his hoarse bark of a voice. "If brewed for too short a time or at too high a temperature, the tea becomes mildly toxic and leaves an unpleasant itching in the throat. If left to stew for too long, the tannins in the tea impart a sickening astringent flavor so potent it may induce nausea." He looked hard at Amana before continuing. "If brewed to perfection, as this pot has been, the tea produced sends the uninitiated into transports of euphoria, a first taste of what it means to be free. The tea relaxes your physical form. But until you learn to sever the link between your painful memories and your heightened state of mind, you will never truly stand on your own. You must detach yourself from your pain, reacquaint yourself with pleasure. Until you have, you shall never know inner peace."

Amana gave a kind of start as he came back into his right mind. It took a moment longer for Shekhar's words to sink in.

"One day, should you achieve True Balance, you may join me in a second cup of pel'lepe," Shekhar said. "For now, you must abstain. The tea is the only variety those who live at the peak ever drink. You will learn to brew the pel'lepe leaf, and to do the thing properly in service to the elders. Take heed. This is no easy task. Do not be surprised if I, or one of my fellows, rejects your first, second, third or even hundredth cup. Accustomed to dealing with pain we may be, but we don't much relish needless suffering."

Amana had been listening as attentively as he could, but all the while as the elder had spoken, he hadn't been able to tear his eyes away from the cup in the old man's hand. The monk noticed his gaze and lowered his voice to a cautious whisper. "And as you work, ponder this, young one: *lasting* happiness is not to be found in the bottom of a pel'lepe cup. All you shall find there are the dregs of a bitter life."

"What do you find in the bottom of yours, master?" Amana asked in genuine curiosity.

"Only the soggy remains of what had been a very fine cup of tea," Shekhar said, pouring another for himself.

FOUR

AMANA WOKE FROM HIS MEDITATION IN A COLD SWEAT, remembering Shekhar's words. He surveyed the scrubbed courtyard and judged his work complete.

"Just in time too," he said to himself as the sky began to lighten.

Mere weeks after having learned to brew the pel'lepe, he'd been sent from the fifth level within the temple all the way back down to the ground floor for his final tasks. As had been the case every other time he'd moved from one rung within the mountain to the next, he hadn't been told precisely what to expect. But he knew whom he was scheduled to meet with and when.

The sun rose high in the sky above, and he was due to meet with Lata. She had mentored him for the last moon, instructing him in the mixing of various herbs and other ingredients. Together the pair had produced a variety of restorative potions, healing salves and other balms. The diminutive master spent nearly all of her time working in the gardens, and she had instructed Amana to clean the courtyard the previous evening. Afterward she had excused herself to a meeting between the other elders which Amana suspected concerned him.

Finally. The moment he'd been waiting for had arrived.

Rejuvenated somewhat by his long moment of rest and invigorated by the prospect of the new day, Amana returned to the center of the courtyard where he had left his cart of cleaning supplies.

He laid his tools in a wooden storage chest near the entrance to the gardens on the south end of the circular meditation ground. He retrieved a large sack he'd left at the bottom of the chest before washing his hands, feet, and face in the crystal-clear waters of a small fountain carved in the shape of a tiger's head.

He pulled on a set of fresh robes from the sack, then walked through the easternmost pathway that led to the topiary maze. He wanted to be early for his meeting at the center of the garden.

As he walked, he felt almost giddy with excitement. The frustration he'd felt throughout his long night of toil had evaporated with the break of day. Today marked the one-year anniversary of his acceptance into the monastery.

His anger and humiliation at the thought of having to return to the lowest level of the temple had consumed his thoughts over the course of the last week. But when the monks had told him that his final test would soon be upon him, his spirits had lifted somewhat, only to have been dragged back down under the sagging weight of anticipation. Now he walked with a sense of purpose, his path illuminated by the light of possibility. At last he would apprentice himself before the monks directly.

To his surprise Lata was already hard at work in the center of the garden when he arrived.

"Have you been here all night?" he asked as a greeting.

Stooping slightly as she worked, she turned away from a willowy bush dotted with vibrant yellow flower buds she had been pruning before his arrival. Her face was impassive, but her eyes shone with light and warmth.

"Sleep loses its luster once you've reached the peak, Amana," she said in answer. "My plants need me more than I need rest."

She bent to take hold of a gnarled bramble as long and unruly as her hair that had wrapped itself around the bottommost stalks of the bush. Using her bare and scarred hands, she gripped the thorny weed firmly and her face remained stoic as she attempted to untangle the wild mass.

Amana stepped forward to her aid, but she waved him off and continued on her own. He watched closely as she went on, noting how careful she was being not to harm either plant as she worked. Dark drops of blood leaked from the palms of her leathery hands and trailed down the length of her forearms to drip from bony elbows, but her grip remained firm.

"Why not just uproot the weeds?" Amana asked, staring at the spots on the ground where here blood had fallen.

As she finished, she straightened her back to stand to her full height. The difference it made for one so short was surprising, and she turned to look him full in the face.

"Uprooting is a last resort, a road to be traveled only when all others are closed to me."

Amana flicked a dismissive hand. "Ah, but it's only a weed…"

Some of the light in her eyes faded away, and she cocked her head, regarding him as though she wasn't quite sure what he was.

He pointed to her hands, his next words more gentle. "It would spare you a great deal of time and pain."

Lata dipped her hands into a basin of water. "Pain is an old acquaintance of mine, and he knows his place. All living things deserve to thrive for as long as they can — whether the ugly weed or the pretty flower. If one threatens another, and can be coaxed, groomed, or separated rather than destroyed, then that would be my preference."

"But it's a weed. It's not in its nature to mind its place or to stop growing. No matter what you do, it will threaten your other plants eventually," Amana warned.

"That may be." Lata bandaged her cleaned hands with silken wrappings. "But one needn't surrender to nature to live in harmony with it."

Amana smiled inwardly and watched as she doddered around the garden, fetching a couple of water skins for the pair of them. A moon ago, when he'd been sent from the fifth floor all the way back down to the bottom of temple, he'd been in a towering temper. He'd been so close! Why had they sent him back to where he'd started? What had he done to warrant such punishment?

But Lata's exercises had been highly educational, and her manner less terse than Vivek's, her disposition easier to read than Shekhar's. Amana thought her more affable, and somehow even more human than her fellows. She had on occasion remarked at the great size of many of the plants she looked after while in Amana's presence.

Over time, he'd grown to suspect the meaning behind the poetry through which she described the little world she presided over. It was peopled by seedlings and saplings that might one day grow tall and mighty under her guidance. Perhaps, Amana thought, that was why the monks had sent him back down to the lowest level for his final test—to remind him of his progress. To show him how far he had come.

Out of respect for Lata, Amana restrained himself from asking about when he would return to the peak to continue his training. After a time, however—his anticipation must have shown on his face—she looked at him pityingly before taking his hand.

"I have something to show you," she whispered as she led him to a portion of the garden he'd never seen before.

She led him through a vine covered archway to a grassy walkway darkened by hedged thickets. The way ahead was so dimly lit that even though the sun had now fully risen the path was only barely visible. After a short walk they reached a large clearing where Amana could see a steady stream of clearest water trickling from a fountain to a planter from which sprouted the most beautiful flower he had ever seen—a large blossom of softly shimmering white that glowed as brilliantly as the new moon.

"It is called *Àyá's* Grace," Lata said, pointing to the fountain. "A particularly thirsty plant, but a picky one. Here, take one of these and crumble it into the fountain."

The old woman pulled a white pellet from a pouch on her waist, holding it up for Amana to see.

"I've seen these before!" Amana exclaimed. "When Shekhar taught me to brew pel'lepe tea!"

"Yes, we craft them here using ancient techniques." Lata nodded. "The powder they break down into settles at the base of the vessel, attracting even the most minute impurities and repelling the water itself. Watch as it swells."

Sure enough, cold clear water bubbled up and over to drain into the planter which Amana now realized held no soil.

"How does the plant survive like this?" he asked in wonder.

"It is dull witted as plants go," she said.

He gave her a questioning look, wondering whether she was joking or not before she continued in a solemn voice. "Who knows what chain of circumstances gave rise to the plant? But it is descended from the Old World. In times gone by, the flower was common. Proud and strong. Perhaps the air today is dryer than it once was. Perhaps the soil is not as vital as it used to be. Or maybe something other than water rained down from the ancient skies. I cannot say, I was not there."

She rested her hands near the base of the large clay pot from which the flower sprang.

"When planted using normal means, Àyá's Grace becomes either infirm or gluttonous," Lata said patiently. "When planted in soil, it drinks too quickly. The flower becomes too strong for its own good and finds itself over-grown. In an effort to balance the scales, the plant will take in water to filter its inner passages. It does this too quickly also and becomes engorged. Pathways saturated, darkened, and clogged, it begins to die. Only by using the purest waters and supplying a carefully apportioned blend of minerals shall the plant flourish and shine."

Marveling at the thought of such a laborious and unending chore, Amana brought the palms of his own hands to rest against the pot.

"It must have great powers for you to look after it like this," he said, speaking more to himself. "But I don't under-stand... why not let it die?"

She looked at him before saying, "If left on its own, the plant would already be extinct. This was the last of its kind in the world when I brought it here. That is the way of nature. But look..." She pointed to two new bulbs lower on the stalk. "New beginnings." She smiled up at him. "When the time for death has come, we accept it. Death is a part of life. But as long as we are here, as long as we can help, we will. Ask for help. Learn to accept it. Encourage three others to do the same. And encourage them to encourage three more. Watch as your light spreads."

Conflicted thoughts raced through Amana's mind and pierced through the flower's calming glow. Had the plant asked for help? Could it have refused aid once it was offered? People were more complicated than that. Some did not know how or when to accept help. Others did not know when they needed it. And more than a few, Amana knew, were beyond help of any kind. Some simply weren't worth such trouble. Some weren't even worth the effort it took to keep Àyá's Grace alive, but Lata would not want to hear that.

"A candle lighting another…" he said, nodding his head slowly. "Why wait until today to tell me all this, master? Does this have anything to do with my final test?"

"I don't know so much about *final* tests." Her lips formed a tender smile. "I find it impossible to stop learning, myself."

Amana weathered the gentle rebuke in silence and tried to look as though he found her remark amusing.

"Go and rest now," she said. "We will speak to you this evening. Come to the Chamber of the Elders at dusk. Bring an open heart and a steady mind. The next leg of your journey begins tonight."

Yes! Finally, he thought as he turned to head back to his humble living quarters. He was truly on his way. He allowed the anger and frustration he'd been feeling to fully slip away from him at last.

A year ago he'd been a desperate wanderer. Now, he was on the verge of mastering destiny itself. The power to seize the future would soon belong to him. Amana had known he was ready for so long, and now the monks knew it too. He was standing on the precipice of a new era. He was about to cross the bridge between today and tomorrow. A great change was upon him. This final test of dedication would mark his passage to the summit. At last he would see the peak and unlock its mysteries. After today, all of his hard work would be worth it.

FIVE

THE SOFT LIGHT OF DUSK BATHED THE LOWER LEVELS OF the temple. Dark clouds drifted across a gleaming sky of purple and orange. And as the sun set, Amana's spirit soared with him as he trotted up the steps to the peak.

He retraced a familiar path through a tall windowless tower which housed the spiraling set of stairs to the fifth floor. It was very long walk in the dark, and he was climbing higher than ever before.

When he had learned to brew pel'lepe tea, he had been largely confined to the meditation chambers that made up most of the fifth level. Tonight, he was bound for the room above all others.

What would he learn? Would he finally be able to see far enough into the future to kill—? No, he couldn't think that way around the monks. They would know his true intentions. They had a way of looking straight through his lies and half-truths. He only needed to keep his face a little while longer. Then he could get back to his real business. A year was far more than enough waiting.

He reached a large wooden door at the top of the staircase and pushed it open. Bracing himself for what awaited him, he emerged onto an outer foyer on the temple's tallest spire. A strange, disorienting sensation surged through him, as had been the case during his guided climb from the base of Mount Junga. An impenetrable mist enveloped his world, and he stared for a long moment at the sight before him.

From a distance, the Council Chamber looked as if it were suspended in the air. In truth, it had been constructed atop a small flat expanse of rock on the other side of a deep gorge. The only thing completing the pathway between the true summit and the rest of the temple, was a rickety bridge of simple wood and rope. He had read about this during his time working in the library, but he had never contemplated what such a sight might actually look like.

For an instant, the view took his breath away. He reached out with his hands and shuffled slowly across the bridge, looking anywhere but down. The foggy sky he glimpsed above him swirled with mystery. Just now, however, only one mystery concerned him. He needed to know how to rescue his future from the cruel grip of chance.

That question, at least, is about to be answered, he thought as he placed a hand on a large bronze door knocker.

Slowly, the doors parted and he entered a chamber at the center of which he found Vivek, Shekhar, and Lata. Vivek stood tall and proud with his hands clasped behind his back. Shekhar crossed his own in front of him, each arm hidden in the opposite sleeve of a voluminous robe. Dressed in garments to match her fellows, Lata had assumed her usual place in the center looking much the same as she had on the day Amana had met her. The only differences were the bandages still wrapped around her gnarled hands.

The elders stood in front of a large hearth in which blazed a miraculous sight. Great flames of purple and silvery white filled the room with light and dancing shadows and burned with unnatural silence. When he was, at last, able to tear his eyes away from the captivating fire, Amana stepped forward, and his footsteps echoed as he continued his approach.

"Masters, I am honored," he said dutifully as he kneeled before them. "Truly, there is beauty here unmatched anywhere in the world. I have seen many strange and extraordinary things during my time here." He nodded toward the fire. "I'm eager to learn so much more."

Looking down on him placidly, hunchbacked Shekhar spoke first. "We can teach you nothing more, apprentice."

Amana's heart leapt, and he fought to stay upright as blood rushed to his head and a fierce pounding filled his ears. How could that be? His sight only extended a few seconds. There had to be more they could have taught him. There just had to be.

"Not yet," said Lata in a gentle voice.

Amana stiffened slightly as he regained his composure. Still somewhat in shock, he blinked at the assembled elders and waited for them to explain.

"There is a village called Aberash a day's journey from the base of Mount Junga," Vivek said in his deep commanding voice. "The nearest river runs with tainted waters unfit for bathing, fishing, or drinking. You must go to them. Help them in the name of M'kahr'ala."

Amana could not believe what he was hearing. Here, on the eve of his anniversary, he was once again being handed another pointless chore. *When will this end?*

Did the monks think he would be content to carry out such menial tasks day in and day out for the rest of his life like Avishal? Didn't the very fact that the elders themselves had risen through the ranks to mastery prove that they *knew* the value of ambition? Surely, they understood what was driving him. Why were they holding him back?

"This is to be the last of your trials," Shekhar explained,

as though he knew perfectly well what Amana was thinking. Not for the first time, Amana wondered whether the old monk did in fact read minds.

Amana kept his thoughts to himself as best he could as he weighed his options. Giving up would ensure that he had wasted a year of his life. Going forward he no longer felt he could trust the monks. Every dreary task he'd performed had been replaced by another.

"They say this will be your final test," hissed a voice in his head.

"Yeah, well, they say a lot of things," said another.

In the end he found the cold emptiness inside him needed filling, and the lone morsel they dangled before him now was the only thing he could hope for.

"What," he asked in a voice of determined calm, "would you have me do?"

Vivek outstretched a sagely hand. "Use what we have taught you to help the villagers."

"Teach them to help themselves," Shekhar intoned.

Moving with grace and deliberation, Lata thrust her wooden staff into the purple-white flames behind her. She paused for a moment, before twirling the staff to bring the burning tip directly in front of her wrinkled face. She spread her arms like a bird taking flight, and the staff stood upright, apparently of its own accord.

"Watch as your light spreads," Lata exclaimed as she clamped her hands on the end of the staff, allowing the flames to spread over her flesh. "And let it guide you back to us, that we may show you the path to Truth." The bandages around her arms burned away, and the flames abated to reveal withered, bloodless, and unburnt hands.

SIX

AMANA'S TEETH GROUND SO LOUDLY THEY DROWNED OUT the sounds of his footsteps as he stormed back down to the fifth floor. He ignored the faces of passersby as he moved through the halls, allowing his feet to carry him forward without conscious thought. After a year of slaving away, he was being trundled off to some inconsequential village on the edge of civilization.

Fuming as he walked, he tried without success to guess at how long his task would take to complete. Weeks? Moons? Maybe even years? And why were they sending him alone on a mission of such importance? If the monks' priority was to help the ailing villagers, surely they would have entrusted the task to a fully fledged master of their order. They had provided no guidance and issued no specific decree. Left to his own devices, how was he supposed to clean the river?

Just as the thought entered his mind, he passed the entrance to the library from which he'd fetched ancient books and tomes for the masters many weeks earlier. Amana bit his lip as he pondered whether or not to go inside.

There's nobody here.

Surely, it couldn't hurt to take a quick look around. Who knew when he'd be returning to Mount Junga—and besides, hadn't he *earned* at least a taste of the higher mysteries so carefully guarded by the monks?

He looked up and down the empty corridor before stepping into the library. The repository of knowledge was among the most elaborately decorated rooms anywhere in the temple. Ancient ladders and spiral staircases linked three stories of glossy hardwood. Enormous bookcases bore thousands of leather-bound volumes, faded maps, and other tomes. Marble plinths bearing tall sculptures of bronze and petrified wood were scattered throughout the aisles. The soft light of hundreds of candles illuminated walls covered with paintings and stone floors lined with carpets of dark red.

A faint musty scent filled Amana's nostrils as he crept around the library, moving with as much stealth as he could muster. He skimmed over an open manual detailing the organization of the library and visited the section concerned with health and medicine, where he hoped he might find something that might aid in his quest to help the village of Aberash.

He thought back to his lessons brewing tea and gardening as he flipped through a dirty guide for the caring of exotic herbs and plants. Taking the manual between his teeth, he shifted books around and examined a few of the assorted trinkets on display before his attention was drawn to a moldy old tome entitled *Herbal Medicines for Maladies*.

Reading while he walked, he moved to another section of the library divided into historical archives on the left and philosophy to the right. He filled a small woven basket with the two books he'd already sampled and continued browsing.

He opened, and immediately shut, an unmarked book

which had turned out to be a collection of poetry from the land of Vaaj. The good that would do him.

He bent low to sort through a large black chest filled to the brim with scrolls of parchment. After several minutes, he found a dusty collection of maps, some of which detailed the area surrounding Aberash, including the nearby Zyeta River. Judging from the name and its description on the map, Amana supposed the Zyeta must have once flowed with rushing white water. Either the ancient Aberashi people had an ironic sense of humor when they named the river long ago, or time had been most unkind in recent years.

Lost in his musings Amana stood up too quickly and bumped his head against the hard wooden shelf above him. Whispering furiously, he cursed himself as he steadied a rattling vase he'd nearly knocked from the shelf. The lingering noise rang ominously through the silence of the vast room, and Amana's heartbeat quickened as he glanced around in all directions.

He stifled the sound of his heavy breathing and rolled his eyes upward as he sighed with relief. Across from him, he glimpsed a single bound scroll stowed apart from the others inside a wall-mounted case. Transfixed by the curious sight, he stashed the collection of maps in his basket as he moved to take a closer look.

The scroll laid on a small plush pillow behind a thin pane of glass. A small tablet bearing an inscription sat at the front of the pillow. Amana's brow furrowed as he read the words: *The Scroll of the Balanced Five*.

What could this be? Was this the key to mastering the Five Paths? Could this be the solution to end his plight? Did this sacred document hold the answers he had been seeking so desperately ever since he arrived?

Moving as quickly as he dared, Amana grabbed a random scroll from the black chest below. He grabbed an old writing utensil carved from reed and pried at the pane of glass. After a moment, the pane lifted upward with a soft grating noise, and Amana swapped the two scrolls.

He took a moment to examine his handiwork objectively, checking for any obvious sign of disturbance. When he was satisfied, he bolted away from the archives back toward the exit. He resumed walking normally, though with a pronounced jaunt in his step once he'd returned to the corridors.

His eagerness to unfurl the secrets hidden within the scroll made the journey from top to bottom feel even longer than usual, but the thought of having something to look forward to had revived him a great deal.

A few minutes later, he had placed the scroll on his sleeping mat and closed the door to his living quarters safely behind him. He unwound the scroll, but in his haste to read it, he'd overlooked the gloomy dark of night outside his window. He lit a candle in the corner of his room and returned to kneel before the miraculous scroll once more.

Before he had the chance to read anything, a feeling of unease shot up his spine and suddenly, his short-sight flashed before him: a withered old hand reached out before him to form a loose fist. As quickly as it had come, the vision had gone, like all the others. If only he could make them last more than a few seconds. But alas, he was again staring at the scroll in his hands, back in the present. Looking around, he found himself in his room, quite alone, but he knew he wouldn't be much longer. No sooner had he stashed the scroll in a pair of old slippers than he heard a knock at his bedroom door.

He took a brief moment to compose himself before answering. As the door creaked open, he looked from right to left, seeing nothing at all.

"Up for a bit of bedtime reading, are we?" came a quiet voice from below.

Startled, Amana looked down to see Lata smiling up at him. "Master! Please, come in."

"Perhaps I misjudged the value of a good night's sleep when we spoke earlier this morning." She hobbled into the room with a wry smile. The shadows of her hair crawled up the candle-lit walls like a gigantic spider.

"To what do I owe the pleasure?" Amana asked as she turned to face him.

"I apologize for calling at such a late hour, but I wanted a word with you before you leave," she said with her hands clasped behind her back. With great difficulty, he quelled the powerful urge to glance at the floppy old pair of shoes in the corner.

"About what, master?" he asked with a steadiness he did not feel.

"Because I am your friend, Amana. I sense in you deep confusion, anger, and impatience. You wonder why it is we have chosen to send you far from here after all you've done. You wonder why it is we do not invite you to the peak. We dare not. Taking you to the peak before you are ready will destroy you. Junga is no friend to the lost." Lata frowned deeply, as though to think of something long forgotten. "Those who are lost must find themselves. And the mountain conceals truths with great ferocity and terrible vengeance. If you are not careful, you will become a mystery unto yourself. But there is more than one path to truth. Your final test will take place away from here, perhaps further than any of us can predict. You shall bear our teachings through the clear light of day. You shall move unfettered by the shroud of Junga's mists. Go back to the world you think you know. And look upon it *truly*, for the first time."

Amana looked at her imploringly. He wanted to make her understand, but he wasn't sure if she could.

Lata broke the long silence first. "You've never said

exactly what it was that brought you to us." He opened his mouth to speak, but she cut him off in her gentle way. "I'm not here to delve into your past. Not all seas are worth swimming in." Her mouth broke into a toothless grin. Amana shifted uncomfortably as she stared at him. "I may not know exactly what you're seeking," she continued, and a note of warning crept into her voice now. "But you have been chasing after it most aggressively."

Amana nodded slowly before responding. "I told you I would do whatever it took to achieve True Balance, and I meant it. My intentions are true. For my life to have meaning... I must succeed."

"You live only for the future... and are captive to the past." She took his strong hands in her veiny old ones. The loose skin and prominent veins belied her firm grip. "As your teacher, I can tell you the path before you is clear. As your friend, I can only ask that you try to stop looking for it. Stop chasing after the future. Let your destiny find you."

He opened his mouth, but let what he was about to say die in his throat as he bowed before her. "Thank you, Master. I will do my best."

"You've had a long day, and longer ones lie before you. Get some rest. Sleep tonight. Tomorrow is a new day."

SEVEN

THE FOLLOWING MORNING, AMANA PACKED A SMALL travel wagon with supplies from the garden. After reading more from his "borrowed" library tomes, he stole a small pouch filled with the cleansing stones the monks used to purify water and several bottles of healing ointments and protective salves. Alongside the silent guide who had shepherded his first climb through the mountainous Junga trails one year earlier, Amana began his descent through the mists back to the world below.

Several days later, they met a pair of young boys at a campsite they'd made near the mountain's base. The children had arrived from the Aberash a day earlier and had been expecting Amana. The two boys had brought three horses and a delivery of spices, grain, and other foodstuffs.

Amana smiled to himself. *So this explains why the temple kitchens were so well stocked.*

His silent guide took hold of the delivery from Aberash, and Amana affixed his own cart of supplies to the horse before mounting it. Taking the lead, the boys set off for their home with Amana traveling close behind them.

The boys didn't speak much to Amana but stared avidly

at him for long stretches of time. They seemed to find him fascinating, but their eyes lacked the light of youth. They looked slightly underfed, but they were good-natured. On a few occasions, he attempted to make conversation by asking them questions about their village. They appeared easily confused and told him nothing beyond what the monks had said to him. He supposed they must have had a very limited education, and instead of asking more of them, he taught them songs to sing as they traveled.

On the third day of their uneventful trek, Amana caught his first glimpse of Aberash from a distance. As he drew closer, he saw the village in greater detail. Vegetable patches and crop fields surrounded the cluster of thatched-roofed topped buildings. Wooden huts and lumpy clay structures made up most of what he saw. As they entered the village square, a half-dozen women greeted them. They collected the children and horses, leading them off to the stables. As the small crowd of villagers cleared away, a powerfully built man of middle age and shorter than average height approached Amana.

"Yemàyá, young one!" he exclaimed with the new moons' greeting, wringing Amana's hand with both of his own. Amana hadn't even known the new moons had passed. But sure enough, as he raised his eyes to the sky, Yem and Àyá's moons crossed one another, denoting the fourth moon of the year.

"My name is Tendaji. Thank you so much for coming!" the man said, looking up at Amana. His accent sounded more similar to the Vaaji's than it did to the monks or the other locals.

Tendaji was balding and had mismatched eyes—both brown, but one darker than the other. He wore simple trousers and a sleeveless vest that did not fully cover his broad chest. His face was kind, but his neck and forearms were covered in deeply lined scars and shiny old burns.

One of his shoulders sagged lower than the other, and Amana's eyes were drawn to the sign of a deep gash, long since healed over. Battle scars. A veteran. Amana smiled down at the man, who was still grasping his hands.

"My name is Amana. Are you the chieftain?"

Tendaji gave a wheezy laugh. "I hope not, for all of our sakes," he said, gesturing around. "I just happen to be too old and useless for the battlefield anymore. I keep a watchful eye out for my villagers these days. Two would be ideal but I've only got the one good eye!" he said pointing at the lighter one.

Amana laughed loudly, but the sound quickly died away as he caught sight of a group of girls hauling buckets of sloshing brown water. Tendaji noticed and shifted uncomfortably as he and Amana watched the girls march toward a large cook pot.

"You've no idea how much this means," Tendaji said quietly. "You've answered our prayers. I have never heard of a group so honorable, nor of heroes more noble than you monks. Ever since coming here years ago, I've spent my days as a friend to your order."

Amana bowed slightly.

"If you don't mind me saying so, you're younger than I expected you to be," Tendaji said after a moment had passed. "How long have you been a Mountain Monk?"

Amana turned to face him. "About one year. But I'm not really a Junga monk—not yet." He glanced around again. It was a dismal sight. Everywhere he looked he saw women with long tired faces hard at work. Livestock were cramped in overcrowded pens and children with muddy faces toiled away in the heat of the midday sun. Perhaps it was only his imagination, but the whole place seemed dull, lacking in color or vibrancy.

Tendaji placed a hand on Amana's shoulder. "A room is being prepared for you where your belongings can be stored. I shall arrange for you to be shown around Aberash so you can get your bearings."

Amana raised an eyebrow. "You won't be coming along?"

Tendaji laughed wheezily once more as he lifted the hem of his trousers to reveal a wooden stump where his right foot had once been. "You'll get along faster without me, young man. Any questions I can answer before you get underway?"

Amana nodded slowly, staring around them at the passersby. "Why are there only women and children?" he asked solemnly. "Where are the men? I see no boy older than nine or ten."

"Fighting on the frontlines against the Vaaji," he grunted. A shadow crept across Tendaji's lined face. "There are some women with them too. The mystic women, that is. The war has already claimed a generation of Aberashi." He pointed to a hut in the distance. "Our healers are there. The few who have returned are in our care. I am the luckiest." The old man swallowed as his eyes misted over.

Amana looked away. He appeared to be allowing Tendaji a moment's silence, but was, in truth, deep in thought. Why would a nation as powerful as Vaaj bother with a tiny spit of land like Aberash. "The Vaaji attacked you? Is the fighting close by?"

Tendaji shrugged. "If the Vaaji have their way, the whole world will bow to them before long. I can't pretend to fathom the minds of those monsters. Heinous conquerors, that's all they are! I got out of there the moment I could. Many other villages to the north have already fallen before their might. All I know is when the Vaaji are on the warpath, you don't want to be in their way."

Amana kept his thoughts to himself. He had only dealt with the Vaaji marginally when he raided their ships in the

Sapphire Seas. Then they were known for their artistry, not their military prowess. Their defeats in Esowon were well known. Perhaps that was why they pushed their front into the east instead of the west. The desert nation wouldn't trouble itself with Aberash or its sister villages without some larger goal in mind. But Amana had enough to worry about as it was and decided to leave the Vaaji mystery for another day.

After catching Tendaji's eye, Amana returned to business. "I've brought a selection of balms and salves crafted by my instructors. Your healers are free to help themselves. I'll take the rest of the day to wander around Aberash. I'll let you know what I plan to do come night." After a renewed outbreak of enthusiastic handshaking and gratitude from Tendaji, Amana took his leave. He'd waved off Tendaji's offer of a guided tour, electing to explore the village for himself.

What he saw was not encouraging.

He visited the healers' huts where his tonics and ointments were being applied to dozens of convalescent soldiers. Most were Tendaji's age, though a few were far younger. None were older. The women's hands worked tirelessly, dressing countless wounds with bandages and healing poultices. As he strode around the village hours later, he bumped into the pair of girls he'd observed carrying muddied waters earlier. He helped them steady their bucket, but a portion of water slopped over the edge and onto the ground.

"Forgive me!" he said kindly. "Did you get this from the Zyeta?" The girls looked at one another before fixing him with confused expressions.

"You mean the Rog?" one of them asked.

Amana stared at them. "I thought the river was called the Zyeta? An ancient and beautiful name. It means white," he explained. To his surprise, the girls laughed.

"There's nothing white or bright about the Rog," said one of the girls as they stumbled off toward the cook pot. Amana followed them and helped them tip the bucket into the cauldron.

He decided he should see the river for himself before going any further.

"How far is the Rog?" he asked.

The second girl pointed to a walkway behind him, which lead away from the village. "A short walk that way."

Amana nodded. "And the broken dam?"

"A day or two away by horse," she said. "To the west."

Amana thanked them and walked toward the Rog. When he finally laid eyes on the brown fetid waters, he fell to his knees. It was even worse than he'd expected. There were no men to help him repair the dam, no elemental mystics to help him shift the rocks. The only ones who lived were away at war or crippled in bed. Between caring for the sick and infirm and running their households, the women were overworked as it was. How was he supposed to fix this on his own? He pulled the pouch of purity stones from his belt and weighed them in his hands. If only he had more of them—or perhaps a few giant stones. But the monks had never shown him how they were made... and then he remembered.

A COUPLE OF HOURS LATER, AFTER RETURNING TO Aberash, Amana was shown to the room Tendaji had set aside for him. As the old veteran had promised, the supplies he'd brought with him from Mount Junga sat waiting for him in the furthest corner of the room. He found what he was looking for in a sack full of spare clothes and shoes. He reached into the bag and fished out the book concerning rare plants and herbs he'd grabbed from the library. He riffled through the pages. Lata had told him she'd brought the last known sample of Àyá's Grace to the temple herself. If she had, it stood to reason she might have left instructions on how to care for the plant... She had!

As he read, Amana's brow furrowed in frustration. Everything Lata had already said about the flower was written there. He didn't need to know how to look after Àyá's Grace. He needed to know how to craft the purity stones. He tossed the manual aside and sank to the floor, gazing up at the bare walls of the room. The sun was setting. Soft amber light shone through the crack under the door. He took a deep calming breath, and the smell of mold filled his nose. Sniffing softly, he looked around for the source of the foul odor and traced it to his bag of supplies.

He emptied the sack onto the floor and gasped. The dirty old tome of venoms lay before him. He had forgotten this one. He flipped through the delicate pages with great care. Surely a book about poisons must contain a chapter or two on antidotes. And there it was: a description of purity stones and their common uses written in the margins. After reading through the early stage of a chapter, he lost a great deal of confidence in his plan. The process involved a dangerous ritual requiring great personal risk. As his finger passed over a foreign incantation, he shook his head hopelessly. This was too much for him. He was no sorcerer.

Still, something about the chapter called to him. He found he did not want to put the book down, and against his better judgment he continued to read. Taking a closer look, he noticed some steps were detailed in an archaic language he did not understand. Was it the Old Tongue? Many of these had been crossed out and replaced by annotations written in the Mother Tongue. He reached the end of the chapter. A smudge obscured the name of the original author, but underneath he read the name Uzoma. *The Lost One?*

Amana closed the book with a thud. The monks certainly wouldn't like to hear he'd literally taken a leaf out of Uzoma's book. He would have to find another way.

LATER THAT EVENING AMANA FOUND TENDAJI BACK IN the kitchen of his farmhouse. The old soldier stirred a large pot of brown bland-smelling stew around which a small crowd of villagers had formed.

Amana wondered how in the world he was going to say what he had to say with all these people around, but after a short time he realized that none of the villagers seemed intent on staying. Each left as soon as his or her bowl had been filled by Tendaji's ladle. From the way they spoke and moved amongst themselves, Amana got the strong impression that this group usually ate with Tendaji, but tonight, it seemed he had made arrangements to dine in private.

This will make it easier, at least.

He stood off to the side, watching as the line dwindled slowly. He stared at the many tired expressions of the women which contrasted sharply against the round guileless faces of the children, wayfaring sailors cast adrift in a sea of youthful bliss. Finally, when the kitchen had been emptied, save for the pair of them, Tendaji motioned for Amana to join him in the next room where a fire crackled merrily within a stone hearth.

Tendaji passed a large bowl of stew to Amana, and the two sat on a tattered rug of purple and gold that must have once looked grand. Amana thanked him and the two ate in silence for a moment.

Amana set his bowl down after only a few mouthfuls and tried, without success, to speak. He knew he was going to have to be the bearer of bad news, but he couldn't summon the words. The old soldier seemed oblivious to the storm raging inside him, which only made things more awkward.

Smiling widely, Tendaji suddenly turned his mismatched eyes to Amana's. "I can't thank you enough for what you're about to do." His quivering voice choked with emotion.

Amana felt as though he'd been stabbed, though no trace of discomfort showed on his face.

"About that..." Amana began, speaking slowly. "I'm not sure the village has the supplies I require."

He found he couldn't hold Tendaji's gaze any longer, so he closed his own eyes to steel himself before continuing. "You lack the manpower required to repair the dam. Even if you did, the process would take many moons. The distance between your village and the new building site would require much time for the transport of materials alone."

Tendaji looked crestfallen for a moment, but Amana went on before the old man could speak. "We could perhaps attempt to fashion new pumps. Running water would be closer at hand and could eliminate some of the constant back-and-forth trips between the river and here. But without the dam, the water is too heavily polluted for even a well to guarantee safe bathing or drinking. You would need to boil water for every last cup. Firewood is too scarce for that to last throughout the year. The problem lies at the source the dam used to check."

With great effort he returned his gaze to Tendaji's. Amana's words came out grimly. "As long as the poisoned tributary flows to your river, nothing I do from here will offer a permanent solution."

A heavy silence settled between them, as thick and obtrusive as the mists of Mount Junga. Something in the fire seemed to die away, and all warmth seeped out from the air.

From beneath his overgrown eyebrows and bushy white

beard, the old man's eyes looked like caves in a hillside covered in snow. For a moment, Amana simply sat and watched as Tendaji's chest heaved up and down. The younger man clenched his fists and braced himself, not knowing what to expect. Anger? Attack? Certainly not tears.

Tendaji's head dropped forward and bobbed up and down as he wept softly. Feeling like an intruder, Amana sat, not knowing what to say or do. He looked on helplessly for a few seconds as Tendaji apologized and began to compose himself.

Amana wished he could turn tail and run from the farmhouse and straight out of the village. He felt as though he were watching something indecent and private and felt disgusted with himself for bringing it about. The uncharacteristic sign of weakness from such a grizzled warrior rattled him. He wasn't entirely sure why Tendaji's outburst had affected him so deeply, but something about it left him feeling squeamish.

He wanted desperately to leave, but instead he stood up and walked toward the older man and placed a hand on his shoulder. Tendaji gave a dry sob and Amana quelled the urge to recoil.

"We cannot leave," Tendaji said, wiping his eyes with the back of his wrist. He continued as his voice shuddered breathlessly. "We have nowhere else to go. I cannot go back to Vaaj. Even if I did, how would we all make such a journey? How would we rebuild? We'd be hated there." He shook his head fiercely as the light of the fireplace danced wildly in his black and white eyes. "No... no... this place is all we have."

Amana thought hard about it, before replying, "There is one other possibility... I may know a way to purify the water at its source. But it will take weeks and I will need supplies... and a guide to the place where the dam collapsed."

Tendaji looked at him as though unsure whether to believe his one good eye. "I know where you can find both."

Amana waited patiently for him to continue.

"There is a marketplace to the west," Tendaji said. "Where my daughter sells what she can. She is the only trader our village has. She can show you where to find whatever you may need, and she knows the road to the tributary."

"What is her name?" Amana asked.

When he spoke, Tendaji's mouth broke into a blinding white grin that outshone the dying fire in the corner of the room. "Manali." The name sounded like butter on his lips. "She will show you where you need to go."

EIGHT

THE SUN SHONE BRILLIANTLY IN A SKY OF PUREST BLUE AS Amana moved through the marketplace on foot. He tied his horse to a post just outside the guarded entryway of a fortified city on the edge of an expansive desert. Dressed in well-worn garments of red and yellow, he walked with head and neck wrapped to guard against the harsh rays of light from above.

Cracked walls of weathered sandstone surrounded a mass of huts, domiciles, and other structures. The cluster of buildings ranged in tones from pale brown and beige to yellow and orange. Tented tables piled high with fruits, meats, and other foodstuffs attracted enormous buzzing flies. Ornamental rugs and carpets lined walls with streaks of gold, indigo, green, and red. Smoke from cook fires and the smells of livestock and their various droppings hung in the motionless air.

Men and women of all ages swarmed the streets, examining goods on display for as far as the eye could see. Merchants and their patrons shouted to be heard as they haggled, while spirited children darted between their legs.

Amana took a deep breath as he savored the noise of the

day. Two days' ride had brought him to the center of what had once been the meeting place for a host of traveling caravans from seven far-flung tribes—or so the story went. The archaic route formed the basis for the name of the now permanent settlement, and Amana strolled at a leisurely pace through the streets of the Seven Serpents.

He took another deep breath as he surveyed the clamoring crowds. The somber mood of poverty-stricken Aberashi had done little to remind him of the life he'd led before apprenticing himself at Mount Junga. His year cloistered away with the monks had been largely characterized by periods of solitude and quiet contemplation. Among both the stoic monks and the solemn-faced villagers, he had felt like an outsider, but here, for the first time in countless moons, he felt like he was truly back among the living.

He walked for the better part of an hour before he found what he was looking for. At the westernmost edge of the market-city, he spotted a short elderly man with a heavy beard browsing at a fish-stand operated by a young copper-skinned girl.

She looked no more than twelve or thirteen, but she was tall for her age, dressed simply in a sleeveless white shirt accompanied by drab brown trousers. On her feet she wore sandals which looked as though they had been inexpertly repaired many times. Her dark brown hair extended to her shoulders in loose curls she had wrapped in a vibrant green scarf. Her smoky green eyes appeared slightly overlarge, set in too thin a face, and glistening white teeth flashed as she spoke animatedly with her single customer.

"When did you say you caught these?" the old man asked suspiciously as he held one fish up by its tail to take a closer look.

"They're as fresh as can be!" she said excitedly in an accent that sounded something between Tendaji's and the locals.

"They stink!" the man cried, waving the fish in her face.

The girl rushed her speech. "I brought them straight from the river—less than a day's ride from here! You can still cure them or smoke them. If you buy two, I'll throw in a third for free!"

The old man shook his head impatiently and threw the fish away from him with such force it bounced off her table and fell to the ground. He walked away grumbling and cursing to himself as he wiped the slime on his tunic. Glaring after him, she bent to one knee to pick up the dusty fish. As she rose back to her full height, she caught Amana's eye, and embarrassment passed over her face.

"See anything you like?" she asked less than exuberantly.

"I think I do, little one," Amana replied as he stepped closer to have a look at her stand. "I see… opportunity."

"That makes one of us, foreigner," she said in a low voice, clearly taken by Amana's island accent. She smirked as she looked up and down the street.

"You say you caught all these yourself?" Amana asked.

"That's the easy part," the girl said, pointing to a horse-drawn cart in the distance behind her, which bore an assortment of barrels, nets, and fishing poles. Amana was genuinely impressed.

"Are they, uh… truly as fresh as you claimed?" he asked carefully.

"Well… yes. Not that it makes much of a difference," she said heavily. Her next words almost came as a whisper. "They come from the Rog."

"And you sell them here on your own?" he asked, allowing his admiration to color his voice.

"I try," she said, shaking a small purse of clinking coins. "This has been a better day than most." She placed a hand on her hip, where Amana now saw a dagger sheathed in her belt. "Even the market thieves know better than to pay me much attention—not that they don't visit from time to time."

Amana placed his hands on his knees and squatted to look her in the eye. "You're too honest, little one." She shot him a questioning look before he went on. "You're a talented angler, and as bright as anyone here." He waved around at the sea of people surrounding them. "But if you're going to succeed, you've got to learn to play to the crowd. Today, you're not a merchant. You're an actor." He waved around at the sea of people surrounding them.

She shook her head like a dog. "What do you mean?"

Amana took a long sweeping look at the many guileless faces milling about.

"Can I show you something?" he whispered.

Nodding, she stared at him as he pointed dramatically from fish to fish counting aloud as he circled the display. When he reached the vendor's side, he stooped to take a look beneath the blanketed table. To his delight, she had nothing stored underneath except for a few empty bowls and plates.

He asked if she minded whether he touched the fish. When she shook her head, he piled all but two of them onto a single large platter.

"You want all of those?" she asked, her eyes wide with excitement.

"Oh, I'm afraid I can't afford all these," Amana said with mock-sorrow as he hid the platter underneath the table. "But I know who can." He gave her a sly smile.

She crossed her arms and regarded him suspiciously as he winked. He caught the eye of a woman wearing robes of deep blue holding the hand of a small boy.

"You there, sweet lady, can I interest you in the catch of the day? Come and sample the finest fish you've ever tasted! You and your son will eat well tonight. A toothsome fish, sure to challenge the experienced palate or enlighten the young and untested. Preconceptions shall be challenged! Minds, broadened!"

The woman stepped forward and sniffed at a fish. Wrinkling her nose at the unpleasant smell, she looked at Amana in astonishment.

"I know the scent may be a bit unusual, but trust me... properly cleaned and cured, these are a highly sought-after delicacy."

"They're *supposed* to smell like this?" she inquired. He had her attention now. He didn't waste a moment in pressing his advantage.

"So high in demand are my beloved fish that I'm afraid stocks are low. As you can see, I have only two left. Let a man rest after a hard morning's work, yes? Buy the last of my catch and make us both happy!"

Shrugging, the woman accepted the fish and tossed a few fat coins onto the table, which he promptly refilled with another two fish once the woman had vanished from sight around a corner.

The girl gasped as Amana turned to face her, smiling widely.

"Keep an eye out for those who have traveled far," he said jovially. "You can tell from the way they move, the colors they wear, their style of hair." He nodded to a couple who wore bright silks of orange and red, their heads bedecked with head wraps sewn with an intricate design. "They're less likely to get wise to us than the locals."

And together the two repeated his trick over the next couple of hours until finally all the funky fish had disappeared. After the last pair had been unloaded, the girl looked up at Amana, silenced by overwhelming gratitude. Her eyes shone with happiness as the money bag jingled merrily in her shaking hands.

"Put that to good use," Amana said in a stern voice, but his eyes twinkled with mirth.

"I can't accept all this... not when you earned it all!" she exclaimed, biting her lip as though in thought. "Split it with me, then."

Amana shook his hand with a small chuckle. "I don't need your coin, little one." He paused for just a moment, as though a thought passed over his eyes. "But there is another way you can help me."

"Anything!" She exclaimed. "Anything at all!"

"I need a guide," Amana said. "Someone who knows every inch of this marketplace, and the land surrounding the old Zyeta dam."

He produced Lata's tome from within his robes and flipped to the recipe he'd memorized the first night he'd spent in Aberash. "Can you show me where I might find these ingredients?"

Her eyes widened as she read this list. "Yes, yes I can indeed, sir!"

"And once you have, will you show me to the site of the collapsed dam, Manali?" Amana asked.

Surprise blossomed in her eyes, and misgiving mingled oddly with the look of joy on her face. "You know my name?" Her hand moved toward her dagger once more.

Amana placed his palms on his knees and bent to look her in the eye. "I have a bit of a confession to make. I know your father Tendaji. He said you may be able to show me the way to the site where the Zytea dam collapsed. Given the bounty of fish you caught on your own, I can see this must be true."

She stared at him for a long moment, but the fingers gripping the knife at her side relaxed a little as Amana spoke.

"I am sorry for deceiving you. Our meeting was not by chance. I came to the Seven Serpents to find you. I have helped you. Now please, help me—hey!" Before he could finish speaking, Manali sprang up and bolted away from him with startling speed. Amana ran after her, rounding corner after corner only just barely able to keep up with the girl as she darted left and right, taking advantage of her small size as she moved through the crowds.

As they passed into a large square, he lost sight of her. When he finally emerged from the sea of people flooding the center of the city, he faced a fork in the path. He came to a stop, panting slightly. Ahead of him lay two barren streets. At the start of one, he saw a green scarf lying on the ground, in front of the other, a pair of mismatched dirty sandals.

The girl has talent.

Staring around, Amana gave thought to his next course of action. Logically, the girl would have to return to Aberash. He supposed he would just have to beat her there. Hopefully, her father would help make her see sense. Grumbling to himself at this latest disruption to his plans, he retraced his steps.

As he walked, his vision flashed before him, pulling him back to the entrance of the marketplace. As his vision returned to the present, he sprinted with greater urgency than ever before. Manali would recognize her father's horse... If she got there first, he'd he stranded here.

He scaled the side of a small building and covered the distance by leaping from rooftop to rooftop, much faster than he ever could winding his way through the maze of streets below. As he reached the gates of the Seven Serpents, he jumped from the rooftop of a four-story building to a long ladder that reached the top of the market-city's walls. From the top he spied a small figure shooting across the sand, heading straight for his mount.

He tore the head wrappings from his own robes and draped them over a rope drawn between two guard towers. Holding onto both ends with one hand each, he jumped forward, sliding along the line. After a few exhilarating seconds, he let go, allowing himself to drop down to the desert below and landing between the horse and Manali just as the girl reached for the reigns.

"Now," he said, panting heavily. "As I was saying, I'll be needing a guide."

The girl reached for her dagger, but Amana was too quick for her. His short-sight giving him the split-second warning he needed. Placing a foot behind her own, he pushed out against her shoulder. Though she caught herself as she tripped, the move bought Amana enough time to grab the knife from her sheath, and in one fluid motion, he cut the money purse from her belt as well.

"I think I'll be keeping this for now," he said, looking down at her. "And in return for the trouble you've put me through, I'll take a small cut out of your profits, after all. Don't worry though, the rest can still be yours if you only do as I say."

Manali gazed up at him, mouth agape. "Who... who are you? What do you want with me?" Fear and suspicion had fallen away from her face, replaced by a look of confused curiosity.

"My name is Amana. I've come to save your village."

NINE

THREE DAYS LATER, TWO TRAILS OF FOOTSTEPS, ONE small, the other large, traced the banks of the Rog. The languid waters of the river ran brown, and a cool breeze carried the fetid smell of vegetation and swamp life.

Amana kneeled in the muck of a large deposit of earth, filling large buckets of clay. He had spent the previous day carrying clumps of clay from the riverside to a small clearing nearby where Manali had built a roaring fire. Promising to return the money after receiving her assistance, Amana had gained Manali's reluctant cooperation.

The two had returned to her stand in the marketplace to collect her own cart and mount before completing their shopping at the various apothecaries spread throughout the market. Manali's knowledge of the various shop-owner's wares had assisted greatly in the procurement of every ingredient Amana needed for the purity stones.

Using a mortar and pestle, Manali had ground the herbs and pastes into a fine powder, which Amana had bound, using more clay, before smoothing the substance into an orb the size of his head. As Amana continued his work in the clay deposits throughout the day, Manali had repeated the process eleven more times. Now they had a dozen stones, ready for sanctification. The rest was up to Amana.

Still, he hadn't let Manali return to the village with her payment. The girl had her uses. She tended to their campfire while Amana was hard at work. Though she no longer trusted him as fully as when they had first met, keeping an eye out for wildlife or potential intruders worked to her own benefit as much as Amana's.

Unfortunately, the girl wasn't much for company, begrudging as her services were. Amana understood. He'd felt much the same during his time with the monks on many occasions. However, while he could empathize with her given the nature of their working relationship, he felt no guilt for the way he handled the situation. She stood to gain a handsome reward for her part in this deal, and he had, after all, only been acting for the good of the village.

"Come here and help me with this," he said to her as he brought in a final haul of clay. He emptied the buckets onto a large heap he'd been gathering since their arrival to this place.

"What are you building?" she asked huffily as she joined him in shaping the clay into a large dome.

"A kiln. We need a large oven to bake the stones. The stones must burn in the intense heat of a Blessed Fire for seven days. Long enough for Yem and Àyá both to smile upon them. Of course, the kiln itself needs time to dry out and harden before it will serve our purposes."

"Seven days?" she cried in shocked disbelief. "We have to stay here for seven days?"

Amana nodded patiently as they continued their work. "That's why I used my portion of the money to buy so much food. We'll be here for a while, and as good as you are with your fishing pole, I don't plan on eating anything that swims in the Rog. Not just yet, at any rate."

She piled some clay haphazardly on the slowly forming kiln with a haughty look on her face and smoothed the lumps over with unnecessary force. She was threatening to do more harm than good. Amana thought for a moment about dismissing her and continuing on his own, but if he could get her to care about what they were doing, the job could be completed so much more quickly.

"Remember why I'm doing this," he said with as much excitement as he could. "I'm trying to help your village."

"No, you're not," Manali spat.

"Excuse me?"

She fixed him with a cold penetrating look which bore the suggestion of wisdom too deep for her age. Something about it reminded Amana of Vivek.

"You're not just here to help the Aberash," she said. "You wouldn't be doing this if you weren't going to get something out of it."

Amana rocked his head from side to side. "True enough, I guess. But does that really change anything? You're still getting what you need, aren't you?"

Her look softened somewhat, and she nodded. "Yes, I suppose I am. But my parents are honest folk. They taught me not to lie. You're not trustworthy," she sneered, picking at a spot of dirt on her cheek.

"You didn't mind that when you had something to gain yourself," Amana reminded her.

She adopted a thoughtful expression and shrugged before joining him in the work. Her hands moved more gracefully across the clay formation as she mimicked his actions. This was good. He had her attention, and she was making the effort. Before he began his ritual though, he knew he would need to gain her trust—if he wanted to survive.

"You never mentioned your mother before," Amana said, speaking tentatively. "You spoke of her as though she is alive. I had assumed, well, you know... Why isn't she back at the village? Why doesn't your father talk about her?"

"She left," Manali said sadly, though she continued working diligently as she spoke.

"For... another man?" Amana asked. He didn't want to pry too deeply into a sensitive subject, but curiosity had gotten the better of him, and the earlier mention of her parents seemed to have a softening effect on Manali.

"Absolutely not!" she spat in a renewed bout of fury.

"Forgive me," Amana said earnestly. "It's just... well, you were a bit vague."

"She left to find my brother," she explained, resting her hands for the first time.

"You have a brother?"

"Had one..." Her voice went low. "He left to fight in the war when I was nine. He had to go far away and... and..." Tears welled in her eyes but did not fall. Instead, she sniffed them back as though it were a frequent habit. "Anyway, my mother couldn't accept his loss."

"And she was confident enough to travel alone?" Amana asked.

Manali spoke through her tears. "She can touch the elements. She can handle herself. She's... not in her right mind. Father says she's on a journey she'll never complete."

Amana frowned. "I'm sorry." He turned away from her. "I'll... I'll finish this on my own. Go and rest a bit. Have something to eat."

"No!" she said brightly, sniffing as she wiped her eyes. "I want to get this over with. I'll stay and help."

Night had fallen by the time their work was complete and after tending to their mounts they settled on opposite sides of the fire. Amana stoked at the flames with a long stick as Manali stared at him. Her green eyes shone brilliantly in the soft light.

"What is it?" she demanded. Apparently they'd maintained eye contact longer than he'd realized.

"Sorry," he said quickly. "It's just that... you remind me of someone."

"Who?" she asked, far more gently than before.

"My daughter... Sanaa," Amana said without really meaning to.

Manali shook her head. "What sort of monk has children?"

"Not a very good one," Amana admitted, deciding not to delve too deeply into his past prior to joining the monks.

Silence fell between them, disrupted only by the croaking of frogs near the river and the crackling of the fire. She turned her face away from his slightly, but her eyes remained fixed on his own. She seemed caught between wanting to look away and not feeling able to.

"Where is she now... your daughter?" she finally asked.

Amana tore his eyes away from hers at last and stared at the blackened logs burning between them. "Far away," he sighed heavily.

Manali nodded her understanding. She stood and circled around the fire, taking one of his hands between hers. "Maybe she's out there somewhere, holding hands with my brother."

For the first time in a long, long while, a genuine smile spread across Amana's face.

Manali's brow furrowed as she brought a gentle hand up to touch his face. "You look so sad when you smile."

TEN

THE FOLLOWING MORNING, AMANA INSTRUCTED MANALI to forage for firewood. While she was gone, he went over the process for summoning Blessed Fire described in the volume on healing poisons. When Manali returned, he piled up the wood she'd collected inside the kiln. Once the job was complete, Amana turned to face her.

"Manali, there is a reason I needed you to stay with me after you brought me here," he said.

"Yes?"

His tone became suddenly grave. "I'm about to summon a Blessed Fire. The ritual will involve a sacrifice from me. I will be weakened when we're done. It will be up to you to complete the process." He locked eyes with her. "You must do exactly what I tell you to do. I'm placing my trust in you." He pulled the money purse from his belt and tossed it at her feet. "Just so you can see the only one with anything to lose is me. Please... don't let me down. I need this to work. It *has* to work."

"I won't, Amana," she promised, fear laced in her eyes.

"Grab a branch from the campfire," he said. "When — and only when I tell you to — use it to light the kiln."

Manali nodded dutifully and Amana drew her knife from his belt. Gripping the blade with his left hand, he slid the knife across it in a swift cutting motion, leaving a deep bloody slash in his left palm. He ran his injured hand across every piece of wood piled within a shallow pit, leaving long bloody streaks on each log as he went. Speaking in a tongue he did not understand, Amana recited a prayer he'd read from the book as he gripped one of the logs firmly.

Gradually, the log lost some of its color and grew engorged. Though Amana had researched the ritual, he hadn't expected to be weakened so quickly. Amana stared as the log sprouted roots that dug deep into the earth, his spirit like a ravenous weed watered with his own blood. As he held the log in his still bleeding hand, he signaled for Manali to light the fire as he continued his strange prayer. Shocked, the girl shook her head in horror at the thought.

"Not with your hands in the fire!" she screamed.

"It will be all right, Manali," he barked. "Now do as I say."

He said the prayer again, and again the logs grew larger and paler. He raised his voice as he continued and motioned for her to do it again, and again she shook her head.

"Manali, you must light the fire!" he shouted.

"I can't! It isn't right!" she cried.

"Do it! Now! Come on! Do it or I will die!"

"No… no… no," she sobbed.

"Manali, please!" he screamed, eyes bulging. "Do it for your mother! Do it for your brother. Do it for my daughter! Light the fire!"

And she dropped the branch.

Purple flames erupted in a dazzling blaze that engulfed the pile of kindling and traveled up Amana's left arm. He turned his head away from the blinding flash of light and slowly crumpled to the ground. Manali rushed and heaved him on this back. She bent low to examine his hand and found the injury had healed—no sign of blood or burns anywhere on his arm. She stared at him in wonder as he smiled weakly up at her. "Place the stones in the flames and cover the pit with the kiln."

"What then?" she asked, as a wave of relief passed over her face.

"Make sure I don't die," he said in a slow lumbering voice as he passed out.

———

AMANA SPENT THE NEXT TWO DAYS SLIPPING IN AND OUT of consciousness. Manali prepared food and drink whenever he awoke, and by the third day, his strength had largely returned. On the seventh morning of the burning. Amana brought a hammer down on the kiln. Three heavy blows was all it took to shatter the clay dome. The twelve purity stones glistened in the sunlight. The largest pearls in all the world.

"They're beautiful," Manali gasped, passing her hand over the flawless white surface of one of the orbs.

"Yes, it seems almost a shame to sink them in the river," Amana agreed.

Together, they loaded the stones into Manali's fish cart and brought them to the place on the river where the dam had ruptured. There, they wove her assortment of nets together, forming an enormous pocket in which they stuffed the precious stones. They scaled the slabs of rubble which were all that remained of the dam and heaved the bundle over the side. They heard it splash as they ran as quickly as they dared back to the shoreline. A needle like geyser of spouting water rushed over the jagged rock, quickly replacing the murky brown waters with a powerful stream of pure blue-white.

As they surveyed their handiwork, Amana pulled a

second pouch of goods from his robes and handed it to an awestruck Manali who looked as though she had never seen clean water before. Perhaps she hadn't, Amana thought.

"Thank you for your help, little one." He smiled down on her. "I really couldn't have done this without you."

She took the bag from him but didn't look at it. "Aren't you coming back with me to Aberash? My people... my father... they will want to thank you for what you've done!"

"I'm afraid I must be going. My assignment here is complete, and I'm eager for its reward. I've been waiting a long time." Amana stared off into the distance. Though he could not see Junga mountain from where they stood, he knew it was just on the horizon. "I've spent the last few weeks in the service of your village, but I've spent the last year in service to the monks. It's time for me to return to Mount Junga."

Amana looked at her bare feet and remembered how she had ditched her shoes on the market streets several days earlier. "I have one more thing for you." He pulled a floppy set of leather-bound shoes from his travel bag. "They'll be a bit large on you, but they'll make your journey back to Aberash more comfortable."

She smiled warmly, and her green eyes watered as she accepted his final gift.

"Is there anything else I can do for you before you leave?" Manali asked.

"If, by chance, the monks should ask how well I served your people, tell them the truth," Amana said with a twinkle in his eye as he swung one leg over his horse. Once his horse broke into its first trot, Manali called for him to stop. He turned to face her as she came running up to him.

"Wait! I found this in the shoes you gave me!" she said.

In her hand she held the *Scroll of the Five Paths* Amana had stolen from the temple's library. He stared at her in wonder as he took the forgotten scroll from her. He wanted to open it here and now. Here was his reward. Who gave a damn what the monks thought now? But no. Now that his job was complete, the monks were finally going to accept him into their ranks. He had completed his mission more quickly and with greater success than they'd had any right to expect. Was he really about to trade the opportunity to learn everything the monks knew for a simple scroll?

"Thank you, little one," he said as she placed the scroll in his bag. "You've given me more than you could ever know."

She didn't look as though she understood, but she grinned all the same.

"Be well, Manali!" He shouted over his shoulder as he sped away. "One day I hope we meet again!"

ELEVEN

THE NIGHT WAS COLD, AND THE COUNCIL CHAMBER SWAM
with purple-white light just as it had on the eve before
Amana's departure for Aberash weeks earlier. He inhaled
the scent of burning incense and brewing pel'lepe tea as he
stood waiting alone in the center of the room.

All told, twenty-four days had passed since he'd bid
farewell to Manali on the banks of the Zyeta River. His
return journey back to the base of Mount Junga had been
largely uneventful but had seemed to take an eternity. Upon
his return, the guide who resided at the start of the trail had
been standing ready to receive Amana.

Just as had happened a year earlier, Amana had
embarked on a five-day-long journey up the mountain with
his silent guide leading the way. This time around, however,
the mountain seemed far less intimidating than it had
before. The climb was still physically taxing, but the spells
of madness he'd experienced in the past did not return, and
he was able to keep pace with his guide without the need to
stop for rest.

When he returned, a pair of masters provided him with
sleeping quarters on the fifth floor. They told him the elders

were locked in conclave and would send for him when they were ready for him.

That had been fourteen days ago.

Amana had expected to be sent for long before now, but he had nevertheless reported to the council chamber after having received his summons earlier that same morning. Now he stood staring at the great hearth with his hands clasped behind his back, ready to face the elder masters.

A quartet of masters entered the room, and he turned from the fire to face them. They all looked much the same. Long shaggy beards and great locks of twisted hair hung from their scalps and faces, and all were clad in shimmering robes of purple and white to match the fire before which Amana stood.

"A feast has been prepared for you at the summit," one of them said. "Please, come with us."

Surprise and delight filled the creases in Amana's impatient face. Feeling buoyant, he strode over to join them. The beating of drums thumped lightly ahead, and the soft sounds of woodwind instruments echoed against walls as they steered him through a corridor opposite from the chamber's large heavy door, which led to a dining area perched on an outer plateau he had never seen before.

Torches burned silently with the same purple flames that lit the chamber, and the night air felt impossibly warm. Platters piled high with food and jugs filled with water and pots of tea covered a table carved from a humongous slab of black stone. Twenty or so chairs surrounded the table, and each was occupied by a master. Amana was directed to a seat at the center of the table opposite Lata who was, as ever, flanked by Vivek and Shekhar.

Lata smiled gently as he approached. Amana adopted a friendly expression but felt slightly uncomfortable as she peered up at him from where she sat. Perhaps it was only his imagination, but Amana thought she looked even older than he had remembered, and she looked unusually tired and frail.

Amana inclined his head in a respectful bow. "Masters, this is a great honor."

Vivek regarded him blankly as the young man took his seat. Shekhar poured a cup of tea and handed it to Lata before pouring a second for himself.

"How fare you from your travels?" Shekhar asked.

"I must admit, it was a pleasant experience living among people like the ones I once knew. In many ways, it served as a powerful reminder of what brought me here in the first place. I want to live a life of dignity. I want to make a difference. I want to feel as fulfilled as I did on the day I saved Aberash. I want to carry that feeling here within me for the rest of my days." He placed a hand over his heart. His words were true. He did want to go back to such a life, but not before he achieved his revenge. Then, and only then, would he allow himself a life of peace.

Vivek raised a curious eyebrow. "Really? You seem unchanged since your departure."

"I remain as resolute as ever," Amana agreed, "but I feel steady and more sure of myself than I used to be. The journey taught me a great deal. I see the practical value in your teachings more clearly than I could before."

Vivek cast a sidelong glance at Shekhar, who spoke next. "This is good. Tests are meant to demonstrate greater understanding. Fortunately, even failed tests provide further opportunities to learn."

What did that mean? Amana didn't quite know what to say to that, so he remained silent. He looked from Shekhar to Lata, who appeared not to notice him as she sipped her tea. To fill the mildly uncomfortable pause in the conversation, he reached for the nearest plate of roasted vegetables tossed with grains, but Vivek held up a hand to stop him.

"We have something special for you," he said in his

familiar, calm baritone. He clapped his hands twice, and a pair of apprentices Amana had not noticed approached from behind.

They placed a covered platter in front of Amana. Vivek stood and removed the cover, revealing a platter filled with pungent smoked fish. Amana glanced around in confusion. The monks did not eat meat or fish.

"What is this?" he asked, voice laced with confusion.

Vivek gestured with the cover, his voice ominous. "I was about to ask you the same thing."

Amana shook his head in true bewilderment. As Vivek resumed his seat, the rest of the table, save for his fellow elders, rose up. Amana watched as the masters slowly filed from the room in silence. Soon everyone, even those who had been playing music had gone from the plateau.

With his eyes closed, Shekhar took a deep breath before cutting his gaze to meet Amana's. "I purchased this fish from a trader in the Seven Serpents sixteen days ago." He paused to let his words hang in the air. Amana looked pointedly at Lata, whom he now felt sure was purposely avoiding his eye. He watched the old woman swallow, with her lips pursed as Shekhar went on.

"Why is Tendaji's daughter still selling rancid fish now that the Zyeta runs with clear water?"

Amana lowered his head in genuine sorrow. The girl must have still been selling her old stock. But why? The river had run clean.

He stared at his hands as Vivek leaned forward to address him grimly once more. "Amana, you and I have never seen eye to eye. Not since you first arrived here, and this is exactly why." There was a fire in his eyes Amana had never seen before. "Take heed, young one! There is no such thing as an inconsequential action. You are talented and strong-willed. You show great potential. But you are reckless and impatient. Your example has set in motion a chain of events that cannot be undone. We sent you to cleanse the river for the village, and you taint a young and open mind. You did this in our order's name! We cannot have renegades. Never again! Not after Uzoma…"

"She was only selling some old fish she probably still had," Amana said defensively. "She doesn't have any more, I'm sure. What does it matter anyway? I can just tell her to stop…" Amana trailed off as he caught Lata's expression. She was looking pointedly away from him.

"You taught the villagers nothing," Shekhar said, his voice thick with disappointment. "We advised you to empower three so that your light can spread in them. But instead you've corrupted one of their youths. You have made them reliant on purity stones, which they lack the ability to create. In a few years, when the stones you dropped at the base of their river are finally dissolved away, what will they do then?"

"What should I have done?" Amana shouted, unable to bear any more. "Would you have had me stay there for the next ten years waiting for boys to grow into men, just to rebuild a dam?" He thundered as he leaped to his feet slamming a furious fist on the stone table. "Should I have boiled the putrid waters for every villager, before filling their cups, or before every bath?"

"If that is what it took, yes," Lata said at last. Amana stared at her. Somehow the softness in her voice quelled the fire kindling in his chest. Even if only for a moment.

"You are selfish," she whispered softly. "We have always been aware of your faults. When it was just you, we hoped we could tame your wild side. We thought we could help you. *I* thought we could help you. I was wrong."

The elders stood up and walked away from him back toward the corridor.

"Wait!" Amana cried out, desperately following after

them. "You can't leave me like this… not after all I've done. Not when there's so much left for me to learn."

The trio came to a halt on the edge of the plateau between two sets of stone stairways. One led up to the mountain's summit. The other led down a winding path through the mist.

"We cannot teach you what you want to know," Lata said simply. "I am truly sorry, Amana."

"Wait!" he begged, pulling *The Scroll of the Five Paths* from inside his robes and placing it at her feet. "Here, at least… let me return this. I stole it, but I never read it. Let me do something right. Let me atone for something. Please, take it back."

Lata looked down at the scroll expressionlessly. "There are none here who need it. We know our paths. It is time you found yours."

Amana fell to his knees, too angry too argue, too guilty to plead. The light from the torches fell away, and a chill wind swept over the summit. Amana shivered as Vivek turned to leave.

"One obsessed with the future lives too fully within the past," he called over his shoulder. As he left, the night seemed to grow darker, and a dense fog filled the air. The sound of the elders' footsteps faded more quickly than they should have.

"Remember, there are many paths to truth," Shekhar said kindly as he too vanished into the mist.

Amana looked up to face Lata directly. Even on his knees, he was a finger's length taller, and now she looked him straight in the eye. Her expression softened, and she surveyed him as she had on the day they first met. As a light entered her kind old eyes, Amana thought he finally understood what Manali had meant when she told him he looked sad when he smiled.

"The way forward is not always the way ahead," she said.

And on that enigmatic note, she disappeared into the night. The fog had swallowed her whole. Amana collapsed on his back, unable to see anything above him but mist. He couldn't say how long he lingered there. It felt like the end of his world.

His eyes found the scroll on the ground beside him, and a fire rekindled within him. He would prove he could be taught. He would master the Five Paths. If the monks would not teach him, then he would find someone who could.

Amana stared at the parchment in his hands, reminded of the annotation left on the ritual... Uzoma. Perhaps this "Lost One" could complete his training properly.

Perhaps the monks were right after all. There was more than one path to truth. The path in front of him was not the way ahead. Taking the scroll in hand, he rose to his feet and walked away from the summit. He started down the stone steps which were illuminated by the now brilliant night sky above. He looked down the winding road that led to the base of Mount Junga.

The way ahead was finally clear.

Amana

A NOTE FROM THE AUTHOR

Thank you for reading *A Servant's Work*. This novella is my first published work, and I couldn't have picked a better way to make my debut.

The chance to get in on the ground floor of the world Antoine Bandele is building was one I just couldn't pass up.

Antoine placed a great deal of trust in me as I worked to help shape the backstory of Amana, the protagonist from the novel: *The Kishi*.

For this opportunity, I shall always be very grateful. Amana was the anchor around which I crafted the various other characters, magical items, and locales. I'll be curious to see how many return as Antoine continues his exploration of Esowon and the surrounding territories.

If you enjoyed *A Servant's Work*, please leave a review on your favorite retailer or social media.

HEARTS IN THE DARK

Lost Tales from Esowon

CALLAN BROWN

BANDELE
— BOOKS —

PRONUNCIATION GUIDE

Characters

Baa·ko - bä′kō

E·na·ke - ē′nä′kā

I·ken·na - ē′ken′nä

I·man·i - ē′mä′nē

Ka·sa - kä′sä

Ko·jo - kō′jō

Ny·a - nī′ä

N·ye·we - en′yeə′wā

Sha·na·ki - shä′nä′kē

U·zo·ma - ü′zō′mä

Terms & Titles

A·ya - ī′yä

I·lan·ga - ē′län′gä

I·lo·pa - ē′lō′pä

O·fe·a·la - ō′fä′ä′lä

O·go·a·la - ō′gō′ä′lä

U·kuh·lu - ü′kü′lü′

Locations

Ba·jok - bä′jōk

E·so·won - e′sō′wän

Go·lah - go′läh

Gue·la - gwe′lä

Ya·se·ti - yə′se′tē

Southern Reaches of
THE GOLAH
EMPIRE
(FORMERLY)

LEOPARD'S
GORGE'S

THE BLACK ROCKS

Uzoma's
Homestead

THE PLATON OF PREDATON

THE

R I V E R

N Y O K A

FARMLANDS OF BAJOK

The Great Village of **BAJOR**

"Are you the boy?" Neema turned her nose to
    Ikenna, examining him up and down. She
    nodded her head approvingly. "You're certainly
    a looker. You're one of them, aren't you?"
"I am," Ikenna confessed without hesitation.
"Why is it you have not yet killed my daughter?"
    Neema took a small step in front of Shanaki.
    "I spoke with your Elder-Chiefs. Your kind
    aren't supposed to be able to handle themselves
    around pretty girls."
"I'm quite unlike most of my kind." Ikenna caught
    Shanaki's raised eyebrow. "But your daughter
    had a lot to do with that."

— EXCERPT FROM *THE KISHI*

PROLOGUE

IKENNA

ILLOPA, OF COURSE SHE'S BEAUTIFUL. WHY CAN'T ANYTHING ever be easy?

Ikenna lay prone amidst the tall reeds of a sweeping riverbank, his chest and legs pressed into the cool, damp mud. The last trace of early-morning moonslight cast a dim glint of silver across the rolling waters before him, and he tensed with waiting purpose, eyes narrowed for the hunt. Ahead, not fifty paces away, sat one of the most beautiful women he had ever seen.

One of. He would give her that much, but she was no Imani.

Her eyes were too cold, her shoulders and back too poised. She lacked the casual, comfortable grace of the girl he had longed for from afar. That sweet, wonderful woman that had made him smile—almost laugh even, sometimes— and that he would never see again.

The thought brought with it both anger and tears, but he was used to that now and let neither flow free. He held them deep within, where they would build and roil, a tumult to feed the beast that would soon run free across these waters, that would soon take its revenge. He felt the stirring of a harsh cackle in his mind. Quickly, he brushed a hand across the back of his head, pressing farther down in the muck as he soothed back the snout rising from his skull to sniff at the air. It wasn't time yet; he was getting too eager in his anger. He had to remember that his second self could taste it too.

The bastards will know what it feels like to have their hopes ripped out from under them, Imani. I swear.

He narrowed his eyes at the thought, and carefully tracked his target.

She sat sideways atop a boat, oars at rest, with a long rod of bamboo cast into the current. She was still, stalwart against the gentle ebb of the world around her, seeming at once at peace with herself, and yet also troubled. Restless. As though fighting the urge to break the solemn quiet about her—with no true want to do so.

Two men clad in hard leathers and iron helmets sat at the rear of the boat, each with a rod of their own. They seemed unsure whether to let the silence rest themselves, shuffling like nervous gazelle at a watering hole. They were clearly aware of their charge's disquiet but had no clear notion of how to ease it. The younger of the two looked ready to approach the woman, break her from her reverie with a question or comment, but he didn't move.

The woman let out a sigh, leaning her head back and opening slow eyes to the dark sky above. Ikenna's own gaze followed upward; the stars were just now fading from view.

He released a silent breath and rose to a low crouch, tension rolling off stiff shoulders and riding out with the waves at his feet. Even from his hiding place in the moistened mud he could smell the soft scent of perfume carrying through the air. The scent of Ya-Seti spice—just the kind he liked too. He shot another glance skyward and saw the last hour of night fading fast in the skies above. Ilanga's dawn was waiting, ready to crest the horizon.

A soft keening sounded, scraping at the back of his skull.

Just a little longer.

ONE

SHANAKI

COOL AIR CARESSED SHANAKI'S FACE AS SHE RESTED, HER boat drifting through the first light of early dawn. She had come to the river—in the face of much complaint from her guards—to escape the bustle and noise of the Bajok village markets. Recent events had left little time for respite, and she craved the peace of her Ya-Seti streams. With hope of home far from her, she had settled for what the locals called a river: this muddy, shallow thing with banks beset by weeds and silt dulling the moonlight glow against the water's surface.

Yes, I am far from home.

Shanaki, Princess of Ya-Seti and second heir to its people, sighed. When she had learned of this land, and had been told she would journey here to secure new alliances for her family and her people, she had been excited. Long had she yearned for a chance to escape the tiresome routine of palace life, for a chance to actually *see* the world to which she belonged. She could finally spread her wings and sample the different wonders life had to offer.

Instead, she had spent weeks confined to a caravan, traveling along dirt roads and dirt plains. When she had heard the tale of the great Bajoki lands and their rich heritage, she had expected... well, she wasn't sure what she had expected. Certainly more than *this*.

The same could be said for her husband to be. Baako was his name, first heir to Bajok: a striking man, chiseled and strong... and a dreadful bore. It really was a special talent for someone to manage that with her. She had long taken personal joy in listening to others and hearing their stories. It was the only way she ever got to really see life beyond the palace walls.

Not that it had always been that way of course. She had originally set out merely to test herself, practicing skills on her servants and guards that would prove useful for the dignitaries and diplomats to follow later in life. All those fake smiles and false words. But she had quickly grown to appreciate the brief glimpses of life they all had to offer. They had such freedom, yet they seemed to take it for granted. Her personal guard especially. Their stories helped pull her from the pits of boredom she so often found herself trapped in. The bonds she had gradually forged through hearing their tales were all that kept her sane these days. At least, they usually did.

In your own time, Kasa. I can feel you itching to say something back there.

The two she had brought with her this morning were not especially vibrant characters, but they were interesting enough in their own simple ways. There were keen differences between them—their age, for one.

Enake was one of her longest-serving guardsmen, steadfastly loyal—to a fault, she would say, though her father would not. He'd been with her since she was a babe, barely out of her mother's belly. Kasa was a recent addition to her retinue and had been very enthusiastic whenever they shared in conversation.

Shanaki waited with bated breath until the shuffling behind her stilled suddenly, and she sighed.

Damnit, Enake. He had an irritating habit of holding the younger among her personal guard back, telling him in no uncertain terms to "stop bothering the princess." There were times when that was appreciated. After all, *too* much familiarity from the striplings simply wouldn't do. But she'd give anything for someone to break this current silence. It was worse than the noise of the village.

"Where's Nya when I need her?" she asked herself softly, stretching her head back on her shoulders and looking up at the waning night's sky. True dawn would be upon them soon. Then, not long after that, a return to Bajok.

"I'm sorry, Your Highness?"

Shanaki sighed dismissively. "It's nothing, Enake."

She sat there a long while, simply staring out at the canvas of stars. Her patience ran dry as her neck began to strain. It seemed she would have to take things upon herself again today.

"So, what do my royal guardsmen think of the great plains of Bajok and its people?" She did not turn to them, instead leaning forward from her recline to make a show of setting her rod back in its hoop, her eyes fixed on the waters ahead.

It was beneath her as conversation starters went. She knew perfectly well what the two of them thought of the Bajoki. They thought them boorish, uncivilized, and beneath the Ya-Seti in almost every way. They just had a knack for holding onto the old magics, that was all. They had some secret way of clinging to the powers of their empire past, the way a creeping vine wraps around a sturdy *baobab*. She knew they knew this, and they knew she knew it too, but they would never voice such thoughts aloud without prompting. They were well trained. Enake, however, took her question for the invitation it was.

"Princess, I—"

" 'Shanaki' for today, I think, Enake. It's just us friends here, after all."

"*Princess* Shanaki," he continued. Shanaki laughed to herself. He'd never change. "I think you know I had hoped for a more… illuminated new home for you than this." She could hear the deep frown his words were working through without having to look. For Enake that was practically an enraged curse.

She had to stifle her smile—he'd hear it in her voice as well as she had his frown. "You don't want to move you and your wife out here, then?"

"Princess! I am your sworn protector. Where you go I shall follow, for as long as I am able and you allow it." His voice was indignant, as though she might doubt him. As if she ever could.

Twisting around and giving him a warm smile she responded, "And what of T'Nota? I'm not sure she'd appreciate being uprooted so. Least of all to live here in this… *unilluminated* place."

Enake faltered at that, just a bit. "She would understand. She knew who she bound herself to a long time ago. And she is most fond of you, Your Highness."

Shanaki's smile widened and warmed further still; she was fond of T'Nota herself. She was an aunt to Shanaki, in name, if not by blood. Family.

She turned her head to Kasa, who was sitting dutifully quiet as his senior and his lady spoke of bonds he was far yet from forging for himself. She raised an eyebrow, and he sat silent for a moment, clearly growing uncomfortable under her questioning gaze. She relented as she felt the twinges of awkwardness herself and turned back to her vigil at the boat's bow.

"I don't think it would be so bad here, Your Highness— Shanaki." She heard the young man cough briefly and pictured a nervous sidelong glance from a disapproving Enake. He continued, "But I—I've not made my vows yet, and while I'd be honored, and willing, truly, my family…"

She was slightly surprised at the nervousness; Kasa had always been confident and bold. This was a new color on him.

"You need not worry, Kasa," she said. "As you say, you have not yet made your vows. You are not sworn to me. I would not force you to follow even if you were. Your place is back home where little Temsi and Balo can grow tall and strong and bright." She looked across the water to a patch of brown brush, its dim branches lilting in the rising sun. "They would wither here." She paused again, pondering whether to continue. "Besides, I do not think I shall be staying in Bajok for long, I—"

A splash of water erupted at her side. She glanced left before—

"Princess!"

A blur of black rushed at her from the riverbank. Running, not through the water… but *atop* it.

What?

The figure leaped overhead, cold droplets of water raining down on her face as she followed its shadowed arc. It twisted impossibly in the air, limbs darting every which way, blurring the last of the dawn-defiant stars still above.

The boat rocked as the figure landed: a man, dark skinned and wrapped in the yet-darker skins of some unknown beast.

The scream of two *shotel* blades leaving their sheaths sounded behind him, followed seconds later by two splashes as both her guards were sent overboard in a single twin-legged kick.

The assailant lifted his body with just the one arm that

had carried his sprung attack. No sign of strain betrayed his body.

Shanaki saw only the swiftest blur of this, her instincts focused on escape. She already had one foot on the boatside and was leaping overboard in a jump she hoped would carry her at least halfway to the shore. Before her first foot had fully touched the water's surface, the man had caught her, holding her up by one arm with terrifying ease.

She could see the splashes of her guardsmen already swimming toward her, and she made to cry out, but a powdered hand clamped tightly over her mouth and her voice was cut off by a suffocating stench. It crawled down her throat and clawed at her senses. Immediately, her world began to darken. The last thing she saw, as all light faded, was the thud of a sandaled foot against Enake's face.

TWO

SHANAKI

SHANAKI STARTED AWAKE WITH GULPING BREATHS AND A hammering heart. Everything was a haze of dull aches and darkness and her eyes held tightly shut against a throbbing pulse in her skull. For a moment, she lay still, resting on her back, spine pressing hard into what felt like bare rock, and she tensed against fresh waves of pain.

What... what happened?

Through the thunder of her heart in her ears she could hear the slow dripping of water somewhere close by, an odd echo carrying in the air. She shook her head to clear it, but the pain that stabbed at the backs of her eyes quickly returned her to stillness.

Minutes passed before she braved moving again. This time she tried to reach out her limbs, leaving her head as still between her shoulders as she could. She felt strangely disconnected from the rest of her body. Any motion she tried for was sluggish and weak like she was pressing through warm mud. Panic prowled at the edge of her consciousness, readying to pounce, and the darkness did nothing to steady her nerves.

Shanaki took in deep gulps of air, trying to calm her

mind and re-center herself. Her instinct called on her inner powers, but the throbbing in her head slowed their response. She could feel the warmth of her healing and suppression lingering at the tips of her fingers and she tried to draw them close, a blanket of power about her. But the ache from whatever had been used to subdue her made it a threadbare one at best.

Gradually, as feeling in her weary limbs stirred once more, she became aware of what felt like roped restraints binding her arms and legs. She could feel the rough texture of the rope scraping her skin. That and the stone, cold against her shoulder as she rolled onto her side. She forced her eyes open through the pain, managing a brief squint before the ache became too much. All she saw was utter blackness; she may as well have not opened her eyes at all.

Fear started to set in, then. Her limbs were waking more and more, and her inability to move them properly despite the fact had her railing against her restraints. One hard kick of frustration sprang loose, and her leg screamed in burning agony as it connected with something painfully solid. Worse, the sudden jolt had jarred her head to the side with a crack and her eyes watered with the pain of both hurts.

The tears that followed did not help her frustration.

In an instant, she was flailing with everything she had, pulling and twisting at the rope around her. Miraculously, they came loose. She slowed for a moment, wondering what kind of incompetence it took to leave a prisoner so poorly tied. Then her heart leaped up her throat and pounded in her ears as a sudden voice came at her from the dark — alarmingly close by.

"Here, I... take care for you... yes?"

Shanaki twisted between heartbeats and kicked with her freed leg. Her head swam, and the pain holding her eyes shut lanced again. That was *Mero-Set*, her people's

tongue; it had been poorly spoken, but Mero-Set none-
theless.

Her kick had missed, and she desperately pulled herself
back, wriggling as much as she could to force herself away
from the disgustingly calm voice in the darkness.

"Easy, Princess." She felt a firm grip pull at her arm.
"You not bound, not tight. It is small bind. We had little
climb—watch it!" She felt her latest kick graze something
with more give than a wall. "You want untie or not?
There."

She felt a firm tug on the now loosened rope and the last
of it flew from her shoulders. The moment she was free she
sprang back from where she had last heard the voice. The
calm in it was infuriating, and the soft, throaty rasp ruining
his intonation would have told her he was no Ya-Seti
without the broken wording.

Yet still, that he knows our tongue at all... Who is he?

More than anything, it unnerved her that she could hear
nothing of his movements between words. There was no
rustle of furs or scrape of feet against stone; he was as silent
as the shadow of the dark.

Slightly to her right, and farther away this time, she
heard his low voice again. He sounded *amused.* "Would tie
better if want you bind. Me not idiot. But me sound like one
in tongue of you... away people?" The last of his words
came to him in a rising tone, as though he was questioning
her on his phrasing.

He was no fool. Mentally marking his position, Shanaki
crawled back farther still, until her scrambling hands found
the rough rise of what felt like natural wall. She wasn't sure
which she hated more right now: the ceaseless pounding of
her heart in her ears or the throbbing of her head. Neither
made straining through the darkness any easier to bear.

"You no see me now. But me make—making—Ya-Seti
peace gestures with hands here." His broken Mero-Set was

grating her already-stretched nerves. To hear her people's words used in all the wrong ways, and with such sickening silk besides... It sent shivers down her spine.

She ignored the jesting tone he seemed to be reaching for and took a deep breath. "Do not sully our tongue with your bile, wretch," she spat in the Bajoki's own tongue, Golah.

"Oh good, you'd prefer Golah. As you might have noticed I'm gods awful with Mero mouth," the voice replied. Shanaki parted her lips. In his own tongue he sounded far more intelligent, more refined. That sensuous voice of his was elevated all the more without every other word butchered by error. He still clearly intended bemusement, but his sickening joviality sounded a mocking jab to her ears, and she felt as far from friendly-minded as she ever had.

Shanaki let silence hang in the air between them. She moved to rub at her eyes, and she felt her pain spike a brief flinch of weakness across her face.

"Oh, sorry, Princess, I forgot. Here." Without the slightest trace of a warning—no shuffle of movement or any sound at all—Shanaki felt a wooden bowl press against her lips. On instinct, she clamped her mouth shut and threw her head to the side, knocking the bowl away from her face.

How the hell is he sneaking up on me like that?

A splash of ice-cold water fell down her front as the bowl spilled. Shanaki heard a slight breath of surprise from her captor, and she enjoyed the momentary sense of satisfaction as his composure cracked, even as she fought back a shudder at the chill. He quickly steadied the sloshing of the bowl.

"Will you calm down, woman? It's to get rid of the pain! Essence of *julan* is pretty strong stuff."

Without a word, she swatted a hand between them, knocking the bowl from his grip and sending it clattering to the ground. He gave a shudder as the icy liquid came down around his feet. She had been splashed again, of course, but the satisfaction of the rebellion, however small, was worth it. She forced a snarled smile as her eyes searched upward for the voice's face.

"Well, that's that then," the man said. "I guess you'll just have to sit there in pain for the next few hours."

He seemed to pull back, his voice rising in the darkness up and away from her. After a long moment's pause she heard him sigh heavily, and she sensed a decision in it. She pulled herself back as subtly as she could, refusing to show fear, but readying herself for whatever punishment her rebellion had sparked. Another moment dragged on in the dark, before...

"Get some rest, Princess. I'll be back soon."

White-hot anger raced through Shanaki at the dismissal. "What? Wait! Who are you? Why have you brought me here?"

Silence was her only response.

"Answer me!"

THREE

SHANAKI

SHANAKI RAGED AT THE DARK UNTIL HER ANGER BURNED down to a hissing simmer. Her shouts echoed, bouncing back at her from what had to be solid stone. She had heard no sign of her captor leaving; there had been no retreating footsteps, no movement or sound at all besides the dripping of water and the beating of her heart. She realized she was holding her breath, and released it in a rush, quietly as she could manage.

She waited and listened, letting the seconds pass to minutes with nothing but her heartbeat and breathing to mark them. Her anger drained, Shanaki started to feel sick. This couldn't be happening...

She thought of Enake and Kasa, both likely dead, and a stab of pain far worse than the physical aches ran through her heart. They should have been there with her, Enake with his stern orders guiding her through the darkness, and Kasa set protectively at her back. She tried *not* to think about Nya, her closest and most capable guardian—and friend—and simply hoped beyond hope that no more of her own had fallen back at the village.

Oh gods, what if I'm the only one left?

Her soul shivered at the thought. She wouldn't go there. Not yet, not until she knew without doubt. Her people were strong. *She* was strong. They would not so easily fall.

I am Ya-Seti. We do not cower from the darkness.

When it became clear the man would not be immediately returning—if she could trust through the silence that he had even left at all—she set her resolve to work. She had no idea when he would return, and she needed to find her bearings before he did. Fumbling around in the dark was far from a good plan, she knew, but it was better than nothing. Ya-Seti did not sit and squirm in the face of fear, and she was their princess. Things were expected of her, and she expected them of herself.

Half numb from the sulan, head throbbing and utterly blind, she didn't much like her chances, but she had to do *something*.

Pushing to her feet and slumping back against the wall behind her, Shanaki took stock of her strength. Now that she stood, she could feel the blood pumping through her lower legs properly for perhaps the first time in hours. Her head still swam with every harsh jerk, but as long as she kept her shoulders set and didn't jostle too much, she could handle it.

She had to.

She pressed a hand to the wall and pushed off to stand fully under her own weight. Judging by the texture of the rock beneath her fingers, the faint echo of the water droplets, and the sheer pitch of the black around her, she had to be underground. The air was tinged with the slight damp of wet earth, and a fresh drip from somewhere to her left brought her mind back to the water she had heard before. For a moment, the sheer primal fear of being trapped beneath the ground gripped at her mind, and she forced herself to take a few deep, calming breaths.

Steady, Shanaki. First thing's first, where are we?

Her captor had mentioned a climb. If he had spoken the truth, then perhaps she was in one of the mountain caves. The thought brought hope and horror both. The Black Rocks were the only mountains near Bajok and they had a dangerous reputation, but they were only a league from the village. That meant they would be the focus of any search party sent to find her. Her people knew the threats the Bajoki talked about lingering there as well as she did after all. However, the rocks were infamous for their labyrinthine turns with who knew how many nooks and holes to hide in. If she didn't find a way to get out and give her people some sort of signal, she knew in her heart that no one would ever find her.

Resolve set in despite her desperation and lack of any real plan, and Shanaki pressed on. She felt her way along the cave wall's edge with one hand, waving the other in front of her in search of any obstruction. More than anything, her senses were strained for any hint that her captor might be returning. She knew in the back of her mind that she wouldn't sense anything from him until it was too late, but that didn't stop her from trying.

I am Ya-Seti. We do not cower from the darkness. We face it.

The mantra ran repeatedly through her mind as she made her slow but steady progress. Every breath and heart-beat seemed to draw out time in her mind.

She was reminded of her childhood years spent playing with her siblings. Blindfolded, they would take turns moving through the palace chambers, dancing about grace-lessly as their unblinded playmates tried jabs for the ribs. The aim was to grab one of your tormentors' hands before they could get away, then give them their turn at the blind-fold. Even then, the fear of the touch you never knew when to expect had her heart beating violent drum beats in her chest.

Now, the game had taken a far more sinister turn, and

she found herself yearning for the stifled sound of children's laughter and the 'tut-tutting' of the disapproving hand-maidens walking the palace halls. The unnatural silence of the cave, save for the occasional dripping of water, was suffocating.

The wall soon curved to the left, and the drip was now ahead of her and growing louder the closer she stepped. She lowered the hand she held outstretched, dropping down almost to a crouch. As she leaned forward, still holding her right hand pressed against the wall to keep her bearings, she felt a cold shiver shoot up her spine.

The tips of her fingers had pierced a water surface she had not been expecting, and she yanked her arm back. Shanaki cursed herself for the childish jump. Her every sense was amplified by the blinding darkness, true, but she had known to expect the water.

I am Ya-Seti. We do not cower.

Reaching out, she cupped her hand into the pool of water. Its surface was raised up from the ground, some sort of basin set into the wall that came just below her waist.

She brought her hand up to her face and winced at the soft splashes of water spilling through her fingers to the floor. When no sudden voice barked at her from the shadows, she raised the remainder the rest of the way and brought the water to her nose. She didn't smell any stagnancy. That was good.

Satisfied, she took a sip. It tasted fresh enough, and the first splash on her tongue drove home how thirsty she really was. But she had learned her childhood lessons well, only drinking enough to moisten her mouth. If she failed to escape today—tonight?—and she felt no sickness, it would be safe to return for more.

Shanaki felt her way to the rim of the pool. It seemed almost like a naturally formed trough, with the cave stone jutting out from the wall to catch the water dripping down from above. Judging from its freshness, the water could not have traveled far from whatever source fed its stream. She knew it was a desperate hope, but it might mean she was closer to the surface than she thought. With her body as pained as it was now, that would be a welcome relief.

But blind hope would get her nowhere, so she discarded it and moved on. She rose back to her feet and sidled farther, her hand running along the basin's rim until it curved back to join the wall proper. She kept her hand pressed against its worn-smooth surface and stepped deeper into the darkness.

She had taken perhaps twenty careful steps when her forward arm caught on something solid. She jerked her hand back in an instant, but noted with satisfaction that her breathing remained calm, and her heart had only slightly quickened its pace at the surprise.

Better, she thought, before reaching out once again to feel the cold breath of an open tunnel.

Well, that's one possible way out.

She continued, working her way along the wall and feeling for any openings or features. She didn't know how long it took, but she was feeling comfortable with her pace, now that she had built up some momentum and courage. Soon enough she had moved through what seemed the entire space of the cave.

She had found only two openings, which settled her nerves a little. Images of a maze had been stretching out in her mind from the moment she had found the first tunnel. It was still possible, of course, but for the moment the signs were good.

The room was roughly oblong in her mind's eye, if she had judged the curves of the walls correctly. The space was likely a few times as wide and long as the average Bajoki hut-home back in the village, and a fair bit taller. How tall, she couldn't tell, but it was farther than she could reach, even when she stretched up and leaned against the wall. It didn't really matter how high the ceiling was, of course, but testing the height had given her a reason to put off her next step.

It was a shamefully long while before she found the courage to push away from the wall and move across the open space of the room she had fixed in her mind. She crouched low, keeping one arm pressed to the floor as the other swung ahead. She thought she must've looked a great fool, but better that than stumbling blindly into a pit or gods knows what else. Anything might have waited for her in the middle of the untested darkness.

The only thing awaiting her, it turned out, was a single column roughly central to the room. A narrow strut of rock that, as far as she could tell, rose to the ceiling still out of her reach. She pushed away from it, guided by the call of the water's drip, and leaned back against the wall at the pool's side.

Shanaki felt very small just then. She fought the urge to slide to the floor and pull her knees to her chest. It was hard. It had taken her a long time to find the shape of the dark world around her, and now that she had, she was left with the prospect of yet more blind searching, this time through narrow tunnels.

Sometimes, the only way to get a thing done is to just do it.

Nya's words came to her out of the distant past, comforting her and helping to fight back the cold of the dark. They were good words, true words. There was no use sitting here waiting for her captor's return—she'd face him here waiting where he left her or out there in the tunnels, trying for an escape. Her pride and her duty left her with only one real choice.

She moved toward the first tunnel and into the unknown.

SHE HAD TRAVELED AT LEAST THREE TIMES THE AREA OF the first room, judging by the count of her steps. The tunnel was long and winding, and she kept her hands against its sides to ensure she missed no branches or forks in the path. She could feel moss growing on the walls, moist to the touch, and she realized by the third patch that it was growing at the edges of smooth, protruding crystal.

Shanaki knew the texture well from years growing up in the halls of the royal palace, where uncut crystal from all across Esowon was collected for decoration and prestige both. She used to steal some of the smaller displays and hide them in her room, once upon a time.

She had long since given up on counting her strides by the time the next feature caught her attention—rather horribly. Her bare foot alighted on what she had assumed to be a bump in the floor—right up until it gave way beneath her weight with the sickening crack of bone.

She stayed there a while, frozen in place with visions of great bone piles rising up before her. She pictured the discarded corpses of long-dead creatures that had found their demise at the hands of whatever beast called these tunnels home.

I am Ya-Seti. We do not cower. I am Ya-Seti. We do not cower. We. Do. Not. Cower.

It was the hardest yet, that next step. Her mantra, which at this point had burned itself forever into her mind, was the only thing driving her forward through the dark. Her courage was rewarded with more smooth stone, and she let loose a deep sigh of relief. It was just the one—whatever it was—and she could let go of the visions of blood and bone.

Or at least, she tried her best.

THEN CAME THE STAIRS. WELL, SHE COULD CALL THEM stairs, but if that was their purpose they had been made for the giants of the Old Days. Shanaki clung to the latest in a long line of the despicably tall steps, and hauled herself upward. Sweat poured down her face and arms as her muscles screamed in protest, her head throbbing in an ever-constant pulse.

She rolled over the corner of the ledge and lay there, staring up at the endless abyss of black above. The first "stair" hadn't been so bad, and her spirits had soared at the prospect of ascent. Walking through the winding tunnels, she had feared she was only moving down, farther into the depths of the mountain. The decline too slight for her blinded senses to detect. When she had reached the apparent dead end and instead found a chest-height ledge, she had leaped up with renewed vigor.

That vigor had died a painful death with this last one, ledge nine. Most of the steps had grown taller and steeper the higher she climbed, and Shanaki found her strength flagging far sooner than was comfortable for her pride. She decided she would leave this part out of the story if she ever made it back to her people alive. Nya would never let her live it down.

She imagined her lead guardswoman's face smirking down at her from the dark, perched atop the next ledge lazily, like a wildcat sprawled out in the midday sun. Nya would be mocking her, no doubt about it. She was always the most impertinent of her royal guard. It was one of the things Shanaki liked most about her. She wasn't so stiff and guarded like—

Shanaki shook her head, welcoming the distraction of the piercing pain. She refused to think of her fallen guardsmen. She wasn't even sure that they *had* fallen, and now was

208

not the time to dwell. Now was the time to escape and bring the furious vengeance of the Ya-Seti down on her captor's head. Exhaustion be damned, she would see it done.

She heaved herself to her feet once more and felt for the edge of the next ledge up. To her dismay, it had to be at least a foot above her head.

Cursing the gods for their little tests and sighing inwardly, she took a deep breath. She braced one foot against the "step," her toes searching for whatever tiny nooks they could grip in the dirt and stone, and leapt up.

Her hands pressed into the stone, and her palms shook as she hefted her weight up onto her chest. She swung her legs back in an ungainly arc for some desperate, extra momentum and wriggled forward. It took everything she had, but ten ledges later—at least she thought it was ten, she wasn't really focused on the counting anymore—she had finally reached the top.

Every muscle ached and her breathing was harsh and labored. She didn't even feel the throbbing in her head anymore; it had been replaced with a constant, biting stab at the base of her skull four or five ledges ago. Yes, it had taken everything she had, but she had made it.

And now I just need to give even more…

She crawled at first, just pulled herself along the ground with her numbed arms, before rising to her hands and knees. Shanaki was pushing herself too hard, and she knew it. There was a limit to how much the body could take, and she had left hers behind halfway up the climb. But when the choice was push or die, one pushed. Simple as that.

And so she did, hefting herself, *again*, to her feet. Her shoulder slapped into the wall with a grunt as she took a shaky step.

It was at that point that the sun dawned before her.

A blinding, piercing light streamed through an opening crack ahead. Shanaki spun on the spot and covered her eyes. As she blinked rapidly into her arm, the harsh scrape of stone echoed down the tunnel behind her. It was a slow, grinding tone, like the grating of an enormous whetstone. As she heard the opening widen, more light leaked through the gap and shone over her shoulder, and Shanaki saw for what felt like the first time in days.

She could see colors returning to the world, but they ran and washed together; they weren't sticking to their lines as they were meant to. Whether it was because of fatigue, hunger, or the remnant sulan, she didn't know, but her spinning head was the least of her problems. She turned back to the cave entrance, now fully open where the curve of a large boulder had rolled halfway to one side.

A dark blur stepped into the light and reached for the rock, its shadowed silhouette dimming as it entered the tunnel. The vibrant colors spilling through Shanaki's vision began retreating back to their lines, and she froze in place. The figure paused, turning from the boulder and looking down the tunnel her way.

She stood, still as a statue, and every fiber of her being tensed. It was possible that he hadn't seen her—she was a ways back from the entrance. With her back leaned tight against the wall, she had to be impossible to see, right?

Then his smooth timbre came. "Maybe I *should* have tied you up."

FOUR

SHANAKI

IT WASN'T FAIR. SHE HAD BEEN SO CLOSE, *SO CLOSE*. SHE couldn't be taken now, not ten paces from the light and its freedom.

His tone carried surprise, perhaps even alarm, amidst the amusement. Had her heart not stopped beating from her fear and exhausted desperation, she might have taken pride in it. He had clearly underestimated her.

Good. Use that.

The thought woke her limbs and untangled her terror. Adrenaline seared through her veins and she turned on the spot, sprinting back into the darkness. Her mind raced to catch up to her instincts, her thoughts pounding through her head to the beat of her footfalls.

She couldn't just run—she had nowhere to run *to*. Before her conscious mind had even considered it, her mystic power flared. It was dangerous to draw on it in her state, but so was being captured again, and she put as much energy into it as she dared. She felt the pulse of power cast out behind her, the faintest ripple in the air that would latch onto whatever mystical traits her pursuer was using and seal them away. She felt a twinge at her core that told her she had him. She didn't know *what* she had locked from his grasp, but it was done.

The drop of the first ledge was just ahead, and a desperate idea took her. It was stupid, and she knew it wouldn't work, but it was her only shot.

"Wait!" her captor shouted, and she threw a glance behind to see how far he'd come. Her heart skipped a beat in shock—he was already half the distance away, arm outstretched toward her.

He's that fast, even without powers?

Shanaki threw herself forward, leaning into her run. She had to reach the stairs before he caught her—she was almost there. She'd have no firm footing, but this was her only chance, she—

She stumbled.

Her feet had caught beneath her, her exhaustion wrapping them in an awkward twist before she could begin to right her fall. She plummeted through the air, her vision awash: half with the tears of frustration, and half from the blur of the sudden light.

Time seemed to slow down as she saw the abyss reaching back out to her, the light of the cave's opening swallowed by its darkness. She had been one step from the stairs. She had meant to spin, use her attacker's weight against him, unbalance him, and push. She'd seen the move on flat ground a dozen times; it was one of Kasa's favorites. He had even gotten Nya with it once. And Shanaki hadn't even been able to set her stance. Pathetic.

She was going to die here.

Halfway over the edge, she felt the strong grip of an arm at her wrist. Her body jerked back, not enough to halt her fall, but enough to twist her in the air and glimpse the silhouetted frame of her captor.

He pulled her to him, gripping tightly and kicking from the ledge. He had no purchase, and he was falling now as surely as she, but his kick had knocked him farther down and twisted him beneath her. She lost sight of him and flinched as he pulled her into a crushing hug.

Time sped back up, and she felt more than saw the blur of the world around them; all was darkness and rock as they fell. A cracking snap sounded and a lance of pain shot through her arm and leg. They had caught on the first ledge down. She felt a horrible twist half-way to her elbow and tucked her chin to her chest, a scream catching in her throat as she braced against the inevitable.

Shanaki felt the air driven from her lungs as the two of them crashed into the ground and her head smacked into her captor's shoulder. Darkness crept at the edge of her vision as her consciousness faded, but she fought it back.

Both her legs were limp and unmoving and she could feel one hanging over what must have been the third ledge down. As she tried to lift her head, she found she couldn't move that either. Her tired body had finally given out.

She felt movement against her back and slumped sideways, her head lolling to the left. She was glad it was the left, she didn't want to see what horror she would find should she look at the right.

Beneath her, a long, rumbling groan sounded, and her captor began to stir, his arms loosening their grip on her frame.

She tried to roll farther, to slide to the side and free herself from the man that had killed her guardsmen. She shifted, lifting her weight from his chest. She heard him take a deep breath and he turned his head side to side, as though trying to shake awake his senses. Running out of time, she heaved with all her might and managed to push herself up and away from his body. In her weakness and haste, her hand slipped on his shoulder and her torso slumped forward as she moved to find balance with her other arm. A jagged stab of agony was the last thing she felt as the darkness took her once more.

FIVE

SHANAKI

SHANAKI DIDN'T KNOW HOW LONG IT HAD BEEN WHEN she next rose to consciousness, or the time after that either. She kept fading in and out, lulled to rest by the comfort of warmth and the rhythm of a strong heartbeat at her ear. She couldn't seem to get her eyes to open properly.

It was only by her third stirring that she realized she was being carried, held against a broad chest with her legs lain over strong arms. She had not been carried like this in a long time, not since childhood. Enake used to carry her like this. He would bring her back to the palace whenever she had stayed too late in the grounds and fallen asleep by the Ipe River.

Enake.

His name brought with it a sadness, but she wasn't sure why. Why would —

Shanaki jolted awake. The strength and warmth about her, far from comforting, was as welcome as the touch of a constrictor snake. She flailed feebly, worn limbs slow to catch up to her frenzied mind. She swung her head out from her captor's chest and slammed it back again, trying to force herself room out from under his grasp. Almost immediately his grip tightened, and her struggle moved from weak to utterly futile.

Refusing to give in, she gathered her strength and pooled as much venom into her words as she could muster. "Un—Unhand me!" No response. "I said, let me *go.*"

"Calm down, Princess. I'm not going to hurt you. You've broken your arm. I need to get you back so—" He faltered slightly with what sounded like a wince of pain. "So I can look at it."

He paused in his walk and she felt herself jostled slightly as he hefted her upwards into his arms. She heard him take a deep breath before continuing, his stride more off kilter now, as though his words had cost him dearly.

Shanaki was about to spit back a scathing remark that she was perfectly capable of walking by herself, but as she readied to force her legs down from his arms, she realized that they still weren't obeying her commands. Each felt as though they had been bruised as black as the dark about them, and for all she could see they were. Her broken arm was deadened to her, and she was caught halfway between gratitude and fear for the fact.

She decided that, for the moment, she would relent. She was whittling her captor's strength and saving her own with the same stroke after all. Nya would call that a result.

It was a while later, with a few pauses for breath and rest by her bearer along the way, that she felt herself being lowered to the hard stone floor of the cave room she had first woken to. She would have felt disheartened by the realization, if it hadn't been marked by the familiar drip-dripping of water. She was terribly thirsty.

Set back against the wall—roughly the same position she had been left in before going by the sound of the water —she raised her good arm to hover over the bad. Gingerly, trepidation shaking her hand, she lowered it to touch against her shoulder, gradually working it down against her sweat-ridden flesh. She lost the feel of her fingers a little way down her bicep, the numbness leaking the hint of a pointed ache as she pressed her hand against her skin.

"I wouldn't do that if I were you, Princess." And there came the voice again, as sudden and bodiless as ever. They were right back where they started. Almost, at any rate, she could still hear the hoarse breath in his voice. He hadn't yet recovered from the fall.

She ignored him and continued her hand's journey downwards, feeling for the break. She felt a twinge shoot up through the numbness when her hand reached her elbow. From the stick of the substance too thick for sweat coating her fingers, she knew the bone had pierced skin. Taking a deep, steadying breath, she felt it. It was pierced clean through the flesh of her elbow.

She raised her head to look out into the dark—she couldn't see him of course—but she preferred to look him in the eye as best she could regardless. "The numbness. What did you give me?"

There was a brief pause before he answered, his voice held as though braced against his own pains. "Essence of *tosi*. You dislocated your knee too. I fixed that up by the steps. Give me just a moment and I'll set the arm for you."

It occurred to her then that her captor seemed particularly invested in her well-being. He had saved her from worse damage with the fall, had numbed the pain of her arm, and now offered to help treat the break, however able he may or may not be.

He needed her alive, that much was clear. She would have to figure out why, later.

Knowing your enemy is one of the most important steps in beating them, her father had always said.

She wondered where her father was. Would he be out with the search party, desperately trying to find his first daughter? Probably not. He would be back in the village, trying to save face with the chief and keep the treaty alive. He was, first and foremost, a pragmatist, she thought bitterly.

Shanaki used to admire that about him, tried to emulate it even, but that was before she realized "first and foremost" came before even love. She had long discarded any notion that her father truly loved her. She was a negotiating tool to him, an asset to be traded away for greater power and influence for Ya-Set, nothing more.

Shanaki gave herself a mental shake. Her mind was drifting entirely too much of late. Now was not the time to be dwelling on past hurts, she had plenty enough to be getting on with here already.

She heard the shuffle of feet against stone, her captor approaching from the dark.

He must be suffering. I heard nothing before.

The shuffling stopped a few feet away and she heard a faint groan, akin to an elderly man kneeling to pick something from the floor.

"Sorry, Princess. Needed a minute there. Here, let me see your arm."

Shanaki heard his arm reaching by the tone of his voice, and she pulled back into the wall. "I'm fine, leave me be."

His voice came incredulously, "You can't be serious. Your arm's almost broken in two. If you don't let me set it, you could lose it forever."

She kept herself pulled back and held her hand to her shoulder. "I don't need your help. I'll deal with it myself."

He exhaled in a sigh that reiterated his bafflement. He said nothing for a moment, as though pondering how best to approach her stubborn refusal.

She left him to his stupor and focused on her arm. She would need every ounce of focus she could muster for this. It had been years since she had had to draw on her regeneration for a serious injury, and never anything close to as serious as this. She should have taken her training more seriously. She had always spent far more time on her suppression abilities, trying to increase its strength and reach. At the time she thought herself clever. She had mastered the basics of healing after all, and past that her suppression would serve her far better. In the end, any force that could break through the palace guard was going to be capable of more harm than her powers could ever hope to heal.

That had seemed sound reasoning before; now though, she could see how foolish she had been. Her justification had been little more than excuses, attempts to sidestep the guilt of her laziness. She had been far more interested in the stories of far off places and life beyond the walls than learning the skills that would help her survive them.

She would suffer for her youthful arrogance now, it seemed, and deep down, Shanaki didn't mind. She had been young when she had started to drift from her studies, but she had had years to correct her mistake. She believed in fair balance and this punishment matched the crime. She would have to labor for hours just to close the surface skin, and it would take she didn't know how many days to work the inside of her arm whole again. It would be painful too, no amount of numbing could stop that.

Shanaki sighed. It was the bone that held her attention for now. She had spent time in the medica as part of her training, understanding of the mundane ways was always encouraged no matter the strength of the mystic. If you could heal without your power, you should; it was almost always easier. Getting the splinter of bone back inside the skin would have been extremely difficult even if she could see and it wasn't her own arm she was dealing with. As things were, it would be almost impossible.

The voice came at her again, as though reading her mind. "How are you supposed to work the bone back in half numbed and blind?" Surprisingly, she felt no condescension, he spoke with simple curiosity. His falseness galled her.

Through gritted teeth, she shot back "Doesn't matter, I'd sooner cut it off than have your aid."

"Wha—Why? I only want to help you." He seemed genuinely surprised.

Shanaki spat a vicious snarl his direction. "*Help* me? You call abducting me and tying me up in a cave *help*."

"I told you, I didn't tie—"

"Enake and Kasa," she interrupted him, her pain driving the names from her lips before she could catch them. "T'Nota and Iidra. Temsi and Balo."

"What?" He questioned. More feigned surprise. Was he *trying* to provoke her?

"The men you killed kidnapping me, and the wives and children left to mourn them." Her voice was ice, and she stared into the dark with eyes like knives.

She heard a heavy sighing breath, one of relief, sounding around a smile. A pulse of rage ran through her and her hand clenched, ready to strike at the dark. How dare he, how *dare* he?...

"Your guardsmen are fine," he said, almost too cavalier. She faltered, thrown off by the sudden response. He continued, "Their pride might be a little bruised, but to be honest, I don't much care for Ya-Seti pride right now."

Her hand stayed clenched by her side. She didn't believe him. It was a lie, it had to be. The last thing she remembered was the bastard's foot stamping down on Enake's face.

"You lie," she managed, brow furrowing.

"Why would I want them dead?" he asked, but faltered, seeming to sense that the question would not be enough to sway her. "If I was the man you think I am, why would I leave you unbound, ungagged, and free to wander whenever you chose?"

Because you're an arrogant fool, Shanaki thought, but she held her tongue.

"You underestimated me." Her cool gaze slipped into a sneer.

"You, with those eyes? Not likely," he said it matter-of-factly, and his apparent earnestness brought her up short.

His words had her at war with herself. Pride and good sense fought against hope in a desperate struggle. She so wanted to believe that her guardsmen were alive, but how could she just trust this shadow in the dark?

She glanced down in thought, before looking back up. "Swear it. Swear it on something that matters."

"Well, I don't follow the gods; they haven't done a damn thing for me. But Yem and Àyá have always meant a great deal to me. I'll swear it on them if you like."

There was a pause before Shanaki asked, "You didn't kill them?" She hated how pathetic she sounded, but she needed to know.

"I swear on the twins. I did not."

Her eyes flickered as she breathed in, her relief as true as the moons he swore by. She could feel her eyes watering. She sat up straight, cleared her throat, and shifted tack. "Then you're a fool. They saw you; they know your face. The entire village will be out looking for you."

"Probably. Would you rather I had killed them?" He sounded slightly sullen now, as though disappointed she had spurned his swearing. "Anyway, they can look all they want but they won't find us. Not here..." he trailed off, and she heard what sounded like a thrown stone skittering across the floor to the far side of the room.

She calmed then. Maybe it was his frank tone, or maybe it was just that he had not shied away from her chances of rescue. But something inside her told her she could trust his words. Enake and Kasa were alive.

Her thoughts raced, her heart at war with her mind. Pain and weariness were flowing free now, as her anger left her, and with the weight of numbness lifting, resolve settled. Slow and steady as a sand snail, Shanaki took her broken arm in hand, and raised it to the dark.

For a moment she got no reaction, and when she did get one it was clear by his surprise he had not been looking at her.

"Oh, okay, here, let me have a look," he said.

Her arm was still numb to the touch, but she felt from the rise of her shoulder that he had grasped her lower arm. He was surprisingly gentle. She had seen his strength first hand, and now she saw he knew how to control it. It only made him more dangerous, in the long run, but for now she was glad. This was going to be painful enough without him botching the job through sheer force. She heard him move closer, muttering something to himself as he examined her injury.

Deciding she didn't want to just sit idle as he poked and prodded, she asked the obvious question. "Do you know what you're doing?"

"The white bit goes on the inside, right?" He laughed. She balked, reaching to snatch her arm away. But he intercepted her good arm by the wrist and held firm. "It's a joke, Princess. Yes, I know what I'm doing."

She frowned in a frustrated pout and he let her go.

"I'm no medicine man, just so you know," he continued. "But I've learned my fair share of healing lore over the years. That's how I knew what herbs to give you for the sedative and to numb the arm."

She nodded her head gently; the ache of the sulan *still* had yet to lift. "Why have you brought me here?"

"To keep you safe." This, he said with definitive confidence, as though it were the most obvious fact in the world. It caught her off guard.

"Safe?" She couldn't have kept the incredulity from her voice if she had tried. And she didn't try. "By abducting me and locking me away in a cave?"

"I said safe, I didn't say anything about comfortable. Speaking of which…" he tapered, and she felt her shoulder rise up as he lifted her arm.

She stilled her expression, refusing to reveal an ounce of her creeping fear. She had seen this done to others, had helped it done even, and she knew whatever anesthetic he had given her would not be enough for what was coming.

To hide any nerves that might have slipped through her wearied mask, she tried for a matter-of-fact tone as she said, "Once you set the bone, I shall take care of the rest."

"You were serious before, then?" he asked as he straightened out her arm. "All right, not much I can do for it once it's back in place anyway. One way or another, it's up to you to do the rest." He paused as if in afterthought, just as she had thought herself prepared, lowering her arm again. "Do you want something to bite down on?"

Her urge to scream in frustration at his delay died back. It was a fair question, and to be honest, she was grateful for the chance. She gave a terse "yes."

"Here, bite this," he said. She smelled something foul placed at her mouth. "It tastes as bad as a warthog's ass, but better that than biting your tongue off and never tasting anything again, right?"

She didn't reply, she simply opened her mouth and tore whatever *it* was from his grip. It tasted about as bad as he had promised, like tar and chalk all at once. She hoped her eyes were lit with the defiant fire she was aiming for, as she readied herself for the inevitable, but in her current state they were probably just bloodshot and dry.

A moment passed, then two, before…

Shanaki screamed into whatever she had clenched in her mouth, glad of the gag as her teeth clamped down harder than she had ever thought possible. She thought she had felt pain in her life, thought she had felt pain since waking in this cave. She hadn't. She was a fool for believing otherwise. This was the most painful, nerve splintering agony she had ever felt before, and this was *with* the numbness clouding its reality.

Her eyes were streaming and her nose pulled in air with the near-bray of a horse's muzzle. She fought to hold herself still as hard as she could, as she felt her consciousness slipping from her.

Don't black out, don't black out.

And then, the pain was gone. For a second Shanaki thought she had given in, that her mind had slipped her grasp and escaped into the retreat of sleep. From the tightened grip of her captor against her arm, only just loosening, it couldn't have been for more than a second if she had.

"There," he spoke with cautious confidence. "You can, well, do whatever you're going to do with it, I guess."

She expected to hear him backing through the darkness, but he remained crouched beside her. She couldn't really blame him for doubting her, she thought, as she slid herself back up from her slump against the wall, she was doubting herself and she knew what she had at her disposal.

She hesitantly moved her hand to the bend of her broken arm, breathing soft and slow as she lowered it to her skin. It was warm and sticky to the touch, her blood and sweat squelching unpleasantly as she pressed against her wound hard.

"What are—" he started to say. Shanaki ignored the cry of shock, holding her hand firm against her arm and concentrating intently on the flesh beneath her fingers. She thought back to all the techniques she had been taught for focusing the mind, bringing her senses down to the pulse of her blood through the arm, to the beating flow of her heart.

She remembered the lessons she had been given on the body and its magic within. How cuts knit, tears sealed, how even broken bones bled, in their own way. The last would help her here. She pressed harder, using the jolt of pain to bring her focus in, work her mind deeper, until she could feel the shifting of the split bone halves touching together. She took a deep breath, then another, before pushing her energy into the bone with all her might. She felt a great chill climb her spine, the heat of her back seeping through her numbed arm. She immediately felt the numbness burn away and her pain climbed harshly, but she pushed through it, focusing the new heat on the wound beneath her hand.

It took time, more than it should have done, even for her. Shanaki was exhausted and this sort of magic took more energy than most. She had to be careful not to draw too much too quickly, or she would pass out, leaving the injury worse off for the half-finished job. She opened herself to a steady channel, only a trickle at first but soon building to a stream.

She had never healed anything this serious before. It was an unusual sensation. She could feel the bone blood flowing, faster than was natural, spreading from the split halves until the fluids touched. She tightened her grip on the arm, and the fluid grew harder. It wasn't the full strength of bone, that would take days even with her healing, but it had the pliant firmness of a callus.

As far as the bone was concerned, Shanaki could leave it at that and let nature take its course. If she was careful with her movement, the callus would pull the two halves back to the right position and solidify from cartilage to bone. That would leave it weaker than it was before, though, and would take months, not days. She would need to continue working on it later.

She felt a wave of pride at her success as she moved on, but she knew she shouldn't. She had learned from her lessons how bones were one of the easier components to heal, and she had the far more complex musculature still left to go.

Components, she thought with the slight turn of a smile, *that's what Healer Dun'aa called them. 'Like the wheel of a cart or tip of a spear, bones, muscles, flesh, they are all merely component parts of the human whole.'*

She could hear the steely tone of her old teacher even in her own thoughts. Back then, Shanaki had dismissed the woman as cold and uncaring, but with her hand pressed against her arm, moving her mind from bone to muscle sinew, she felt she could appreciate what little warmth the woman had shown more and more. Even this token effort had the cold creeping up her back. If she'd needed to spend her days working on wounds like this and worse, Shanaki doubted *she'd* be able to spare much warmth for inattentive students either.

She made a mental note to thank her tutor personally when she returned to the capital; to thank her, and apologize. She would visit the temple and ask to continue her long neglected education, mundane and magical both.

Yes, *when* she returned.

That's the spirit, Shanaki...

Once again, she had no real way of knowing how long it took to work her arm back to a stable state. The muscle took far longer to work together and the skin kept unsealing before she could get it properly closed up. If she were anyone else, that would have left an unpleasant scar, but with a helping regenerative hand, that too would fade.

By the end she was exhausted more than she had thought possible, slumped back and held up only by the wall behind her, her thick hair fluffing around her ears. Her arm was a long way from fully functional, but the hard work was done, and the rest of the healing process would require far less focus and attention. She would continue later, after she had rested. Shanaki tried to lift her head from the wall, but she was utterly spent. She brushed her tongue over dry lips and spoke into the darkness wearily.

"You can stop gawking now."

She heard the slight scrabble of rock, a sure sign she had surprised him again. "How'd you know I'm gawking? You can't see."

Shanaki's head rolled sideways slightly, holding it steady was more effort than it was worth right now. Pride be damned; she was too tired for it.

She shifted her legs, letting them extend limply along the floor with a sigh, trying to get more comfortable. "People always stare the first time they see it. True healers are rare these days." She reached her good arm to massage her opposite shoulder gently.

"So... I'm safe here, am I?" she asked.

"Yes," the voice replied.

"Safer with you, a complete stranger in a dark cave, than in Bajok?" She stifled a long yawn with the crux of her arm as she worked her hand into her shoulder. "Safer than surrounded by my royal guard, the best Ya-Set has to offer?"

For a moment he didn't respond. She could almost *feel* the look of derision through the darkness but she held her tongue and kept her face passively inquiring. She felt less threatened by her predicament with every passing moment. How much of that was sheer exhaustion and how much was reliable instinct she still had yet to determine, and she had to do it soon. She could feel herself reaching the end of her tether.

"Yes?" he finally answered in a question. "I mean, I took you easily enough, didn't I? And I'm not —" He cut himself short, as though worried he might give something away.

She rolled her head back from the wall. "Not?" she prodded quickly, waking to attention again.

"Not the greatest fighter around…" he finished.

She paused in her massage, lowering her head to level a stern gaze at the dark. "That's a lie and twofold insult both. My guards are not wheat before a shotel blade. You think I would believe you a mere midling after you defeated them so swiftly? You claim to hold my eyes in high regard. So listen well when I tell you they are not so easily fooled, even blind in the dark."

"Right…" He offered no apology.

Leaving it alone for now, Shanaki hurried on to her next question. She was fading fast.

"Where are we… exactly?"

"Well…"

Shanaki listened as the voice broke into a telling of the history of this place. A mountainous region, with tunnels and caves running all throughout, holding all sorts of unsavory secrets he didn't deign to share with her here. The mountains had been the source of much storied history in Bajok for generations.

As she listened, it dawned on her slowly how young the voice seemed. There was an eager edge to it, a haste to get all the words out before they lost their place. She had heard that in others before, from nervous retainers as they hurriedly spilled their stories to her, wary of straining her attention. There was more confidence to this tale. The man, the markedly *young* man, wasn't concerned about her reaction at all. But it was clear he had little experience with such long-winded tellings.

The more she heard, the more the tension drained from her body. She wouldn't lower her guard with him, she wasn't stupid, but her instincts were telling her she wasn't in any immediate danger for now.

She might not be able to take him on his word, but she

did know that he had every advantage over her right now. He could clearly see for one — if the lack of blind pawing at the rope or her arm was anything to go by. To say nothing of the fact that this was apparently his cave, his space. If he wasn't already using his advantages, he must have a reason.

She would need to learn it, of course. It was essential she do, but for now...

SIX

IKENNA

WELL, THAT COULD HAVE GONE BETTER.

Ikenna slumped against the far wall, sliding to the floor and clutching at his side with an inward groan. He never expected this to be easy, nothing ever was, but he had hoped for a better start than this.

That fall had done a real number on him. His back was bruised black, and he had a wide, shallow scrape across his lower left. He wasn't sure, but it felt as though he might have cracked some ribs as well. It was an unfamiliar experience for him, feeling fragile. He touched at his ribs gingerly, and looked across at the princess, asleep on the opposite side of the cave.

She had done something to him as he chased her. He hadn't recognized it at the time, but the unnatural chill that had run down his spine as she fell had been more than simple dread. She had thrown a glance his way before she tripped, sent out some unusual wave of power. It had snared him without him even realizing. As they had fallen, he had called to the beast within, coaxing his hyena free to harden his hide and take the brunt of the fall. But he had heard no response. For the first time in his life, his second self had been silenced.

Ikenna didn't know how the princess had done it, and he wished she hadn't at that precise moment—he would have been saved from his injuries, then—but the fact that she could, sent a surge of hope racing through his heart. He had never in all his life had the chance to live without his hyena. The heckling cackle always lingering at the edges of his mind no matter what he did, no matter how hard he tried to fight it back. He had never known the peace of not even having to try.

He had to know what she had done.

He looked down at her arm, the blood from her pierced skin stemmed by the thin layer of flesh closed over the wound. He wasn't sure what he had expected from the young woman when she first woke. He hadn't put much thought to her as a person at all before he actually got her to the cave. She was a target, a goal—a means by which to strike out at his clan. He supposed he hadn't really expected much of *anything* from her. She was just some pampered princess from a foreign land, a silly, scared little flower that would wilt at the first sign of danger. That's just how royal whelpings were.

Except... she wasn't.

In the short time it took him to scout the area for more tosi, she had somehow managed to make her way, completely blind, to the den exit and almost out onto the hills. If he hadn't returned at that exact moment, she would have been one stone's press away from freedom, out wandering The Black Rocks where anyone could have found her.

And then, exhausted and half drugged, she had taken her broken arm in hand and casually sewn it back together with nothing but strength of will alone. He knew such power, mystic healing was something the Bajoki had been using for centuries—though through group ritual, not any one healer's power. And hell, inherent, natural healing was something his own kind had as part of their intrinsic bloodline.

But it was one thing to brush away scrapes and cuts. Healing away the worst of the damage from an arm as mangled as hers had been, practically unaided... *that* was something special. It was no wonder the others wanted her blood.

Ikenna shook his head side to side with an angered hiss, stifling the gibbering moan fighting its way from his hyena's throat at the back of his head. He had to be more careful. The others would be out in force searching for her. He couldn't afford to mess up again.

He turned away from the sleeping princess and scratched at the back of his head. He was glad of the cave's darkness. At least until the twinslights lit up for the night, his hyena could slip free without Ikenna worrying the princess might see. It helped him keep the beast calm, letting it taste the open air. It chafed constantly beneath the bindings of his flesh. There were other benefits too. The keen sight of the creature was one of the few traits his demon bloodline offered him that he didn't despise by default.

He scratched at the furred hide grown out behind him, feeling the quivering shake of the raised hairs as his hyena's senses flared.

Quiet, N'yewe.

Ikenna soothed the beast absently, his thoughts dancing listlessly in the dark. Most kishi, well, *none* of the them gave names to their hyenas. His father, Uzoma, had chided Ikenna when he first let slip that his beast had been given one. Ikenna learned quickly to keep such "queer" customs to himself.

With the thrills and fears of the hunt for the princess, he

had been focused, set on the path he had chosen. The path his clan had forced upon him. The rage that had driven his rebellion still bubbled within him, but now that he actually had the princess here, locked away where the scum wouldn't find her, he didn't know what to do with all the hate.

He had learned early in life that misspent emotion could cost dearly. The beast within wanted to run wild, free, always and forever. If he let it think it could, riding on the back of his rage—even for a moment—all the leashes and chains he had worked so hard to fasten through the years would slip away. And then he would never get control again.

It won't happen. I won't let it.

He felt the chuckle of his hyena. It nibbled on his hand as he stroked the maw still stretching from the back of his head. The creature was a fickle thing. It fed on his emotion and delighted in his frustrated attempts to battle back the anger. It had been a long time since he had struggled like this, he had thought himself an adept by now. He'd spent his entire life trying to control his demons after all, literal and figurative both.

He had to let the rage go, to turn to acceptance of what his family had done. He would destroy them for it, but he couldn't do it with hatred in his heart.

But every time he thought about his brother Baako biting into Imani...

He clawed his hand down the hyena's skin, his nails grinding against its iron hide. Just thinking about it made him want to howl and rake at the wall. It wasn't his anger at Baako that had him. His hate of his enemies was strong and pure, but he had dealt with that all his life. No, it was the anger at himself that bound him tight. It was the frustration of knowing the source of his imbalance and yet still failing to purge it from his mind. He was supposed to be better than this. He *was* better than this. But his baser, primal side... just didn't care.

His hyena cackled quietly again in a sickly chuckle and Ikenna sighed. This is why he couldn't do things like throw himself off a ledge to catch falling princesses. His instincts were not always his own. He could never be sure of his own heart until he had calmed his mind and stilled his senses. In-the-moment instincts left no such pause.

Ikenna gently tugged at the tuft of one upward ear, willing his hyena to stay silent. In isolation, the two of them got on well enough. It was in how they dealt with outsiders that their wills crossed most often—and to them, all *besides* themselves were outsiders. The pack offered them nothing. Strangers offered them nothing.

But she's different, Ikenna forced through his mind with fierce determination. *The princess is different.*

He gripped the twitching maw of his hyena firmly and ceased its shaking, forcing it to look at the girl on the far side of their den. *She offers vengeance and retribution for Imani.*

The hyena threatened a growl, and Ikenna released his grip. He understood. He knew now that that wasn't all the princess might offer him, and N'yewe knew it too. The hyena had no desire to be locked away at the back of Ikenna's mind. He had made his displeasure clear the last time it had been tried all those years ago...

Ikenna pushed to his feet and rubbed at his back. His kishi healing was doing its work, but much too slowly. His injuries should have been halfway healed by now. The fact that they weren't meant his hyena was holding back, relishing in the pain Ikenna was suffering for his, as N'yewe saw it, stupidity.

He could handle the pain—he'd dealt with far worse—but his partner's petty rebellion needed putting in its place. He needed both his heads on straight if he wanted to keep the princess safe. He closed his eyes, all four of them, and held them shut against the will of his beast.

When he opened them again, awake to his inner self, he saw the den around him in an old light. He saw the pillar he had danced around as a child, the same one he had chased around and scratched at as a pup. He saw the moons' pool set into the wall that mirrored a reflection of the twinslight shine when the cavernous crystals woke to the night. He remembered splashing in the pool and howling up at the chasmed ceiling. The large splinter of layered rock would catch his cries and echo them higher, like a small, skyward canyon.

He fought the canine urge to shout those cries now, biting them back and turning his gaze again down to the den walls. Upon those walls he and N'yewe beheld the ruin of their shared youth. They found more anger, but not the splayed and separate hatreds of today. There, was a unifying rage; red-hot anger replaced by the icy stab of old betrayal. As their gaze circled the room, they saw great tracts of rockwall scratched away, chunks of broken stone scattering the edges of the cave. Between the worst of the damage, he could still see the edges of their art. Paintings and carvings ran along the wall, some simply rough-hewn shapes, others fully formed pictures of mountains and flowers and rivers and waterfalls. The shared work was the first collaboration between Ikenna and N'yewe.

The pack had ruined it. The pack had taken their pictures and their colors and destroyed them forever. It was the first great betrayal, but it wasn't the last.

Resting a clenched, trembling hand against the pillar splitting the cave he walked around the spindled strut, looking back at Shanaki.

She is our revenge. She must be protected, he begged the beast as it sniffed the air with a tilted curiosity.

After a moment, Ikenna felt a tug at his neck, and he

turned his head to follow N'yewe's urging. Across the room, he saw the remains of one particular painting. The hind paw, the tuft of a front ear of a hyena cub, and across from it the snout of a second pressing close to where the first's head should still have been.

Yes, Ikenna thought eagerly. *Ours. Kin. Protect.*

He felt the concept settle in his second mind, and the pain of his back dulled, his ribs aching a little less. The subtle, distressed shifting of N'yewe's snout stilled.

Ikenna sat back down and leaned against the cave's pillar, tired from his latest struggle with the demon, and waited for Princess Shanaki to wake once more.

SEVEN

IKENNA

HER EYES ARE LIKE HOT COALS, IKENNA THOUGHT AS SHE stirred awake hours later. The princess had fallen sideways in her sleep, and had to sit awkwardly on her side until the feeling in her good arm returned from where she had lain on it. The smoldering heat of her gaze seemed to give off a faint light all its own as her eyes traced their way through the gloom.

A few moments passed, and Ikenna found himself unsure of how to break the silence. He could see a shift in her eyes; they had been searching, straining for any sign of him they could find. Now they held a question, one that he could tell by the rest of her face she was fighting the urge to ask.

Ikenna considered, for a moment, leaving the unasked question unanswered. It would be interesting to see what she did when she thought herself alone. Perhaps he'd catch a glimpse of the cunning nature that had, in the brief time he'd known her, almost granted her escape. In the end he decided against it. If he was aiming to build a foundation of trust here, he needed to make honest first steps.

"Did you sleep well?" He cursed himself the moment he said it.

Of course she didn't sleep well, you idiot. She was sleeping off a sulan hangover with a half-healed broken arm at her side—in the cave you've abducted her to. Did you sleep well? Honestly…

"Well enough," came her reply after a moment's thought.

Ikenna was surprised at the calm of her tone. It was still cool, and her eyes had lost none of their edge, but she seemed more guarded than hostile as she rubbed the sleep from her eyes.

He had left the pause too long. He uttered a quick "good," and ushered in a fresh silence.

He didn't want to let this less-hostile air slip away. He cast about for something to move the conversation past awkward etiquette, but came up short. Eventually, he remembered that neither of them had eaten anything all day, and it was almost nightfall outside. With the exertion of her injury and climb, the princess was bound to be hungry.

He asked the question, and she nodded a firm yes.

"I'd rather have some light, though, if possible," she said. "I grow tired of talking to a shadow in the dark."

Ikenna glanced up at the twinslights. "I would have lit a fire for when you first woke up but, you know, the smoke and all." She wrinkled her nose in irritated acceptance. "Don't worry though, we'll have some light soon. The moons will be out in an hour or so."

A look of confusion crossed her face then. "And how will that help us here?"

"You'll see. Give me a moment. I'll grab the food." He climbed to his feet and jogged to the second tunnel way on the far side of the room. He clutched at his ribs as he went; the last of the cracks were still only just on the mend now that his hyena was back behind him. N'yewe sniffed quietly at the air, eagerly following the scent of food as Ikenna lead them down the passage.

The room off from his main den had been turned into a paltry storeroom of sorts. When Ikenna had decided that he would bring the princess here, he had gathered what supplies he could in a hurry and stashed them.

There wasn't much, only enough for a few days—weeks if they could stomach staling bread and turned meat—but it was better than starting off with his next resort. At least this way he'd have time to win the princess over before feeding her rodent and cave moss.

He took a fair chunk of the bread and some cold peanut soup and turned back to the main den.

The princess started with a small jump when he called out that he had returned. She tried to hide it at first but quickly gave it up for a lost cause.

"You might consider making a little more noise when you approach a lady blind in the dark," she said through gritted teeth. He could hear her heart hammering in her chest.

"Sorry, Princess. Very old habit. I've spent most of my life trying to go unnoticed." He wasn't sure why he told her that. Even as he said it he regretted the words. He expected her to prod for further explanation, but instead she simply looked away from him, or where she thought she had heard him at least.

She turned her head down and ran her hand over her half-broken arm, testing the stretched skin gently. "No matter."

He moved to sit in front of her, pointedly scratching his bare feet along the stone and giving a light sigh as he lowered to the ground. She gave no sign she had taken note of his efforts; she simply looked back up from her arm and waited for him to speak.

He reached out with the bread and gently nudged it

against her good hand. She took it from him without preamble, holding it in her lap and continuing to watch his way.

"It's not poisoned, before you ask," Ikenna muttered as he tore away a bite of his own portion loud enough for her to hear.

"I wasn't going to. It seems to me that, for whatever reason, you want me alive." She gave him a look before taking her first hungry bite, gulping it down and adding, "At least for now."

Ikenna swallowed his own mouthful quickly. "I do, I —"

"You *claim* to have brought me here to keep me safe," she continued, interrupting him. "The question that leaves me is why? What are you supposed to be protecting me *from*?" She bit into her chunk of loaf again, chewing steadily, her eyes fixed only slightly off from where he actually sat, as she waited for his reply.

It didn't come quickly. There was a long, drawn-out silence, broken only by the tearing and chewing of more bread. Ikenna honestly wasn't sure where to begin. He tried desperately to think of an answer that wouldn't just lead to more uncomfortable questions, but none came to mind. How was he supposed to convince her of the danger she faced, without leading her to the obvious follow-ups that would reveal who and *what* he was?

He could see from the narrowing of her eyes and the longer gaps between bites that the princess was growing impatient for an answer. She wasn't going to just let the question lie. In truth, he had wanted her to know as soon as possible himself. He needed her on board if he was going to have any hope of keeping the two of them hidden after all. But now that she had actually asked him, he didn't know how best to get the words out. It wasn't an easy thing to say.

He took a deep breath and started at the beginning. "What do you know of the kishi?"

The princess swallowed her latest bite and frowned. "Not much," she admitted. "The villagers back in Bajok spoke of them as demons they had faced many years ago. But they wouldn't explain any further when I asked. It was about the only interesting story any of them had to tell too…"

Ikenna gave a murmur of acknowledgement. "I'm not surprised. It's not a pleasant story."

"The interesting ones rarely are." The princess tore another mouthful from her bread, shrugging her good shoulder casually as she dismissed his ominous tone.

Ikenna sat there for a moment watching her eat. He pushed the bowl of peanut soup toward her, and she bent down to dip her bread. She didn't understand just how real the demons were. He felt a wave of irritation from his partner, felt his urge to snap at the air and show her the truth of things. Ikenna could understand his reaction; no one liked to be dismissed as insignificant. He couldn't begrudge the beast that. But the princess didn't know who they were, or anything about the kishi at all. He had to make her understand.

"The kishi are real, Princess. And they're monsters. Half-human, half-hyena demons. They're fast, faster than you can believe, and strong too. They'd tear your best guardsmen to pieces, and they'd do it with ease. But worse, they're clever. They don't just kill you—they manipulate you into killing yourself. They twist your emotions until you just walk like a hapless puppet right into their open maws." Ikenna spat the explanation in disgust, pushing on before he could falter. "Their favorite prey are the weak that think themselves strong. They twist their spirit and play with their inner selves until they'd happily dance through fire if they asked them to. And the kishi do this all in the name of a more satisfying meal."

He finally relented, swallowing back the bile from his tirade and forcing himself not to continue.

The princess paused her eating and looked out through the darkness thoughtfully. She swallowed the last of her bread and set the bowl she had been pulling from down by her side, wiping her hand on her silk skirt.

She pursed her lips briefly before speaking. "What is your name?"

"My name?" he asked, surprised at the abrupt change of subject.

"Your name. Captor or savior, I should like to know it."

He hesitated a moment, though he didn't know why. He supposed he felt a strange comfort in his anonymity, but she would see his face soon enough. The time for hiding in the shadows was past.

"Ikenna," he returned quietly.

She nodded. "*Weiya*, Ikenna. I am —"

"Princess Shanaki, second heir to Ya-Set," he interrupted swiftly. "I know who *you* are, Princess." He realized his mistake immediately; the look of surprised irritation she shot him, a stern chastisement. That said, it felt like she was holding herself back, still trying to avoid hostility.

"*Shanaki*," she voiced in a deliberate tone. "My name is Shanaki. I'm not one for needless formality where I can avoid it, and *Ogó'ala* knows we've no need of it here."

"Shanaki, then."

There was another pause. Shanaki seemed to be weighing something up in her mind, so he left her to it, taking back her discarded bowl and scooping the peanut soup to his mouth with his hand.

"How do you know so much about the kishi, Ikenna?" she asked. He froze, his latest scoopful halfway to his mouth. She pressed on. "How do you know they're targeting me?"

Her eyes were fixed on where she thought she would find his own, her searching gaze unblinking. Ikenna thought to lie, to come up with some story about how he had overheard them making plans when he was walking in the hills, but he knew it was pointless. She already suspected something. Lying would only burn away what little cautious trust she had.

"I know because... because I'm one of them." Ikenna took a deep breath and let it out in a rush, a great weight seeming to lift from his shoulders. It was the first time he had ever revealed his secret to anyone outside the clan.

Shanaki sat still, watching him, her eyes unchanged. They still held to their search, sensing for any hint of deception or threat.

"Why, then? Why help me? Why betray your people for a stranger?" She spoke the questions softly. It was the first time he had heard her voice free of its underlying edge.

This, he could answer swiftly. "Because I'm *not* one of them. They're not my people and they never have been; you can't betray what you were never loyal to." He turned his head to the ruined walls she couldn't see. "I've hated them since I was six years old. We share nothing in this life but the demon's blood running through our veins."

He considered leaving it at that, but he had come this far. He may as well run the full gambit. "They—they killed someone important to me, and—and I want to make them pay."

The princess stayed quiet for a while then, picking out chunks of her remaining bread and lifting them to her mouth slowly. She seemed to withdraw deep inside herself, the way he did when his hyena was being particularly ferocious. She was coming to a decision in her head, he could see it in her eyes.

"Thank you, Ikenna," she finally spoke up minutes later. "Thank you for your honesty and for your courage."

It was almost too much to hope for. "You believe me? Really?"

She smirked around her last bit of bread, a hint of something new flashing across her face but gone before he could put a name to it. "I do, actually. I'm not really sure why, but my gut tells me you're telling the truth, and it's served me well thus far." She wiped at her mouth and brushed stray crumbs from her chest. "Besides, if you *are* lying, playing some grand part to lure me into trusting you, I'm not sure what you expect to get out of it. No matter what, I'm still stuck in a dark cave with a dangerous stranger. Cooperative or not, I'm not getting out without you letting me."

He supposed she was right. The perspective certainly made things a lot more simple.

"Right, I guess that's true." *Smooth, Ikenna.* "Well, I'm glad."

Silence followed then. Not the tense silence of potential hostility that had reigned before, but the slightly awkward silence of unfamiliar companions reaching for fresh somethings to say.

Shanaki broke it first. "So... what's the plan?" She sat up a little straighter and rested her good hand over her injured arm. The tension of her brow told him she had begun her healing again.

Ikenna didn't want to answer, didn't want to tell the princess—whose confidence he had only just earned—that there was no plan. He really hadn't had time to think much beyond stealing her away and getting her to his den in the first place. His clan hadn't given him any.

So instead, he took the easy dodge. "Should you really be healing your injury again so soon? You weren't asleep that long, barely a nap, and you only just got some food in you."

"I have strength enough for this much. I dealt with the worst of it before. I'm mostly just strengthening what I already healed now." She looked up from her arm, unfazed, her expression expectant.

Ikenna glanced to the side, nervous under her stare. It was amazing how she could do that, make him feel like she was staring into his soul even through the dark. He dreaded what she could manage under the glow of the twinslights.

"What?" he asked.

Her expression dampened fast, her eyes slating over in annoyance. "The plan?"

"Right... Long and short of it is we wait here until my clan gets lazy in their search for you, then make an escape north through Guela. Unless my..." He hesitated. "Unless I get word otherwise. Either way, we'll figure out the best way to get you back to Ya-Set."

Shanaki didn't look happy with the idea. "You would have me cower and hide, and then when we've had enough of that just run back home with my tail tucked firmly between my legs?"

"I wouldn't put it like that," Ikenna remarked dryly. "But essentially, yes."

"Ya-Seti don't run from danger, and I am their princess." Shanaki held her expression firm and unrelenting, her grip on her arm tightening slightly in her obstinance.

"From *this* danger you need to; you don't know the kishi like I do. Your people can't fight them, they'll tear them apart." Ikenna was gesturing with his arms, desperate for her to understand, futility through the darkness be damned.

Shanaki bristled. "Are you so sure?"

"Yes, I'm sure. I already told you, I'm far from the strongest kishi out there, and I didn't exactly struggle with your guard."

"You took them by surprise. Had they—"

"Had they been prepared I still would have beaten them. I'm just *faster* than they are, Princess—"

"*Shanaki*," she hissed in irritation.

Ikenna sighed. "Sorry. Shanaki. I'm not trying to insult your guard. Really, I'm not. They're good, better than anything I've seen out of Bajok by a league and a half, but they're fighting demons. It's not a fair competition." He pushed on, wanting to cover every base he could, "And they won't be prepared. They'll be just as ambushed as your men were on the river, it's how we—*they*—operate, how they *hunt*."

He paused to see if any of it was sinking in. Shanaki had taken on a stubborn but contemplative posture, clearly bristling under the weight of her pride. But she didn't strike him as the type to linger in that headspace for long, and from the softening of her expression after a few scant moments, he had guessed right.

"All right, so my people are at a disadvantage, I'll grant you that." She looked at him, her healing hand lifted from her arm slightly in her distraction. "But all the more reason not to run. I can help them fight; my power can hold them back long enough to have a fighting chance!"

She really, truly cares about what happens to them...

Ikenna sat quiet for a moment, slightly in awe and watching as the princess hung in anticipation of his reply. "You used it on me before by the stairs, didn't you? I didn't realize until afterward what you had done. What is that power? I've never heard of anything like it before."

Shanaki leaned back, clearly not happy with the change in direction, but glad to have avoided outright dismissal all the same. She returned to her healing and answered carefully. "It's part of my magic. I'm Twice Blessed. I can heal and I can suppress other mystics' Blessings—or curses I suppose, in your case." She focused down at her arm, shame darkening her face. "I'm usually much better at it than when I used it on you. I was panicking, acting on instinct instead of intention. It was sloppy."

"It was amazing," Ikenna corrected sincerely. He had to get what this meant for him across to her now, while he had the chance. "I couldn't call on my hyena at *all*."

Ikenna shifted his back a bit with a groan and tried to lighten the mood a little. "Not going to lie though... I wish you had held off on it just a few seconds longer, that fall would have been a lot easier on my back if you had."

Shanaki smiled a little at that, just a small smirk, but he saw the fires being stoked behind her eyes once more.

"But seriously," Ikenna continued. "You don't know what that was like... to have my power stripped completely away like that."

He saw her smile drop, a flash of defensiveness crossing her expression. "I didn't exactly know you were trying to help me at the time—"

"That's not what I meant," Ikenna spoke quickly, his hands pointlessly raised again to calm her. "It wasn't a bad thing. For the first time in my life, I was free of the hyena, free of its gnawing, biting, cackling hell in my head. It was unbelievable!"

She looked up from her healing, her idea clear in her face. "I could do it again—"

"Don't. As unpleasant as most of it is, there are some benefits to my kishi blood. I need my night's eyes while it's still dark, for one, and if I concentrate, I can sense if any of my clan are nearby. It's safer this way." He paused, then added, "Besides, I—I don't think it's a good idea to get too comfortable with that."

"Why not? You're allowed some peace of mind. It's not your fault you were born with demon blood in your veins, you know." She was being earnest. It surprised him how little she seemed to care what he was.

"It's not that... it's... it's..." He paused again, unsure

how to get across his true fear. "I don't want to grow comfortable with the quiet, just to end up losing it again when you leave."

"Oh."

They fell silent again. Ikenna could tell she was looking for something to say just as much as he was, but after a while she returned to focusing on her arm. He could see the hairs on her skin raised around the touch of her hand as they reacted to the steady flow of magic.

She looked up suddenly, a question clear on her lips. "You said you could see through your 'night's eyes,' and that kishi are half-man, half-hyena. Tell me, what does that look like? If I had the light of sun to see by right now, what would I be looking at?"

Ikenna's heart beat heavy in his chest. There was no fear in her question, no trace of hidden malice; she was genuinely, honestly curious.

Who is *this girl?*

He looked down at his hands and back up at her. "You would see a man, just a normal man, with long locs of dark hair and golden eyes."

Shanaki frowned. "Well, that's disappointing. No mottled fur? No serpent's tongue or bloodied fangs?"

Ikenna couldn't help it, he smiled. "What hyenas do they have in Ya-Set that you would expect a serpent's tongue?"

"Well, I don't know, do I? You say hyena, but you also say demon. Maybe you were just exaggerating with that second part." Shanaki leaned back against the wall behind her. He could see keeping up the constant flow of energy to her arm was starting to drain her again.

He considered her words. He was tempted to leave her with them, but it wouldn't be right. She wouldn't be sitting here so matter-of-fact about it all if she knew the true darkness of his kind.

He let the silence fester a little. Maybe the hint of drama would help him convince her. "It's not an exaggeration, Shanaki. Kishi *are* demons."

"You say that, but I—"

"Know nothing about them," Ikenna cut her off. "One look at us and we ensnare your senses, creeping into your mind and turning it against you. We eat men, women, and children as easy as boar. Hells, our first act in life is tearing our way through our mother's belly. We are literally *born* children of Dulagi, Shanaki. Born with a taste for blood."

Ikenna had his head in his hands, his locs falling in curtains around his face. N'yewe mewled silently from the back of his skull, his voice held tight by Ikenna's mental chains.

"It's *who* you are that matters, *ukuhlu,* not what," Shanaki said. "You are Ikenna. And while I admit I have only just met him, if he has been true of himself thus far, then he does not strike me as the evil type." She smiled, raising her hand from her arm with a tired sigh. "Trust me, I'm an excellent judge of character."

She raised her slightly swollen arm before her face, squinting as though she might suddenly be able to see it through the darkness. She clenched her hand twice, testing its strength with a look his way.

"I am not afraid of the kishi, or *any* demons that would threaten my people. Don't think I'll just give up on going to help them because you've got horror stories to tell." She lowered her clenched fist and shrugged her good shoulder. "That said, I'm in no state to help anyone like this. We'll do things your way for now, at least until I've had a chance to heal properly."

Shanaki nodded, the matter clearly settled as far as she was concerned, and moved swiftly on, jerking her head to the air above.

"When am I going to get this special moon lighting, then?"

"Any minute now." Ikenna set the small chip of stone he had been fingering in one hand down on the ground, resting his hands on his knees and looking up. He could sense the faintest, imperceptible glow of the twinslights starting to come to life.

"Good. I should like to see this face that promises to 'ensnare my senses.' " She smirked, sitting up a bit and shuffling until she was comfortable against the rock.

EIGHT

IKENNA

IT WASN'T LONG BEFORE THE FIRST OF THE CRYSTALS
began their glow. Ikenna drew N'yewe back within his head
at the first sign of the cave's curtain of darkness drawing
back. The pitch black faded and the faintest of blurred
outlines became dim silhouettes, shifting into shapes and
shadow as everything started to take form before their eyes.

Most of this went unnoticed by Shanaki, Ikenna saw, as
she stared at the chasmed ceiling above. Her eyes were
alight with radiant sparks of silver blue, deep mirrors
soaking in the luminous, lunar light shining down on them
both.

As her eyes cast up, Ikenna's own were drawn down.
The new light had drawn stark attention to her beauty: the
soft hue of her cheeks, the fullness of her lips. For the first
time, his human eyes took in the quiet grace of her posture,
the swell of her curves, her long legs carved from dark
marble smoother than satin silk.

"I thought you were supposed to be the one ensnaring
my senses." She canted her head, her golden earrings
resting atop her shoulder.

Ikenna snapped his eyes upward, startled back to

himself by Shanaki's voice. She was smiling bemusedly at him, her gaze twinkling from more than just the crystals above. Ikenna could feel himself blushing and he jumped for some excuse, a reason for his stare.

"I was checking your leg—I..." He swallowed, moistening his dry mouth. "I thought there might be some swelling."

"Of course," she agreed with enthusiastic and mocking earnestness, before mercifully dropping the jest and nodding up at the crystals. "I've never seen so many natural light stones in one place before. They're beautiful."

"They are," Ikenna said, following her gaze. "I call them twinslights. For a long time they were the only light I knew."

"I like that," Shanaki mused. " 'Twinslights.' After twilight and the twins."

For a while they passed into light conversation. Ikenna told Shanaki the story he had been taught about how the twinslights had been sung to life by his ancestors and rooted in the kishi dens. She spoke of how, back home, the Ya-Seti had mastered the art of growing their own. They used enchantments to store light over time and keep their stones glowing regardless of sun or moon.

Ikenna was fascinated by her tales of Ya-Set, and Shanaki seemed eager to share them. She clearly missed her home. She had spent much of her life hearing of its wider regions from servants and guardsmen—maybe the occasional merchant trader if she caught one out on her rare, secret walks through the streets.

The more they talked, the more he noticed how little effect he was having on the Ya-Seti princess. Ikenna would never call himself a conceited person; he prided himself on holding to his humility. But he had long grown used to having to fight off the attention of women. He deliberately distanced himself from the villagers and farmhands he encountered, knowing that his demon nature lured them in just by his very breathing.

He had tried, once or twice, to talk to some of them. He had wanted some practice to see if he might one day approach Imani. But every time he tried, forcing all his inherent, mystical instincts back beneath his skin, he still ended up drawing them to his words like fireflies to a flame.

He hated it. He wanted a real connection with someone, someone to talk openly to and to share thoughts with on an even footing, not a spellbound slave hanging on his every word, every motion.

But as much as he wanted it, he had never expected to actually find it—not from a human girl at least. Yet here Shanaki was, conversing with him freely, her senses as sure looking at him as if she were looking at a wall. It shouldn't have been possible.

He had become lost in his thoughts, and didn't immediately realize that Shanaki had stopped talking. She was looking at him with a question on her face.

"Sorry, what was that?" he asked apologetically, hand rubbing the back of his head.

"It doesn't matter," she dismissed with a wave. He noticed she seemed to turn inward a little, like he had disappointed her somehow.

They both spoke at once, cutting off and waiting for the other to resume. Shanaki drove ahead faster.

"I've just seen something far more interesting." She pointed her good hand over his shoulder to the wall opposite her own. "What are *those*?"

She was pointing to one of the larger pieces of undamaged stone. A small collection of scrawls and painted pictures were scattered across it, lit by the silver glow of the twinslights.

Ikenna had mixed feelings about that spot. It was the

largest section of art that had survived his clan's savagery, but only by virtue of it being where he had cowered before their attack. N'yewe detested it, the memories it invoked stunk of weakness and failure. But Ikenna saw the lesson it represented and appreciated what little had been saved, despite the reasons why.

"Oh, that," he said. "Just some pictures I made when I was a boy."

Shanaki left her arm alone for the moment and stood up, walking toward the opposite wall and running a hand across the carvings and painted shapes. "How old were you? They're pretty good."

"Seven. Not much to do when you're stuck here in the dark with only your*selves* for company."

Shanaki raised an eyebrow at that. "Selves?"

Ikenna shrugged, turning away and walking to lean against the cave's pillar.

Shanaki looked back at the art. "Why did you destroy it all?"

"I didn't. My clan took exception to me 'shirking my training,' and wanted to teach me a lesson."

"No wonder you're not close." She moved closer to look at a painted paw-print. While she was focused on the wall, Ikenna moved behind the pillar and called to N'yewe in his mind. From within his locs he felt the hyena stir, poking its snout out to sniff at the air. Ikenna was surprised, and his concentration slipped for a second, long enough for the beast's mewling to escape its throat.

He heard Shanaki spin toward him, and he quickly pulled the hyena back within. He used the pillar for cover as he pushed at the back of his head and forced the frustrated maw through his hair.

"Ikenna?"

"Sorry Princ—Shanaki, I was just curious." The hyena

fully drawn within and his hair back in place, he stepped out from behind the pillar.

"About what?" Her head was tilted in curiosity of her own, her gaze guarded.

"Just, I thought you might be suppressing some of my power, is all." He shrugged, trying to show her she could relax, and that it wasn't something he was concerned about.

A look of realization shifted her expression. "Ah, right. Wondering why your 'irresistible charm' hasn't swept me off my feet yet, is that it?"

"To be honest, I'm not used to women turning away from me when they have the choice not to."

"Well, maybe Ya-Seti women just have higher standards than your usual Bajoki stock." She smiled and rose from her crouch, walking out to the middle of the cave and scratching at her arm. "You're not *that* handsome you know."

"But you think I'm handsome though?" Ikenna joked. "Seriously, how are you —"

"I'm just keeping my guard up, that's all. I don't have to spread my power out all the time, you know." She rubbed at the scratch marks on her arm, massaging the raw skin. "Though I admit I'm curious to see what you look like with my guard lowered a little."

"Have you always had such dangerous curiosities?"

Shanaki shrugged. "Nya always says it's probably for the best that my father keeps me locked inside the palace as much as possible. Not that that stops her sneaking me out from time to time."

"Nya?"

"The captain of my personal guard." She took on a wistful look. "And my friend."

Ikenna knew what that look meant. She was worried for her people back in Bajok. He saw where those thoughts would lead her and tried to steer them clear.

"She's the captain of your guard but she sneaks you out the palace?"

"I can be very persuasive." She gave a half-hearted attempt at a canted smirk, but her heart clearly wasn't in it. Her thoughts were far away and down the mountain.

Well, she likes stories...

"I bet you had fun," he said.

That was all it took, she was clearly as keen to escape her thoughts as he was to steer her from them. Ikenna spent the next few hours learning more about Ya-Set, its culture and its people—the smaller details she had left out of her earlier tales.

Shanaki continued her healing on and off throughout. He could see the process was taking a lot out of her, beads of sweat were starting to run down her forehead and arms, and the occasional shiver would shake her shoulders. The reprieves between her healing began to grow longer with each passing hour.

When Ikenna felt the twins reach their zenith, by the light of the crystals' glow, he spoke up. "You should get some rest; you're looking a little worn."

Shanaki feigned indignation. "Excuse me?"

Ikenna had grown used to their back and forth by now, and waved her off. "I said I'm tired. I need my sleep."

Shanaki nodded indulgently. "Oh, well in that case we had better get some rest."

Ikenna smiled and sat down to sleep.

THE NEXT FEW DAYS FOR THEM WERE SPENT sporadically switching between talking, eating, and sleeping. Ikenna grew to know Shanaki rather well: he learned her passion for debate, that one of her favorite pastimes was fishing, and that she had a particular pride for her country.

Ikenna shared things about himself as well. Things he had not shared with anyone before. It was a comfortable companionship, and Ikenna found he liked the princess a lot. She was interesting; she knew much of the world beyond Bajok—far more than he did—and yet she had the same yearning to see it that he held himself, as most of what she knew came from stories.

They shared their pasts, Ikenna abridging less and less of his own as he began to trust Shanaki's strange tolerance for his darker side.

They spent some time trying to improve his Mero-Set. Shanaki claimed he was a fast learner and that his knack for picking up the vocabulary was "surprisingly" good. It was just his pronunciation that needed work for the most part.

It took a few days for them to shift their body clocks, but eventually they had themselves set so that they woke with the glow of the twinslights. Shanaki was especially grateful, she had grown reasonably familiar with the dark now that she trusted Ikenna with it, but it still frustrated her to be so completely blind for so long.

Her frustration was made worse by the difficulty she was having with her arm. She had woken on the third day to a throbbing at her elbow, and by the fourth her skin had darkened as though halfway to a bruise.

Ikenna was worried. He feared the wound might have festered from within and picked up some sort of infection. Shanaki was stubborn about it though, insisting it was just a part of the process and that she'd work through it with her power.

That day's "night," Ikenna stayed awake, watching Shanaki's form sleeping restlessly in the darkness. The healing was taking more out of her than it should have. He was no expert on mystic healing, but it stood to reason that the farther along the process she was, the less strenuous the healing should have been. The body could be relied on to heal itself more, for one thing.

By "morning" of their fifth day together, Ikenna had made his decision. She was beginning to show signs of a fever, and her arm had turned a true blackened purple. None of the herbs or salves he kept in the cave would do anything for her, this was an internal sickness, it needed the *iwosani* herb. He had to go back out onto the hills.

"Shanaki." He shook her shoulder gently. "Shanaki, wake up."

She moaned an unintelligible complaint, which was unusual. He had learned early on that Shanaki was the definition of an early riser. It normally took barely a motion to snap her fully awake.

He tried again. "Shanaki, you need to wake up." He looked around for the water bowl she had been using the previous night, finding it empty and propped up against the wall. He went to draw from the corner pool and returned to the princess, dipping his fingers into the bowl and flicking a splash over her face.

It had the desired effect. Shanaki woke with a splutter and a cough, cursing him with her eyes as they focused on his face. "What was that for?"

"Sorry, Princess. You wouldn't wake up." He pointed at her purpled skin. "Look at your arm."

She did, glancing down and raising what was clearly a very stiff limb. She frowned, and he could see the faint spark of fear deep in the corners of her eyes. There was only one reason the Princess Shanaki of the Ya-Seti he had come to know would show even that much fear in her eyes.

That settled it, then.

He was going out into the hills.

"You said it was too dangerous to go just outside the cave when I asked for a little sunlight, but it's okay for you to go all the way out roaming for medicine?" Shanaki was holding her darkened arm with her good one, strain showing in the creases of her eyes and forehead. Yet still she managed to look imposing as she towered over a sitting Ikenna.

He was seated against the pillar, wrapping rope over his shoulder in case he needed it for his climb. "It's not so bad if it's just me. I know my way around and I can stay hidden easier."

"And if they find you anyway?"

He shrugged. "Then I'll outrun them."

She gave him a despairing look and seemed half ready to roll her eyes. "This is stupid. I can heal it myself." She gripped her arm harder and he felt the channeling of magic again. The hair on the back of his neck stood up at its pulse.

He straightened upright and pressed his hand over hers, lifting her grip gently from her arm. He spoke softly, imploring her to listen with his eyes. "You've been trying. You told me yourself you're not the best at this. Don't push yourself."

As she gave up her half-hearted fight against his hold and looked up into his eyes, he saw for the first time the old and familiar warning signs of his power taking hold of her. Her gaze was locked a little too fiercely on his own, her breath braced a little too tightly.

He released her and turned quickly, moving out of the main chamber and into the tunnel where they kept their supplies. From inside he brought back a large wooden basin and a plain set of wrappings. She had had time to shake herself back to attention while he retrieved them, and again looked her usual self—if ragged and tired.

"You should wash while I'm gone. There are some fresh wrappings here." He held up the cloth for her to see. "Use the basin to get the water from the pool. Don't want to spoil the water by cleaning in it directly."

She was looking at him as though he had grown a second head. The irony was not lost on him.

"What?" he asked plainly.

"There are ways to say these things to a lady, Ikenna. 'You should wash' is not one of them." She looked indignant, and though she was playing it mostly for humor, he could still sense the tinge of actual embarrassment in her tone.

Ikenna almost laughed. "Wouldn't you like to clean up and get out of those sweaty clothes?"

"That's not the point," she hissed, whipping the wraps from his hands and reaching for the basin. She let out a wince of pain as her weak arm strained against the weight of the bowl briefly, but quickly hid it as she tucked the basin beneath her arm.

"Sorry, Princess. I'm just a lowly, uncultured demon. I have a lot to learn about these things." He bent to pick up his loop of rope and threw it over his shoulder. "I'll be back as soon as I can."

NINE

IKENNA

IKENNA WALKED DOWN THE DEN TUNNELS FOR A FEW minutes, passing four bends in the passage before stopping to draw on N'yewe. He bent low, his head twisting and his limbs folding over in a sickening crack as his hyena surfaced and his backside shifted to a thick, furred hide.

He sped to the surface as fast as he could, demon blood pumping in his ears. As he closed the den behind him, the silver glow of the boulder's seals matching the hue of the dying light of the stars above, he thought about the last few days and the changes he had begun to realize in himself. His parting words to Shanaki, for one.

If someone had told Ikenna he would be joking about his cursed blood a week ago, he wouldn't have believed them. Spending all this time with the princess had shifted his perspective. His priorities shuffled to match her uncompromising sense of humor and wit. Shanaki had made clear she had little time for the particular brand of self-pity Ikenna had so often found himself dwelling in throughout his life.

He had learned to deal with his curse as best he could, finding ways to work with his inner beast. It was best when they worked toward shared goals, as they did now, thundering up the hills and rocks toward the flora-rich terrain at the center of the range.

But he had never been able to shake the weight of his burden from his shoulders. He had always felt its presence bearing down on him. The temptation to just let Shanaki lift it with her power had been overwhelming these past few days. He had been able to resist it, his will for temptation long tested under entirely different strains, but she had still been able to help him.

He didn't think she had meant to, no more than she might with anyone at any rate, but she had truly made him feel accepted as they talked. There was no judgement in her gaze, no cruelty in her jabbing remarks, even as she openly mocked how seriously he described his people's nature.

After a while, her refusal to accept the gravity of what he was—something that had vexed him at first—became something he was grateful for. In the beginning he had feared, as he had all his life, that any human would be disgusted to hear what he was. He had thought they would all flee in terror, and perhaps that was true. Perhaps he had just gotten lucky with Shanaki; she may have just been an exception to the rule.

Still, even if she was to be the only one he ever met that refused to judge him for his nature, he was glad. He hadn't dared to hope for even that much before.

It took him half an hour to reach the summit of his den's hill. He could hear his hyena panting as it tasted the open air, guiding them to the pungent aroma of the veritable herb garden of the valley below.

It wasn't a real garden, Ikenna had only ever heard of those—seeing the farm fields didn't count. But nature had given its best attempt, especially for the region surrounding Bajok. The "valley" was a rivet in the hillside as it met the edge of the higher mountain. The stream running down from the mountains to the north-east pooled into a small lake at the valley's basin, moistening the soil. That paired with the shade the same mountains offered during the high hours of the sun meant a ground rich with nutrients. The stretches of shrubbery, bushes, and trees scattered about made up a golden oasis compared to the dry grass of the hills and plains below.

Ikenna was looking for one herb in particular, but drew many others he saw of use along the way. *Dawa* root for pain relief and healing, *ashwagandha* for sleep-soothing, he even found some *mbongo* pepper that could be ground down for some spice flavoring he knew they would be needing before long.

The iwosani proved challenging to find. It was a rare herb, in part from its unwillingness to grow in the majority of the Bajoki climate, and in other part due to its value. But he knew that it could be found here. He had made use of the extract from the valley many times before.

The sun had reached its zenith when he finally stumbled upon the plant. His muscles ached from his hastened search. He plucked at the stem, taking care not to disturb the precious and delicate roots.

The hair on his back stood on end suddenly, the same way it had with Shanaki's magic, and he sensed something before he heard it, if he hadn't he'd probably be dead.

"IKENNA!"

He heard the shout as he flew to the side, crashing into the dirt and rolling to a prowling crouch, immediately ready to spring up and shift. Where he had stood not two seconds before, there was now a large spear jutting out of the ground.

Thanks, N'yewe.

Ikenna shot a searching glance around the valley's sides, looking for the source of that horribly familiar voice. Halfway up the nearest slope, he found him. Bulky form held low to the ground, hidden amidst a stretch of bushes, eyes like blackened pits, stood his eldest brother Baako.

For a moment they both crouched still and low, and the silence that fell between them was as a knife to the throat. *Ikenna's* throat.

This was perhaps the worst person that could have found him short of his father Uzoma himself. Baako was bigger, faster, better than Ikenna in all the ways that mattered here. In all his years, Ikenna had never come close to beating him in a fight. No matter how hard Ikenna fought, Baako left him beaten and bloody in the dirt every time. *Every* time.

Ikenna had spent long hours in his den, wondering how his brothers could be as they were, how none could wish for better from themselves. Baako was always the first face of that crowd in his mind, the one they all seemed so eager to emulate. On his better days, Ikenna had dreamt of beating Baako, to assert himself in the clan and lead them down a better path. On his bad days, he just dreamt of beating him.

Today, Ikenna would settle for surviving.

Baako bellowed again from across the way. "What have you done, Ikenna?"

Play dumb, he doesn't know you have her.

"What are you talking about, Baako? What's wrong with you?" Ikenna tried to put as much surprise and affront into his voice as he could muster, but even to his own ears it sounded more a frightened yelp than an indignant shout. Baako had always had that effect on him.

"I know you took her, you stupid pup! Where is she?"

Or maybe he does know.

Baako's question had come in a snarl, his sharp teeth bared. Ikenna could see him twisting at his hips in the crouch, his neck twitching with the tell-tale signs of an imminent shift. Ikenna hesitated a moment too long, and Baako hammered the ground with a fist.

"Why is your den locked to me, Ikenna?" His eyes were slits now, their black a cool, hard slate. His voice dripped like sap from a palm as his tone changed with his tongue.

Ikenna felt a spike of fear, and not for himself. To his surprise, he felt a flare of paired anger from N'yewe. When did that happen?

He shook himself, time for that later if he made it out alive. "You tried to get into my den?"

"Don't play games with me, you little shit." He pawed at the ground, scratching the dirt as his hind legs lowered. It would happen soon.

"It's my den. I can lock it whenever I want." Taking a single step back and feeling his inner beast coil itself within, Ikenna prepared for the worst. "I don't have your damned princess, Baako."

"Who said anything about *my* princess?"

Shit.

Baako lunged forward, the last of his change finishing mid-leap. Ikenna threw himself back, shifting in the same instant. He was prepared for the charge, but not its speed. It had been a long time since he had faced Baako like this, and the older kishi had only gotten faster.

Ikenna felt a surge of panic as he kicked up at his brother, driving hard under his maw and shunting him with his own steely shoulder. The jump bought him a second, but his fear had him flailing, and he failed to take advantage of it. He felt his brother's angry bite snapping at his shoulder, and bent low and away before it could sink deep into his flesh. Red flashed in the sunlight, a shallow line of blood torn from him as kishi teeth met hide.

Ikenna leapt away as Baako drew back from his bite, a snarled smile curling his hyena's lips as it spat fur and flesh from his mouth.

"You're weak, Brother," his human side said in that

demonic tone all kishi had in full form. "You always have been weak."

It was true. Ikenna knew in his bones that he had no chance against his elder brother, not like this. He had to run, but—

He heard a deep, low growl rising up from his belly to his throat, anger pouring through him like a burst dam. Fresh panic rose with the heat, his mind reeling as he felt his inner beast fighting for a hold.

No, no please, you can't beat him—we *can't beat him,* Ikenna screamed into his mind desperately.

In his mind's eye, he felt old memories drift before him. Memories of being run down by the pack, kicked to the dirt and taunted. He remembered how that had felt—for both of them.

There was no chance of fleeing either, he knew that, but it held better hope than fighting. Kishi fought as beasts and Baako was the most bestial of them all. As blood and thunder beat in his ears, more images drifted before his eyes.

He had felt this before. When his hyena was at its strongest, it could drag sorrow and fear and hate into his mind, forcing his hard-fought control back under the weight of memory. But this was different; N'yewe wasn't flashing the usual fears through him, wasn't lashing against him in rage. This was more like… desperate pawing.

It was the last image that did it: Shanaki with shallow breaths and a pained voice, leaning weakly against the den wall.

N'yewe…

Hatred of their family had always been the one thing to unite them, but Ikenna's own anger lacked the blood and bile of his hyena's. He was never able to stand as one with him in his rage. It had always left them imbalanced, always fighting each other for control. Man or beast held the reins whenever they fought, never both. That was their problem. But today, today they stood as one. Selves had become self, and Ikenna felt his maw snapping at the air in answer to the thought.

You're right, N'yewe, he thought sharply, resolve hardening. *This time it's different. This time we aren't just fighting for ourselves.*

He felt the flashing images cease, his vision filled once again with the snarling form of Baako watching from across the way. A rumbling growl of eager anticipation barked from within.

Together, then.

He leapt into battle, maw wide for the kill.

TEN

SHANAKI

SHANAKI LAY WITH HER BACK TO THE PILLAR AT THE center of Ikenna's den, her head leaned against the rock. She couldn't quite remember how she had gotten there. It seemed such a distance from the wall to the middle of the room, now that she thought about it. She had a much better view of the moonstones though. What had Ikenna called them before?

Twinslights. That was it.

She liked that name. Ikenna was good with his words, especially for someone that had grown up in a place like this.

Shanaki's eyes flickered from one light to the next, looking to see which glowed brightest. She wasn't sure why it mattered, and when she caught herself trying to figure it out, the question just didn't seem to matter all that much anymore. They were very pretty lights, she decided.

Somewhere at the back of her mind she heard Nya scoffing, and the thought drew Shanaki back into herself. She shook her head with a start and lifted her good hand to rub at her eyes.

Gods, she was losing it. How long had Ikenna been

gone? She felt so drained, and her injured arm danced between a pulsing, bruising ache and sheer numbness. She had to keep holding off the corruption. She needed to *focus*, but she was just so tired. Sweat from the effort of it all had already soaked through the wrappings Ikenna had given her, and her hair had started to mat. She couldn't remember the last time she had felt so wretchedly filthy. The basin she had used to wash with earlier not nearly enough to truly pull the grime from her pores.

Oh, how she yearned for the river streams of the palace baths. She could lower herself into the warm currents and have Àyá's waters simply wash the dirt away. Shanaki sighed deeply. She wouldn't have to worry about her arm either; the palace physicians and healers would see it mended with ease.

She stilled then and her breath hitched as she caught the flow of her thoughts.

All my life I've wanted free of the palace, to venture out into the world and see it for myself. Now one broken arm and a bit of muck has me scurrying back within its walls. No... no.

She forced her hands to her face—both of them—and slapped her cheeks. Hard. The shock to both face and arm jolted her back to her senses, and she let out a muffled shriek of frustration and pain as she shook her head side to side. There. Back awake, for now.

She grasped her again-numbed arm with her good one and channeled another thread of healing energy within. She could muster little more than a trickle right now, but it was better than nothing. All she could do was hope that Ikenna would be back soon, and that whatever herbs he hoped to collect could, at the very least, take some of the edge off her work.

Shanaki was just beginning to drift again—she didn't know how long later—and was considering having another wash with the basin just to wake herself back up, but froze when she heard a pained hissing coming from the tunnel at her back.

Instinct had her spinning around before her mind could even register her fear, and she leaned heavily against the pillar. She held her breath against her exhaustion and pain, eyes straining at the unlit dark of the tunnel.

The hissing came in short, soft heaves, like the panting of some wounded animal, but it sounded nothing like any creature she had ever heard before.

A few long seconds passed, and she began to see the first signs of movement emerging from the darkness. It was crawling, its long back arched, and seemed to be dragging itself against the side of the tunnel. The grating of the wall sounded like stone on flint, and Shanaki's ears were filled with the heavy hammering of her heart as she held her breath. Suddenly, the creature grew still and silent, and she pulled herself behind the pillar, her head resting against the cool rock and praying to all the gods whatever *it* was hadn't seen her.

A moment passed, then two. She heard a strangled cry from the tunnel followed by a sickening crack, like bone being torn from a socket.

"Shanaki…"

Shanaki's hammering heart jolted and seemed to skip three beats at the voice.

"Ikenna?" she gasped and leaned around the pillar, good hand firmly holding her to its surface and definitely *not* shaking like a leaf in high wind.

She saw, just now entering the glow of the twinslights, the slight frame of Ikenna, down on one knee and struggling to stand. He held a clutch of assorted leaves and shrubs to his side by one arm, the other pressed tightly against his chest. His body was a canvas of cuts and bruises. From the blood pooling at his feet, she could tell the worst of his wounds lay hidden from her, held back only by the will of his fading strength.

"Ikenna!" Shanaki pushed herself away from the pillar and stumbled over to him, her own tired frame barely able to carry her the way. Her world turned, and she slumped down heavily beside her friend.

Somewhere in the back of her head, her mind wondered at that. Was friend the right word? But even as the question passed through her, her thoughts refocused on the injured man. Her weakened arms pried at his own — still much stronger even in this state.

Blood rushed from beneath his fingers and left sticky lines trailing down his stomach and onto the cave floor. The two struggled together for a brief moment, Shanaki trying to work Ikenna's hand away from his wound while Ikenna stubbornly insisted he was fine.

Shanaki found herself wearily beating her good fist against his arm, knocking it painfully down and away to get underneath. Ikenna groaned, his arm raising back to his chest but falling limp halfway there. She placed her good hand against the wound and, in sheer, desperate exhaustion, shouted for it to close. Even so tired and worn, her shout came as a command, and to an onlooker it would seem as if the flesh at her fingers had heard and obeyed. Somewhere from within, she found the strength for one last channeled burst of energy before she collapsed back to the ground, aching all over.

A few minutes passed while she and Ikenna simply lay there, tired and hurting. Shanaki imagined they must make for a pitiful sight, bloodied and filthy, groaning in the dirt of the den. She chuckled slightly, her sickness turning it into more of a gurgled giggle in her throat. She sensed Ikenna turn his head to her at his side.

She smiled tiredly. "You know, it's not polite to one-up a princess, Ikenna. *I'm* supposed to be the patient here."

"Sorry, Princess," Ikenna rasped. "I'll be sure to get only half as beaten up next time."

Shanaki pushed up onto her elbows, leaning her head forward and looking over at her companion. Her smile went wan. "I'd prefer you not get beaten at all, thank you. I'm greedy like that. Don't want anyone else stealing my sunlight."

"Right…"

Ikenna hacked up a cough and clamped a bloodied hand on his barely scabbed-over chest wound. It was a poor attempt at banter, Shanaki thought, but they were hardly at their best right now, they would take what they could get.

Her eyes roamed over his body, and her tired mind made mental notes of all the smaller wounds she found there. Light grazes, shallow scratch marks, deep bruises. All the hurts he had suffered for her. She felt her guard truly lower for the first time, something in her telling her that now, more than before, she could trust Ikenna.

She knelt close and ran her hand over his shoulder, tracing the line of one of the deeper gashes. She could feel the tension in his muscles and they quivered at her touch, the strain in the movement joining with the pain in his chest. She could tell by his unfocused eyes.

Lines of sweat were running down to his waist, curving with the unsteady rise and fall of his breath. A faint sheen of blue-white hue glinted off his brow as the twinslights shone down on him from above. Even in this state, she saw that he was beautiful, despite what she had said before.

He abruptly stiffened, his breath catching and his eyes flickering up to refocus on her. She wasn't quite sure when she had leaned over him, or when her hand had moved to his chest, but it hardly mattered, not when she was so close she could—

"Shanaki!"

The shout startled her, and she flinched back with a push off Ikenna's chest. He heaved out a pained breath as she backed away and he clutched at his wound with a groan.

Shanaki looked away, feeling halfway between a startled antelope and a chastised child as she smoothed over the sweat soaked wrappings at her waist.

She cleared her throat, eyes darting for a distraction before Ikenna could make anything of her blunder. Her gaze fell upon the herbs at his side; the leaves were twisted and the branches bent from whatever Ikenna had been through to get them to her. He spoke as she reached to pick the plants from the floor.

"Sorry, Princess, you were..." He kept his head low as he pointedly examined his wound. "You were glazing over a bit there."

"R-right." Shanaki crawled to where she had left one of their food bowls nearby, bringing it back to Ikenna's side. She sat beside him, placing the bowl in her lap before pulling the largest of the herb branches to her. She ran her hand through its leaves and smelled the scent of it come away with her touch.

Good, the picking's fresh and the plant was healthy.

She cleared her throat again softly and looked back up at Ikenna, now half sitting himself with his elbows back behind him. She took a quick, steadying breath.

"What happened?" she finally asked, as she picked the leaves of the *ponya*.

"Baako happened." His tone was bitter, as though the name alone dirtied his tongue.

"Your brother? The First Son?" Ikenna had made mention of him before. He had been chief among Ikenna's tormentors when they were children, and had destroyed Ikenna's beautiful wall. Shanaki hated him for that. He was also the one to whom she had been betrothed, and the main reason she had, in Ikenna's eyes, needed kidnapping in the first place.

Ikenna looked away. "If you could call him that."

Silence settled again, a familiar companion to them by now, but Shanaki knew her exhaustion would swiftly return to her if she let it sit, and she still had work to do before then. Besides, she had much yet to say.

"Thank you, Ikenna. You've brought exactly what we need. It's called ponya back home, by the way." She smiled. She liked sharing her language with him; he was an attentive student and his skill had greatly improved since their first day in the den.

"Ponya," Ikenna repeated back to her, only slightly off with his pronunciation. He sighed wearily. "Wait, we?"

He looked at her with concern. Shanaki finished her plucking of the ponya's first leaf and moved to grasp the second as she explained, "We don't want your injuries getting infected as well. There should be enough for—"

"No, I'm fine." He pushed up from the ground, wincing at the pain but stubbornly refusing to fall back down. As if to hammer in the point, he twisted at the hip—straining his scab—and stared pointedly at her. "Save it for yourself, Shanaki. I'm kishi. We heal fine by ourselves."

Shanaki scowled, her hands falling still over the bowl. "Less of that. Some of your wounds seem to be closing well enough, but I can still see plenty that aren't. You're exhausted."

"I'm fine."

Shanaki made a noise somewhere between disgust and dismissal before pulling the last of the second branch's leaves and sweeping them into the bowl in her lap.

"I don't suppose you have a mortar and pestle back there, do you?" She nodded to the tunnel that held Ikenna's supplies.

"No. I just used a rock."

"Fetch it for me."

Ikenna paused. He had been lowering back down to the floor and now sat frozen halfway, his face settling—all stony and stoic—even as his eyes spat sparks at the pain.

She could see him about to stand up, could see it in the way the crease of his brow tensed and his eyes turned stormy, so she leaned over her bowl and shoved him hard.

"*Honestly,*" she spat. "You're stubborn as a boar, and only half as smart as one. Lie down, you idiot."

She ignored his gasp of pain and turned to hunt for her discarded spoon. Its flat would do for now...

A WHILE LATER SHANAKI SAT BOWL IN HAND—ASSORTED herbs mulched into a relatively fine paste. She had added fresh water to moisten the remnant leaves for pasting, recalling her past healing lessons. In an ideal world she would have added *karkade* or *gongalez*, but nothing about this situation was ideal. She scooted closer to her patient and leaned over with a scoop of the paste held in her fingers.

"This is going to sting a little," she warned, reaching her hand toward Ikenna's still-weeping chest wound.

Ikenna held up his arm in complaint. "You first. We might not have enough—"

Shanaki gave him a look. "*I'm* the healer here, Ikenna. We have plenty. Besides, the salve numbs after a while and I don't want to be straining just to hold my arm up when I get to you afterwards. Just sit still."

She worked through his begrudging silence, lathering healthy portions of the cleansing paste over the worst of his injuries. She paid special attention to the chest wound that should have been healed by her strength alone.

She was too weak. Ikenna had fought a nightmare from his past for her and he shouldn't have even been out there in the first place. If she had been stronger, *better*, he wouldn't have had to take that risk.

She looked down at the deep cut across his chest, paste freshly coating the angry colors through and around the wound. Glancing up at his face, she could see Ikenna was far away in his thoughts, chewing something over in his mind.

Feeling her own starting to drift again, she asked the obvious question. "So how did you beat him?"

Ikenna didn't say anything at first, but eventually his eyes flicked back to her own, and he sighed. "I didn't, not really."

Confused, Shanaki asked, "You escaped, didn't you?"

"Barely." Ikenna began to scratch idly at the cave floor with his fingers, his attention still focused away from her.

Shanaki leaned farther into his line of sight, brows rising in question. "Will he follow?"

The injured young man shrugged one shoulder, brushing aside some of his loosed scratchings with the back of his hand. "Probably. He can't get in though. Not even Uzoma can break into our dens."

"Really? You told me he was your people's leader. Why would he make it so that any of you could shut him out?"

Ikenna snorted in disgust. "Because it made him look benevolent at no real cost to him. Worst-case scenario one of us hides away in our hole for a few weeks until we start to starve and have to come back out again."

Shanaki sat back, hands resting on the ankles of her crossed legs. "And so what's keeping *us* safe from that?"

Ikenna paused in his scratching and finally looked up into her eyes.

He has such an intense stare, Shanaki mused. *Like an owl's in starlight.*

Ikenna paused a moment and his gaze lowered back to his work, his scratching more vigorous. "Long term? Nothing. He can't spare anyone to sit outside for long right now though—he needs all of the kishi to take on the village."

"So, what do we do?"

"For now, we wait. We wait for our injuries to heal and for Uzoma to make his move against Bajok. When they do, we'll make a run for it and escape before the dust settles." He paused to brush away loose dirt again and looked back up at her once more. "I'll keep you safe, Princess. I'll get you back home. I promise."

Looking into those eyes, their fixed gaze staring intently into her very soul, she believed him. Somewhere at the back of her mind she rebelled against the notion, shouting a refusal to retreat, to abandon her people to their fate at the hands of the kishi demons. But right now, as she looked into Ikenna's eyes, the idea of running away with him just didn't seem so bad.

"You should treat your arm now, Princess. You need to take care of it so you can rest."

Shanaki looked down at her still-blackened arm. The deep bruise along its length had grown harder the past two days, to the point she could barely feel her own touch upon it. Absently, she leaned down to pick up the paste bowl and bring it to her lap once more.

She began to lather the remaining paste onto her arm, running the sticky green of it from the base of the blackened skin at her forearm, all and around to just below her shoulder. She sighed deeply in relief as she felt the numbness of the ponya seep into her skin. Because of the lack of feeling in the blackened flesh itself, she hadn't realized just how much tension had been built between it and the rest of her arm's muscle. The paste drew the tension out of her and forced her arm limp by her side.

Ikenna was watching her closely, and—with the unrealized pain of her injury set aside—a spark of mischief lit in Shanaki's mind. She knew that look. She had seen it in countless men before—even some of the women of her palace home had unknowingly revealed to her *those* eyes over the years.

Slowly, casually, Shanaki leaned back into another contented sigh, her healthy arm behind her to hold her up from the floor, as she reclined her body gracefully in an inviting arc. Not quite as gracefully as she might have had had the use of both arms, but Ikenna was young, he wouldn't know the difference.

Shanaki leaned her head back in an open-mouthed sigh, raising the knee of one leg slowly and rolling her shoulders. Peeking from beneath her lowered lids at Ikenna, she saw him leaning forward, eyes even wider and his mouth half open, a question on his lips. She delighted in this; she always had. The tangible power she could wield, in all its forms, without ever having to give a single royal command. She—

Ikenna sat back suddenly, shaking his head like a wet dog and slamming a hand down on the den floor with a powerful thud.

"Don't *do* that!" he gasped out in urgent warning.

Shanaki's first instinct was to play coy and ask whatever he could mean, but before she could get the words out, her teasing mood left her. Not with the subtle ebb of a tide, as most moods, but with the crash of a wave overhead, leaving her spluttering, shocked, and cold.

What on earth was she doing?

Ikenna was pulling away, shifting himself along the floor toward the nearest denwall with a tension clouding his every movement. It seemed his mood had turned dark as fast as her own.

ELEVEN

IKENNA

WHAT THE HELLS WAS THAT?

Ikenna pulled away from Shanaki, crawling to the den wall behind him before she could get her bearings back. He tried to maintain a cool composure, but inside he was reeling, desperately trying to get a hold on N'yewe's fervor.

This had never happened before. When she had first glazed over, he had thought it was just the passive effect of his kind. The jolt of his shout had seemed to shake her free well enough. But her turn after that was more than just plain attraction. She had been enamored.

He'd never lost control like that, his other self had never been able to use his powers before. The power of the empath was the business of the man, not the hyena. Was it something to do with the fight, was that it? Had their new-found "oneness" brought more of themselves together than he had realized?

Whatever the reason, he had to get a grip. He had just done to Shanaki what he swore he would never do to anyone, least of all someone he admired and respected. It was a betrayal of their newfound friendship. It was *wrong*.

Ikenna held his hand to his forehead and groaned in

dismay. He peeked through his fingers, glancing back at the princess—still sitting where he left her—and saw a look of fading confusion on her face.

With the effect of his power wearing off, he could see her starting to put the pieces together in her mind, and he knew what her next move would be.

Shanaki's eyes narrowed, and his connection to N'yewe was abruptly severed; the hyena was ripped from his consciousness and scraped to the back of his mind in one stroke, like a rake pulled over freshly broken soil.

"What the hells was that?" Shakani demanded, echoing his earlier thought.

"I—I'm sorry, Princess," he stammered, instinctively using her title. "I lost control. I—"

"*You* lost control?"

Shanaki looked torn between disgust and outrage, and it wasn't clear to Ikenna whether it was aimed at him or herself. It was probably both.

She looked like she wanted to say more, her mouth opening partway around an angry question or insult, but she stopped before voicing it.

Ikenna spoke first, breaking the charged silence. "I'm sorry. N'yewe broke free for a moment. I—*we* had a bit of a revelation up on the hills. I think it's made us—"

Shanaki's look could have melted stone. She was clearly as eager for his excuses as he was another bout with Baako.

Ikenna trailed off, eyes downcast. "I'm sorry."

The princess let the silence sit for a long while after that, half turned from him and with a scowl cast firmly on her face. From the set of her shoulders and the wrap of her hands around her arms, he could tell she wanted to pull yet farther away, to turn her back on him completely. But he also knew her pride—and newfound distrust—wouldn't let her do so.

"N'yewe?" she finally asked.

Ikenna nodded. "My hyena's name."

"And is that the power you spoke of, then?" She was trying to sound matter-of-fact, but she fell far short. "The power to 'ensnare' me, to 'lure me in?' " She asked the last like she was embarrassed. Perhaps at having fallen for his power despite having been warned about it before. That'd be just like her.

He hesitated before answering. "Sort of. The ensnaring tends to come from words and touch. The kishi influence just... lowers your inhibitions a bit."

"Yes, well, we'll see how well *N'yewe* does with that from now on." She kicked a stone out from beneath her foot, and Ikenna almost *physically* felt the oppressive weight of her dampening pushing down on his shoulders.

He slumped lower against the denwall and a strange sense of numbness seeped into his shoulders. It felt, all of a sudden, like he had been hauling sacks of stone up a hill-side, his back aching under an inexistent strain.

He couldn't see her now, his head bent low under the force of her suppression, his energy leeched out of him to such an extent that he could no longer lift his own weight.

"Princess—"

And just like that, it was gone. His strength returned and his posture snapped straight once more. His back clicked at the sudden motion, and his head reeled as he readjusted to his returned senses.

He looked up, wondering why the princess had with-drawn her power.

As if in slow motion, he could see the seated form of the princess tipping, her head lulled to one side as she fell away from him. Without even realizing he had moved, he was catching her in her fall, hand held behind her head to ease her gently to the den floor.

A SHORT WHILE LATER, IKENNA SAT BACK AGAINST THE far wall of the cave once more. He had left Shanaki asleep, resting opposite from him with a basin-watered cloth lain on her forehead.

He was confident she was fine. He had checked her arm for any spread of the infection and it seemed to be receding as well as she had claimed it would. She had just reached the limits of her exhaustion, the exertion of her power taking the last of her dwindling reserves. Not even the princess' stubborn pride could fight back that kind of drain.

She would be out of it for a long while.

Ikenna felt the pawing of a snout against the back of his head, and his right foot scraped insistently at the ground without him ever moving it.

He had felt his second self return to him the moment Shanaki's power had been withdrawn, the familiar presence no longer feeling the oppressive burden it had once been. He had expected his partner to come at him with anger, to try to break loose of him again. He expected him to want revenge against Shanaki for forcing him back beneath Ikenna's psyche. But for whatever reason, that didn't seem to be the case here. For the moment at least, Ikenna could feel only concern in his hyena's restlessness.

Taking a deep breath, Ikenna closed his eyes and went to him. His eyes reopened to the deep black of the demon's —if that was even still the right word—sight.

He felt the familiar twisting of his limbs, the bending of his bones creaking in a soft groan as he lowered to all fours. The transformation used to be one of pain, but it came to them much easier now. They still had a ways to go, but they had taken many strides very quickly.

Ikenna felt the urge to go to Shanaki, his front paws taking the first pattering steps before he halted them in their tracks.

No, he thought determinedly.

He felt an answering curiosity drifting through his mind, and his head tilted to the side in a question.

We don't get to be near her right now. You—he shook his head at that, it wasn't fair—we *broke trust.*

N'yewe stopped his forward tugging. His tilted head straightened, lowering down with a snort of disgruntled, begrudging acceptance.

Ikenna released their legs, and the hyena spun them on the spot before lowering to the floor and resting their head on their front paws.

He wasn't sure what to make of this new, docile N'yewe. They had spent almost their entire lives at odds with one another, battling for freedom from each other's constraints. Never seeing eye to eye.

The change in that had come so suddenly it felt false. Too good to believe. Was standing united against Baako, sharing in their fears and fighting him despite them really all it took to bring them together as one?

Ikenna—no, *N'yewe*—gods it was getting harder to even tell their own thoughts apart, snorted in derision.

All right, wise-ass. What is it, then? We've never been this in line before.

N'yewe turned their eyes back to Shanaki again, and Ikenna felt the hyena forcing memories before them once more: visions of defiant eyes atop the den steps, the feeling of stubborn hands forcing them to lay back and take their medicine, the thrill of being thrown back by her power.

Wait, what?

N'yewe cackled quietly before scratching an itch behind their ear.

TWELVE

SHANAKI

SHANAKI WAS FURIOUS WITH HERSELF. SHE COULDN'T
believe how thrice-damned stupid she had been.

Judging by the brightness of the twinslights above, far
brighter than the faded state they had been before she slept,
it had been at least a full day's cycle. For all she knew it had
been two—her limbs were certainly numb enough.

She couldn't believe she had knocked herself out with
her own power like that. She was such an idiot. She *knew*
she was already on her last legs and still she had cast her
field out without a second thought.

And why? Because I was angry.

The last thought came in a mocking snarl, half her own
voice and half Nya's. She deserved it. Careless anger like that
was as pathetic as a childish tantrum. She knew full well
what Ikenna was capable of, he outright *told* her, and still she
fell into his hands. Hells, she had practically leaped into them.

She shot a quick look across the way. Ikenna was sat
against the opposite side of the cave, slouched over crossed
legs with his face propped up in one hand, the picture of
misery. She thought she could see him scratching a finger in

the dirt between his legs, but she looked away before he could catch her looking.

She wasn't even all that angry at him, not really. The same gut feeling that had told her she could trust him in the first place still hadn't given out on her. She could tell he had been earnest before—that he hadn't meant to affect her. And she could see from his pitiful state here that he was sorry for it, almost sickeningly so, like she had played no part at all.

Which, of course, was what really had her angry: that she had been caught by his power in the first place.

How had he so easily enamored her? *Her*? She was better than this, damnit. Even without the defense of her power she should have been able to resist. She wasn't some common village whelp; she was second heir to the throne of Ya-Set. She—

Shanaki forced herself to pause her trail of thought there and took a deep breath. Her usual, comfortable clarity did not come quickly, but it came. She had a lifetime of practice, after all.

Dwelling in her thoughts would change nothing. She had, in a moment of weakness, let her guard down. She just had to accept that, accept it, and move on.

Taking control back is what she did best.

A SHORT WHILE LATER, THOUGHTS COLLECTED AND emotions settled, Shanaki stood before Ikenna with her hands on her hips. He didn't look up as she approached, his shoulders tight as though clenched for a tirade. From the hang of his head he probably felt he deserved it too.

Who knows? Maybe he did, Shanaki thought. *Either way…*

She clicked her tongue, channeling her best Nya

impression. Ikenna looked up slowly, waiting for the hammer blow.

"Quit moping. It's dull and it's a waste of our time. Now, what's for breakfast?"

Ikenna looked for all the world like he had just seen her sprout a second head.

"AND NOW I'M EATING DRIED RAT," SHANAKI REMARKED dryly an hour later. "You really know how to treat a girl, you know that, Ikenna?"

Ikenna, still clearly unsure of himself in the face of such an un-angry Shanaki, shrugged a shoulder and took a bite of his own rodent. Chewing the hard meat down, he spoke up properly for the first time since Shanaki had woken. "You wanted to see the world, Princess…"

Shanaki swallowed her latest mouthful, the taste not so bad in the grand scheme of things, and her hunger more than enough to ignore it if it was. She watched Ikenna appraisingly.

"True," she said. "Though I did have a somewhat different idea for how I planned to actually see it. And for what I ate along the way…" She watched for signs of Ikenna's usual humor dancing across his face, the slight upward tilt of a smirk, the crease of laughter around his eyes, anything that would show her they had made progress since waking. She saw none.

Sighing and setting aside her skewer, she rested her hands on her crossed knees and gave Ikenna a stern look. "Ikenna." He quickly looked up from his meal at her tone. "Did I not tell you to stop moping? You make for a poor conversationalist when you're in a sulk."

She saw a spark of irritation at her words, and dove

ahead eagerly, fanning it to a flame. "Honestly, I've known bratty children less mopey than this."

Ikenna finally started at that. "How can you be so damn calm about this?" With the cramped walls of the cave, his question sounded as a shout.

Shanaki rolled her eyes. "Why wouldn't I be, Ikenna? It's not like getting mad is going to change anything here."

"You didn't seem to think that before."

"Well, what did you expect?" Shanaki half laughed. "You had just made me — I don't want to hear it!" She interjected before he could interrupt with another benal apology. "You had just made me openly flaunt myself like some common street performer. I wasn't exactly going to be praising you to the heavens, was I? But that was then. I've slept on it now, and it's really not that big a deal from the *you* side of things. I'm mostly just angry at myself for falling for it in the first place, and I'd rather not have your incessant moping reminding me of the fact."

Ikenna looked dumbfounded. He seemed to be struggling to accept that anyone could be so blasé about his kind's influence. It was like any reaction but hatred was alien to him. She thought she understood a little of what he felt on the matter himself then, and any residual anger she *had* been holding onto slipped away from her in an instant. "Oh, Ikenna…"

He looked down at his hands, clenched tightly into fists as he sat. "How can you not hate me, even after this?" His voice was barely above a whisper. "You know what I am. I thought that maybe, because you hadn't seen… But now you have. You've seen what we can do, and you still don't care. You're crazy."

Shanaki leaned forward slightly. Her instincts were telling her to reach out for Ikenna's hand, but she ignored them. This wasn't the sort of thing she was good at, certainly wasn't the sort of thing she *enjoyed*. Comforting people was meant for when people needed comforting, and it was a rare moment that Shanaki felt anyone should *need* comforting. That was for when the real crises and tragedies of life laid one low, not some stupid mistake like this.

"Honestly…" She flopped her head back dramatically and ran a hand through her—still disheveled, she now noticed—hair. "All you did was get me a little worked up. It's not like you did anything with it—or that you could to begin with." She hadn't intended to add that last part, but an idea had struck her. One that would soothe her own pride as much as she hoped it would assuage his guilt.

Ikenna looked alarmed at her words.

"You still don't get it?" His eyes were pleading as he asked the question. "Even after feeling it, you still don't see how dangerous I am?"

Shanaki tilted her head to the side and worked a tangle loose from her hair with a finger. "Not really. I was dead on my feet before, for one thing, and even in that state I wouldn't have let things get out of hand if you had tried anything." Shanaki wasn't so sure on that last point, but if the maybe-lie helped her here it didn't matter either way. Besides, belief could be a powerful tool, even unfounded.

"You can't be serious," Ikenna muttered.

"I am, actually." Shanaki smiled. "Look, I'll prove it."

Before Ikenna could so much as squint in question, she dropped her dampening shroud. She knew from the sudden —immediate, really—widening of his eyes that he felt it: her defenses dropping from her shoulders for the first time since she had woken up.

She jolted a bit in surprise as he leaped to his feet and ran, faster than anything she had seen in her life, to the opposite end of the den room. He stood up against the wall behind him, eyes wide and arms spread to the sides, his breath coming in deep, gulping lungfuls. He looked like a petrified gazelle.

Once the slight shock faded, Shanaki couldn't help it, she laughed. Harder than she had in a long time. "Oh wow, gods above. Yeah, you're right, Ikenna. I'm definitely supposed to be scared of you. What a truly *dangerous* threat you are." She couldn't stop laughing. He was such a pup!

When she finally had herself back under control, a stitch half formed at her side, she waved Ikenna over. "Come on, get over here, you big idiot."

"No." His tone surprised her, and she thought, belatedly, that she might have offended him with her laughter.

If I have, she thought. *Then he really needs to pick a road and stick to it already...*

"Don't be ridiculous. Come here."

"No," he insisted again. "Not until you're using your power."

"And what if I don't want to?" she asked, eyebrow raised over a slanted grin.

"Then I will stay here."

He seemed adamant on this, and Shanaki's smirk gave way to a frown. He was standing resolutely, calmed from his initial shock, no longer clinging to the wall at his back. His face was half cast in shadow and half lit by the blue light of the twins. Her humor now dampened, she could see the genuine fear hiding behind his eyes. Even as they dazzled in the crystal glow.

It was the *eyes*, she realized suddenly.

THIRTEEN

SHANAKI

FAILURE, SHANAKI HAD REMINDED HERSELF WHEN SHE
had woken, had one constant. As long as one let themselves,
they could always learn from it.

The benefit of having tasted Ikenna's power was that
she now knew it from her own mind. She could recognize
its touch, the ebb and flow of its influence. It was slight, but
for her, that was enough.

The moment her gaze had fallen on his eyes, those deep
wells of fear and sadness, she had understood. That was the
real secret of the kishi power. If they could catch your eye,
they had you.

The tragedy of it was that Ikenna's were so lonely. He
could capture the attention of almost anyone he wanted,
and he never would.

Shanaki could feel the power of the kishi seeping into
her, could feel herself being drawn to those lonely eyes, and
flushed a wave of her suppression over herself. This was
what she had wanted to try, to prove to herself that—now
that she was rested and aware—she was the one in control
once more. She felt a shiver pass through her, felt the pull

toward Ikenna fade from her shoulders, and smiled to herself.

Then I will stay here, he had said.

Fine, then. I shall go to you.

Slowly, Shanaki rose to her feet. She held Ikenna's gaze, moving step by step out into the middle of the den. She kept her distance from him, waiting until she had reached the center of the room. She ran a hand along the pillared strut before turning and walking fully his way.

She could see him trying to decide whether to say something or just move around the cave's edge, farther away from her. But in his hesitation she only drew closer and closer, hands held clasped behind her now and innocently humming a soft tune under her breath.

Shanaki watched Ikenna's eyes, delighting in the awkward nerves now flashing behind them amidst the dancing light of the twins' glow. She felt the soft pull of his power at the edges of her senses once more, and flushed a fresh wave of her own energy through her to brush the influence off. She reveled in this, tipping the balance of power in her favor. It's what she was good at, what she'd done all her life. She had just taken a little longer to figure out how with Ikenna, that was all.

She was finally standing in front of him, noting for the first time that she barely came up to his chin, when often it was she who dwarfed men.

Ikenna tried to turn away from her as she looked up into his face, but she followed him, keeping him in her sight. She gave him her most charming smile, and poked him hard in the ribs.

"Ow! What was that for?" he asked, rubbing his side indignantly.

Shanaki rolled her eyes then turned and stepped away again. "For being an idiot."

Ikenna shook his head. "You're crazy."

"You're repeating yourself." She kept walking away, back to where they had sat before. "And no, I'm very clever."

That earned her a genuine snort of bemusement. *Mission accomplished.*

Ikenna crossed his arms in front of him, tilting his head slightly to one side. "And how'd you figure that?"

She turned a glance back over her shoulder and smirked, feeling smug. "You're not being a miserable sap anymore."

AFTER THAT, IT DIDN'T TAKE LONG FOR SHANAKI TO GET Ikenna settled back down with her to finish their meal. The upside of dried meat, she mused as they ate, was not having to worry about it getting cold.

Ikenna's spirits had raised some, she could see it in the way he tore at his food; it was entirely too casual for someone still in a mope. He was still hesitant, his eyes darting up to check on her whenever he thought she wasn't looking, as though she would fall into his arms if he wasn't paying enough attention. Regardless, it was a definite improvement from before.

For Shanaki's part, she was glad her idea had paid off. Maintaining her passive shroud wasn't overly taxing, as long as she kept it wrapped around herself alone. But concentrating on maintaining it for such lengths of time as she had been was a distraction she didn't need right now, least of all because her arm was still healing from infection.

She looked down at the still-purpled flesh at her elbow. The mass of blotchy skin was receding; the cleansing paste she had mixed together working wonders. Now that she had rested she was helping it along with her own power well enough. It would be a few more days before it had faded completely, but it *would* fade. She was looking forward to having her arm back in full working health again.

The thought returned her to Ikenna, just now setting aside the last of his meal. She had been trying to think of how best to broach the subject of Bajok. How best she could try to convince him to bring her back to her people and help them fight in the coming battle he had spoken of. She knew if she could just get back and warn them, she could be of use in the fight.

Getting Ikenna to believe it too—*that* was the problem.

She knew if she could just convince him that they had a fighting chance, he'd be eager to join against his kind. They were more his enemy than her own, really. For her they were just a threat to her and her family. For him, they were personal, literal demons. He deserved to be rid of them.

Ikenna was starting to watch her more closely now. He could clearly tell she was thinking about something. Shanaki decided she would wait for him to ask and that she would tell him what she wanted as straightforwardly as possible. That always threw people off their guard.

It took a while, and for a moment he reminded her of Kasa, twitching under the watchful eye of Enake.

She missed her guardsmen.

Eventually, he asked. "What are you thinking about?"

"I'm thinking I want to meet your hyena."

"What?" Ikenna responded, looking dumbstruck. "You want to—"

"Yes," Shanaki interrupted simply.

"No!" Ikenna shot back before she had even finished responding herself. He was recoiling as though it was the maddest thing he'd ever heard. "No way! Do you have any idea how dangerous that would be?"

Shanaki shrugged. "I imagine less so than facing someone like Baako without experience."

"The point of bringing you here is to make sure that never happens," Ikenna pointed out.

"And I've already told you what I think of that plan," Shanaki pointed back.

Ikenna sighed in exasperation and leaned back where he sat, rubbing at his eyes frustratedly. "Not this again…"

She pressed on. "You can't expect me to just leave my people to die."

"It's better than going back and them all dying anyway!" He was gesturing wildly now. "I know what you're thinking, and I get why—really I do. But this isn't the same thing as resisting the influence or charms. My hyena side is dangerous!"

"I drove it back on the steps."

"I wasn't already transformed on the steps, we don't know that it'll work the same. It's *too risky*."

Shanaki crossed her arms, half turning away from him and changing tack. "What do you care anyway? You only brought me here to spite your brother and ruin your father's plan."

"What? But… You *know* it's not that simple anymore. I —you're—" He stumbled over his words, seeming all of a sudden embarrassed. "I know your heart now. You're my friend. I'm not going to let you throw yourself to the wolves just for the sake of pride."

Know your heart. It was an expression she'd heard before, but she put that to the side for now, she had an argument to win. "Pride? I want to save my people, Ikenna."

"And you know full well you can't. You're throwing your life away for pride, and that's just the truth of it." He pulled backward, leaning on his arms and mirroring her turned head in the opposite direction.

She turned back to him. "Better to be prideful than pitiful. I'd sooner die, side by side with my people, than live having left them to the slaughter." She could see he wasn't having it, so she turned his own words against him. "If you know my heart, Ikenna, then you know I can't just run away from this fight. *And...*" She continued, twisting fully back around and sliding closer to him. "I know your heart too."

She felt him still as she spoke the words. He tried to hide it, but she had seen. The words were powerful ones, drawn from the Old Ways. They were the acknowledgement of a bond, which could come in many forms, but which was always, more than anything, heartfelt.

He turned toward her, and her breath caught sharply. His eyes were shining with the faintest hint of tears. So faint that she would have missed them in the light of day, but by the starscape of the clear crystals above, the watery orbs were like rippling pools. Shanaki could feel the powerful lure of his beauty as she stared into those golden eyes, but held the instinct to react with her power at bay. Ikenna would feel it if she did, and this was a pure moment, one of trust. She could see his stark loneliness at war with his darkest fears, and she refused to feed either. She wouldn't do it.

Besides, she was pleased that she could feel herself well within the bounds of control, even without her shroud. She was getting more familiar with him.

Ikenna blinked rapidly he cleared his throat and glanced away a moment, collecting himself. When he looked back at her she could see the resignation on his face, but he made one more attempt to dissuade her, his tone pleading.

"I can't show you…"

She leaned closer, keeping her eyes fixed on his, and squeezed his hand gently. She said nothing, trusting to the Old Ways to convey her belief in him. When she saw his nod, and knew he had settled upon his decision, she took her hand away and moved back.

Ikenna pushed to his feet and turned away from her,

taking a few steady steps. His hands were at his side, clenched tightly into fists, and he took a deep breath, one that seemed to roll the weight of the world from his shoulders. Raising his hands to the back of his head, he parted his hair.

FOURTEEN

IKENNA

Ikenna's heart was thundering in his chest as he lifted his arms behind him. The rough weave of his locs, long a curtain of dread, felt like snakes ready to wrap around his throat. He could feel Shanaki's eyes on him, could picture the focused intent on her face, the anticipation of what he was about to reveal.

Was he? *Could* he? He honestly didn't know.

It was a battle to keep his hands from shaking as they dove into the weave of his hair. His fumbling grip found purchase on the knot that kept N'yewe hidden, and cold sweat beaded on his forearms and face.

He hesitated. This was a moment he thought would never come. A moment he had *promised* would never come. His chest rose and fell rapidly; it was getting harder to breathe. Within, his nervous breath was mirrored by the excited panting of N'yewe, ready and waiting to taste the air once more. What else would he try to taste?

"Do it, Ikenna."

It was Shanaki, and it was an order. The utter confidence behind the command settled his nerves in an instant. Shanaki trusted him, trusted him to keep control of the beast, of *himself*. He decided he would return that trust. If she thought this was something that needed to happen, so be it.

He let N'yewe free.

It was an entirely new sensation, joining with his inner beast without the leash of control wrapped around his neck. The two had been gradually bonding for days now, through Baako, through the pain of their shame and injuries, and through Shanaki.

Ikenna let N'yewe pull himself from the back of his head, the locs parting aside and rolling around behind them in a twirl, joining the steeled fur of the hyena's back. There was no snapping crack this time, the long form of the man simply fading to the poised mass of the beast, the brush of fur rising to the air as a whisper. Ikenna's vision dimmed, and he closed his eyes as he fell beneath the hyena's form, reopening his gaze to the sharper, focused vision of N'yewe's own blackened orbs. To Shanaki.

He almost drew away, almost gripped at the beast's control and clawed it back under his command. This was the moment he had feared all his life, the moment of rejection and disgust, the moment she would shun him and cast him away—

"So, you are N'yewe, yes?" Her voice came softly, but firmly. And… and there was no fear in it.

Ikenna opened his eyes behind N'yewe's own, he hadn't even realized he had closed them, that he had drawn back within to hide from his fears. His heart swelled with relief, true happiness that her first reaction had not been one of terror. This was a miracle, not from the gods—damn the gods, this was a miracle from the gift that was Shanaki.

She sat, kneeling, eyes fixed on N'yewe's own, her head tilted slightly in her question. He felt his other self mewl, his head turning in a mirror of her own, and a gentle tugging of his legs toward her jittered through Ikenna's mind. His hyena was asking if they could go to her. Actually *asking.*

Ikenna nudged one paw forward, half sharing in his hyena's excitement at moving closer—and half dreading it. His bestial form pattered forward, an eager spring in its gait and his mouth open, tongue lolling in a contented pant.

To her credit, Shanaki didn't blink at their approach. He'd never understand where she had honed such steeled nerves, harder than any kishi's hide, but he was glad of them. She raised a hand out toward their approaching maw, reaching to pet at their snout.

"It's a pleasure to meet you, N'yewe. I am Shanaki." Her breath hitched as she spoke the last of her greeting, N'yewe's snout pressing into her hand in a firm nuzzle, but she never faltered. Without missing a beat, she brought her second hand—arm healing well, Ikenna noted from behind the hyena's distracted eyes—to scratch behind tufted ears.

N'yewe gave a sudden, keening cackle, and before Ikenna could blink, his world was upside down. Shanaki laughed, bright as the crystals that dazzled above him, her arms pulling from his head and rushing to ruffle his exposed belly.

This was madness. This couldn't be happening; it was too much. Every fear he had held for everyday of his life was being torn away, discarded like imagined nothings. N'yewe—*he*—was cackling in laughter, Shanaki scratching at their underbelly as though he posed no more threat to her than a common pet.

He felt like he should have been insulted, but instead he was only relieved, ecstatic in the face of such unbelievable acceptance.

Shanaki kept them pinned by her assault awhile before reaching back up to ruffle at their ears and sitting back down at their side.

"Well, you don't seem like the big scary demon Ikenna

made you out to be," she said, lowering her hand to stroke a finger under the hyena's chin. "You don't want to hurt me, do you, N'yewe?"

Ikenna felt his other self raising their chin up higher, encouraging Shanaki's efforts, a rumbling purr rolling up their throat.

"Nooo, you don't." An idea seemed to hit her then, her face turning thoughtful and then outright conspiratorial, her expressions played up for N'yewe's benefit. She leaned in close to their face, her smile wild. "Why don't you show me what you can do?"

She kicked to her feet, letting go of the sides of their head and stepping away. N'yewe instinctively moved closer, following the retreating princess, but stopped as she held out a hand in front of her.

She nodded to the side, to the center of the den. "Show me how fast you can go. Go on." She swung an arm out in a beckoning motion. Ikenna felt a jolt of frustration as his head swung sharply to the side, following her motion. He was caught between N'yewe's instincts, thoroughly enamored by Shanaki's leading antics, and his own sense of pride. He marveled at the princess' confidence, her natural strength commanding instinctual respect from his hyena. But the young man in him chafed at the idea of being treated like some common plains dog. It was like she didn't even see *him* anymore, just N'yewe.

Ikenna felt their legs kick forward, launching into a dash along the length of the den, and he understood. Pulling back from the hyena's senses, distancing himself from the physical sensations of the beast, he could see that Shanaki was doing it deliberately. She was acknowledging them both, man and beast, as individuals.

N'yewe seemed to appreciate it. At her urging, he ran them in rings around the den room, picking up speed with every circuit. Ikenna could feel the steady rush of excitement building within his second self. And of course he was excited, Ikenna knew the joy of having finally been accepted for what he was. He didn't blame N'yewe for reveling in the same.

"That's it!" Shanaki laughed again, clapping her hands. "Go on, faster!"

They really sped up then, and Ikenna was just along for the ride. He could feel N'yewe's charged focus, the need to show off what he could do to the princess. The first person to ever truly see him. Ikenna didn't think he could slow them down if he tried.

On their final circuit, they leaped as they passed Shanaki, her eyes failing to track them fully in the blur of motion. They span as they touched off on the wall behind her, kicking their hind legs and launching back out into the den space, before scraping to a sliding halt on the far side of the room. Every muscle in their body shuddered with the rush of the exertion.

"That was amazing." Shanaki was walking toward them, her hand running along the wall they had jumped from. Her voice had taken on a tone of awe, but to Ikenna it felt exaggerated. He could tell by the look in her eyes she was still playing to N'yewe's ego. She was up to something, Ikenna knew, but the hyena didn't seem to notice, practically purring with pride at the compliment.

"You must be strong too." Shanaki continued, the hand running along the wall lowering as she crouched down against it. She moved her fingers lightly over the cracks of the ruined paw print. "Can you break stone like this too?"

N'yewe's mood darkened swiftly at that. Ikenna felt a spasm of anger run through their suddenly tense form, the memory of their art wall's destruction flashing before their eyes. A soft growl worked its way deep from within their chest.

Shanaki looked away from the wall, her hand held in

place over the remnants of the print. Her shoulders had stiffened slightly at the growl, and she nodded a solemn agreement. "I hate that they ruined your art too. I would have liked to see it."

She paused and looked thoughtful again, Ikenna could feel N'yewe's frustration bubbling deep within, it didn't take much for the old anger to stir, and he wondered where Shanaki was going with this.

"What do *you* think we should do about your family, N'yewe?" she asked suddenly. She turned from the wall and rose from her crouch, taking a step toward them with a pensive expression on her face.

"*I* think we should face them, and kill them. For threatening my people and for turning on you. I think that, together, we can do it. That, with your strength and my powers, we have a chance." She turned around again and paced away slightly.

Ikenna couldn't believe she was trying this. He willed his thoughts through to his partner, but N'yewe was ignoring him. Right now, his ears were only for Shanaki.

"Ikenna doesn't think we're strong enough. He thinks we should run away." She paused her pacing and turned back to them. "I was just wondering what you thought on the matter. Are you scared of them too? Do *you* think we should run away?"

Ikenna had to stop this, he could feel the rage roiling inside at Shanaki's words. He knew *exactly* what N'yewe thought they should do, but he knew they couldn't do it. He reached out to take back control, forcing his focus back into the hyena's senses.

N'yewe growled again, his maw an open snarl. Visions of their fight with Baako played before them, the moment they had dropped beneath the currents and kicked him over the waterfall's edge sending a shiver of satisfaction down their back.

Ikenna fought his own snarl of anger. *You can't be serious, we lived through that by the barest thread of chance.*

Shanaki pressed on. "You don't think we should run, do you? You know we should face them. It's just Ikenna we have to convince."

Ikenna's anger sparked at Shanaki's words. She knew why he had refused her. It was for her own safety, damnit! He was desperately trying to take back control from his partner now, who was only getting more riled up as Ikenna fought him.

From the look on Shanaki's face, she could see something of their struggle herself. She looked straight into their eyes, and he knew she was addressing him again now. "See, Ikenna? Deep down, you want to fight them too."

The sheer truth of it, spoken with such infuriating surety, had Ikenna shouting curses inside his own head. N'yewe skipped their front feet in humorous glee, cackling at Ikenna's frustrations, the battle of their wills reaching its apex. Ikenna didn't know how it happened, and he didn't know which of them had started the run, but in an instant, he was leaping at Shanaki.

FIFTEEN

SHANAKI

SHANAKI WAS ASHAMED TO ADMIT THAT SHE FLINCHED. The sudden rush of the half-hyena, half-man toward her had caught her by surprise. Before she had time to even raise her arms in defense, N'yewe's speed had already carried him up her body and tipped her crashing to the floor.

Panic took her as the creature's open maw descended, its too-long tongue lurching from its mouth. She forced a burst of mystical suppression, weak in her stressed state, but enough to tear the power from the hyena—as it lapped happily at her cheeks.

Shanaki shuddered out a breath of relief as the twisted form of the half-beast shifted atop her. As the power of the beast was driven back within, Shanaki felt the presence of Ikenna's own allure pressing at her defenses. The close proximity between them was amplifying their effect and straining her suppression to breaking point.

She *almost* let it, her body telling her in no uncertain terms exactly what she thought of having Ikenna's lithe form pressing down atop her. She fought the heady mix of genuine and demon-induced passion both, struggling for a long moment in a standstill, before finally coming to her senses.

She pushed Ikenna up and away, watching him roll to the side, the two of them gasping out their twin-held breaths.

Seeing the wide-eyed expression on his face as he turned to face her, Shanaki laughed again. She'd been doing that a lot lately, she thought idly, as the adrenaline rushing through her body quickly turned the laugh into a distinctly *un*-royal fit of giggles.

Her head lolled on her shoulders and she fell back down, gasping out her laughter. Beside her, Ikenna choked on his words, no doubt trying to restate her insanity, utter some inane apology, or both.

Shanaki hadn't felt this alive in a long time. She knew she was playing with fire, but the reward was more than worth the risk. To have a creature like N'yewe alongside her...

N'yewe *and* Ikenna. He was young at heart, and would need a lot of work, but Shanaki had a feeling he would prove to be just as much fun before long.

Besides, she liked a challenge.

She turned to him, the last of her laughter giving way to an honest smile. He was looking at her with disbelief in his eyes. Those bright, amber eyes. Shanaki had to admit, they were entrancing even *with* their power held at bay. Ikenna was a handsome specimen, through and through. And the blush rushing through his cheeks had only added to his brand of innocent beauty.

She chuckled again as he pulled away, breaking the eye contact. He opened his mouth to speak, but Shanaki beat him to it. "I'm *crazy*. I know, you've said." She smiled, rolling her eyes.

"Well, you are! What were you thinking riling him up like that?"

"I think I had more than just *him* riled there, personally." She raised her eyebrow, inviting him to challenge her on that. He didn't. "I know you want to hurt them for everything they've done. You have more than enough reason to." She rolled her head toward the wall, nodding at the broken art. "For your stolen childhood." She turned back to him, poking a gentle finger into his palm. "For your friend Imani." She raised herself up on her elbows, leaning to one side and hanging over him, delivering the coup de grace. "For *me*."

His face remained impassive, his gaze turning back to her slowly. *"That's... presumptuous of you."* He spoke the words in Mero-Set, and Shanaki felt a rush as he genuinely surprised her with it.

"Ooh... 'presumptuous.' " She fixed his pronunciation, grinning. "Look at you bringing out the big words." She poked his side, and she could see him fighting a smile of his own.

Shanaki's grin widened as she saw him resisting. She jabbed at his side again and leaned nearer. She could see the cracks forming as he tried not to look at her, and she poked a third, and final time, closer to the underside of his arm.

Ikenna sighed in resignation as his smile finally broke across his face fully, but his expression soon turned serious again. "I want you safe. For everyone's sake. Keeping you away from them is the best way I know to ruin their plans."

"But it's not the only way." Shanaki squeezed Ikenna's side, desperate for him to believe her. "I turned you, didn't I? —Sorry for that, by the way, N'yewe. You startled me," she added.

She heard a soft purr at the back of Ikenna's head in answer and continued to Ikenna. "We *know* we can fight them now."

Ikenna looked deep into her eyes, the gold of his iris glinting his doubt. "I'm just one kishi."

Shanaki rested her hand on Ikenna's chest, his breath retreating from her in surprise. She held his gaze, not looking away for even a second. "You're not alone anymore."

He was conflicted, she could see it, but he was starting to cave. She had stoked the embers of his loneliness and she could see him starting to fill the hole in his heart with her words.

He looked up, a spark of wry humor in his tone as he asked, "Together, then?"

"Together."

"WE'RE NOT LEAVING UNTIL YOUR ARM HAS FULLY healed," Ikenna warned insistently as he paced side to side in front of her. "That's just asking for trouble we don't need."

Shanaki nodded. "Agreed. It'll only take me another week and a half to heal it up properly anyway, a fortnight at most."

"And we're not just charging in and announcing your return to the whole village either. We're sneaking you in quietly, back to your guards."

"I know that Ikenna. I'm going back to fight, not get myself killed."

Ikenna made a face through a tut. "Is there a difference?"

He continued to walk from one end of the cavern to the other, and Shanaki continued to watch him. His pace was frantic, charged with the stress of what he had agreed to do. She found it odd, looking at him now, to imagine the movement of his kishi form. Giving sway to his hyena, he had almost bent backwards before her eyes, his arms rolling in their sockets and twisting round into legs, their smooth skin shifting into hide. Despite the ungainly appearance, the speed and agility he had shown her were nothing short of elegant in their grace. Quite the opposite of what she could see from him now.

He's no good to us like this.

"Ikenna," she said, interrupting his agitated walk. "Sit down. You're making *me* all fussy."

Ikenna looked like he was going to carry on, but clearly thought better of it, moving to join Shanaki on the den floor. "Sorry, Princess."

"It's fine."

"Just nervous, that's all."

"Really? I couldn't tell." She smiled wryly at him, lifting a hand to rest on his shoulder. "We're not going to be able to do this if you're falling apart before we've even come up with a plan. Relax." She gave a little push, and he rocked back where he sat, yielding her a wan smile.

An idea came to her as she took note of his weary slouch. "Sit up a minute." She beckoned him closer. "Turn around."

Ikenna raised a questioning eyebrow, straightening his posture and cautiously turning where he sat.

Shanaki rolled her eyes and moved closer herself, kneeling behind him. "Here, my old mentor in the healing halls did this for some of her patients. It's supposed to help with deep worry." She placed her hands at his shoulders and began to slide them over his bare skin, warming the tight muscles to loosen them up.

Ikenna half turned his head to her. "I don't see how this is supposed to ease me."

"Be patient. I've not started yet."

"Oh."

Shanaki moved from sliding her hands to rubbing with

them, her fingers kneading at the flesh of Ikenna's shoulders and back. "Does that feel good?"

"Uh, yeah." He didn't sound so sure to Shanaki's ears. It was Ikenna being unnecessarily deferential again—and she told him as much. "No, really, it feels—" He flinched, his right shoulder lurching, and Shanaki heard a yelp from beneath his knotted hair. A complicated mix of bruised pride, irritation, and curiosity played through her chest, and she rose up the knot of hair that kept N'yewe's face hidden from view.

"Sorry, N'yewe." She scratched at his ear and he mewled in delight, pain clearly forgotten. Lowering the hair back in place, Shanaki gripped the knot and pulled Ikenna's head to her unceremoniously.

"Ow, watch it!" he blurted.

"Do not lie to me, Ikenna." Shanaki murmured into his ear, her tone light but with a distinct note of warning. His back was warm against her thighs. "It's insulting. My ego is not so easily bruised."

"Clearly." He rolled his eyes, echoing her earlier sarcasm.

Her grip tightened in his woven locs. "*Yes*, Shanaki." She spelled out for him, willing her tone down to a dangerous edge.

He groaned at the renewed pain. "All right, Princess. I get it, gods…"

She let go, patting his back as he drew away. "Close enough."

She heard a soft cackling chuckle from beneath his locs, and the reminder that the bestial mouth that loosed it had lain mere inches from her fingers, and let her make her point anyway, was a thrilling one.

She returned her hands to his shoulders, switching to a different technique. "If you *lie*, I won't know what works best for you."

An hour later and they had used up every technique she knew, to no avail. Shanaki definitely *wasn't* pouting about it.

"Well, none of the patients in the halls ever complained…" she trailed, flopping down beside her wincing victim.

Ikenna gave her a look that said it all.

She blew at a loose strand of hair which was damp with her sweat. "Well, it's not *my* fault they're too cowardly to call out a royal." Ikenna breathed out a sighing laugh in response, and Shanaki nudged him with her foot. "Still, failure of a massage or not, you seem more relaxed now. I'll take that for a victory."

"Heh, fair enough, Princess."

***

Neither of them were in any rush to return to their unformed plan. Shanaki knew that, with her arm as it was, they had the time yet to spare, and Ikenna would be of no use to her with his nerves frayed anyway. Instead, they sat and talked, of small things mostly, but every now and then brushing on something more. Shanaki's most pressing questions were for what would become of their futures, but she let them rest for now, knowing how quickly Ikenna would turn the mood dark if he thought she was assuming the best about the coming fight.

The two of them lay down beside one another, looking up at the twinkling light of the crystal constellations above. Squinting at one particularly beautiful cluster, Shanaki thought she recognized the shape of the True Sky's stars. The crystal formation glinted as a jagged sword, criss-crossing from hilt to pointed tip, just like the sign of Ofé'ala's shotel. She pointed it out to Ikenna.

"I've seen that one before," he said. "I didn't know it had a name though."

Shanaki shifted to look at him. "Do you know any of the signs?"

"I've seen most, I guess. I work late on the farms. It's just..." He shrugged. "I never knew the names." He held his hand up in the air, grasping at the hilt of Ofé'ala's constellation.

"*MA ASA UKUHLU,*" IKENNA SAID A WEEK LATER AS THEY staved off boredom with more lessons in Shanaki's native tongue.

Shanaki smiled and waved her hand out to the side in the passive sign of acceptance that matched the phrasing. "That's good. A little clearer with the *ukuhlu* though. It's a bold phrase; your tone should match."

"*Ma asa ukuhlu*, like that?"

Shanaki grinned at him. "Just so. Or, in Bajoki, 'I am a naïve duckling.'" Ikenna deadpanned, shaking his head as she laughed.

When the light of the crystals had begun to fade, Shanaki had suggested they try for some lessons again, seeing as they wouldn't need to see for that. Well, most of it anyway. They used what little time they had left before the darkness closed around them to run through some of the physical movements that were sometimes paired with the vocal phrases in Mero-Set. It was an older custom, but it paid to know the signs in case one encountered a stickler for tradition—a royal and her cohorts for instance.

Jesting aside, it honestly impressed her how quickly Ikenna was taking to her language. He was a remarkably agile thinker, with a knack for catching the patterns in the various different rules she explained. Shanaki was no teacher, but she felt reasonably sure they had laid a strong foundation in their time here in the cave. She looked forward to seeing how far Ikenna could progress once they had dealt with his kin.

———

It wasn't until the following day—by their own crystal cycle—that they broached the question of their plan. Surprising Shanaki, it was Ikenna that brought them to the topic.

"I think I have an idea for how we can get you into the village." His voice held an edge of scratching dirge to it, and she wondered at how much sleep he had—or hadn't, as the case may be.

Shanaki set aside the bowl she had been eating from—more dried rat—and ushered for him to go on.

"There's a man in the village named Kojo. He's the one person from Bajok I really trust. If I can get a message to him, he might be able to help us."

"How will one man be able to get us through the walls?"

"I don't know. He's smart though, and he's got some well-placed friends—well, students really. There's this whole thing. Point is, he'll find us a way in." He scratched at the back of his head. "Anywhere else I'd just carry you up the walls but the village's magic is powerful—and very anti-kishi. We wouldn't make it ten paces before it shifted me back."

"How will you contact him?"

"I'm not really sure he'd like me to tell you that. But I can—when we absolutely need to."

Shanaki pinched at her chin in thought. "If you have a man on the inside, why not get him to send my people out to meet us?"

"Trust me, Princess. The *last* thing we want is to lead

312

your guard out onto the open plains." He grimaced. "If they're not dead yet, they soon would be."

Shanaki bristled at his casual dismissal of her soldiers, but he had made his point clear before, and she let the slight go.

"So, once we're in the village, then what?" she asked.

"We warn your people." He shrugged. "Like I said, I only trust Kojo. Anyone else in the village could be working with my clan."

"Why would they side with demons?" She saw his eyes flinch a little. "*True* demons, Ikenna. The ones that revel in their evil."

He shrugged again. "Fear mostly. But I know there are some that would want to use the kishi as another step toward rebuilding Golah."

Shanaki scoffed. The Golah Empire had been fractured decades ago, as good as dead in all but name. Especially by the standards of the *real* powers on Esowon.

She waved a hand to the side. "Well, they can't all be so blind. My people will rally any willing to fight beside us. We'll show the demons of Bajok what Ya-Seti archers are made of."

Ikenna grimaced. "Inside the village, we *may* have a chance. With enough warriors..." He trailed slightly, clearly unconvinced by his own words. "But I don't think Uzoma will be stupid enough to let everything go down in the village itself."

"If we force his hand, it's not like he can just wait outside the walls though, right?" Shanaki questioned.

"I suppose..." Ikenna conceded grudgingly.

"Then, let's do it. Your man on the inside sneaks us in, I warn my people who we're *really* allying with if we stay, then we seize control of the village by force. Uzoma will have to face us, then."

Ikenna scratched idly at his arm, his head turned down to the ground. "As easy as that, huh?"

"I didn't say it would be easy, Ikenna. But what else can we do?" Shanaki could see the answer in his face and ignored it. She wasn't running away from this. It was never a choice for her, and it would never be. She had already made that clear.

When he said nothing more, she stood up. "Well then, if you've got nothing more to add, it's settled. I should be good to go in a week, maybe more. Now go fetch us some more rat. I'm hungry and this arm isn't going to heal quick enough by itself."

SIXTEEN

IKENNA

WITH THE WORRY OF THE PLANNING LIFTED FROM THEIR shoulders, the two of them had fallen into a comfortable pattern again. Ikenna could tell Shanaki was still bothered by her arm holding them back, but for the most part they managed to talk around her frustration.

Privately, Ikenna was glad for the delay. He was intent on savoring every moment before they stepped out of that den door and onward to the slaughter. Unlike the princess, he held little hope for the coming struggle, and he made no secret of the fact, taking every opportunity he could to try to dissuade her. He knew they would need nothing short of a miracle to even *survive* what was to come, let alone triumph over it. She thought his battle with Baako proof enough that they had a chance, but she had not been there to witness it. He had lived through that farce by the barest skin of his teeth and he was not looking forward to a rematch with his brother. To say nothing of the rest of his clan.

Not that waiting in the den with Shanaki was entirely stress free itself. No, that brought struggles all its own. N'yewe's attention had been so thoroughly captured by

Shanaki that Ikenna had found it increasingly difficult to keep his mind clear. His own thoughts and feelings were complicated enough, without adding his hyena's eager attachment to the mix.

All walls had been lowered between them now — at least those that he had raised himself. Ikenna felt the deep pull of powerful attraction toward Shanaki. His eyes were endlessly drawn to her, like a moth to torch flame. Her every movement seemed tailored to him, the shimmering flicker of silk-sheet on a soft wind. As the days passed, he saw more and more the sway of her hips, the slow rise of her breast, the light of the moons dancing in her eyes...

Not for the first time, Ikenna shook himself free of his senses. He cursed his weakness as N'yewe laughed inwardly at him. Every time Ikenna's mind started to wander, his idle gaze invariably brought him back to Shanaki. He was starting to think it was N'yewe himself, turning his thoughts deliberately. The hyena was certainly enjoying himself enough.

Was this infatuation what it felt like to be caught by the lure of his own kind? If it was, he felt all the more glad he had never fallen to the temptation of his powers. He wouldn't wish this on anyone; it was maddening.

What made it worse was the rising suspicion that Shanaki was wise to it, that she was aware she had him hanging off her every aspect. His was not the blind, fumbling attraction of some simple farmhand. He had meant it when he had spoken the old words. He *did* know her heart, and it was no pure and gentle thing. Shanaki possessed a cunning and ambition Ikenna had seen in others before, his father chief among them, but where his father would turn to cruelty, Shanaki held to calculation.

He watched her. She stood across the room from him, bent low over her bowl, propped up on the edge of the cave basin, washing her face. Even in this she was careful and

deliberate, every movement of her hand a conscious place-
ment of finger to flesh. The fact that she took such care with
such simple things only further confirmed his opinion of
her. She was like a sphinx, her mind as labyrinthine as The
Black Rocks that hid them both now, her heart: ice.

It was a strange thing, to know the secret held behind
her eyes and yet not feel the chill of it. He didn't know if it
was N'yewe's growing submission to her, or his own quiet
longing for companionship, but the longer Ikenna spent
with Shanaki, the less he seemed to care what her intentions toward him were. Her eyes may be cold, but they
were also clear, and he could see the flicker of a future in
them with every touch of the light.

If they survived to see it.

"Someone's deep in thought again."

Ikenna's attention refocused at the sound of her voice,
and he saw Shanaki rising from her bowl and wiping at her
face, looking his way.

He didn't say anything, and she continued, "Am I going
to have to give you another massage to scour more nerves
away?"

Ikenna shuddered at the thought. It had been days since
she had dug her bruising grip into his back, and he did not
soon want to repeat the experience. It had felt like an
elephant trampling over his every nerve.

Fortunately, Shanaki seemed to surmise as much
herself, clearing her throat dramatically and continuing,
"Well then, cheer up. I've already told you, moping
bores me."

Ikenna blew out a breath and crossed his arms against
his chest. "I'm not moping. I'm thinking."

Shanaki dipped down for another splash of water,
rubbing at the edges of her eyes. "Oh? What about?"

"You."

She paused again and glanced out the corner of one eye,

head still tilted back as she rubbed dripping water from her face with one hand. Her familiar searching gaze was intense, even with one eye covered, but Ikenna leveled his own even stare back at her.

"Care to elaborate?" Shanaki asked, finally, setting aside her bowl.

He thought about how to put it into words and snorted as he realized that that was the one thing he *shouldn't* do.

Ikenna took a deep breath and relaxed. He just let his words loose as they came. "You know exactly what you're doing," he began. "You think I don't see it, but I do. Everything about you is measured, considered." He broke off, his flow faltering for a moment. "I—I don't know what I think about that yet, but I want you to know that I see it. I'm not blind, and—and I meant what I said before..." he trailed off, unsure how to continue and distracted by the look on Shanaki's face.

She was watching him with steady, unblinking eyes. His thoughts raced, his mind trying to glean any hint at what she might be thinking, what she might say.

It took Ikenna a moment, but when no response was forthcoming, he gradually realized that Shanaki had none to give. She was looking at him in disbelief, like she was only now seeing him for the first time.

Ikenna's thoughts raced, unsure what to make of this non-reaction. It was a little insulting that his insight had apparently come as such a shock to her, and he noted that mild insult seemed to be a running theme with Shanaki.

Well, she is Ya-Seti. They're not known for their humility.

He saw her step toward him and he unfolded his arms from his chest. He watched as she walked straight toward him, dropping down to sit crossed legged at his side. She looked like she was trying to solve a complicated puzzle in her head, and he patted his knees idly while he waited for her to finally say something.

Eventually, she spoke, her tone as nonplussed as her expression. "You know my heart, huh?" She turned her shoulders to him, looking on him full. "Prove it."

She was looking at him with the utmost seriousness, her command carrying the weight of a royal decree. There was a new, keen-edged, glint in her eye. Her gaze fell to his lips, a slow smile spreading across her own.

"Go on," she urged.

Ikenna sat watching in alarm. Panic rushed through him, his instinct sensing the change in mood before his mind had time to explain it to him.

Shanaki was challenging him, testing him for some unknown quality. He could feel her leveled gaze searching him for it.

She prompted him further, her eyes darting back up to his own as she stared in bared hunger. "What do I want you to do now, Ikenna?"

Ikenna knew what she wanted him to do. He wanted to do it too. He could feel himself leaning closer, his eyes held to her own, both their gazes unblinking. N'yewe had fallen surreptitiously silent; his very quiet tolled bells in Ikenna's ears. But for the life of him, right now, Ikenna couldn't quite bring himself to care.

They were getting closer. He could *feel* her drawing near. The air was sparking with a new tension—as foreign to Ikenna as the girl before him—and it held him transfixed. He knew what she wanted him to do, he *knew*.

They were suddenly very close and Ikenna felt a shiver up his spine. Was this really happening? Could this really—

Their lips were a hair's breadth from touching when Ikenna jolted back.

Shanaki gave a hiss of frustration, sucking at her teeth —but Ikenna only half heard it. His gaze had shifted to the den ceiling above them and he had jumped to his feet. Chilling fear crashed over him in waves, all excited tension washing from his mind as an icy grip clenched around his heart.

He gasped aloud and then Shanaki was in front of him, grasping him by the shoulders with confused panic. She tried to hold him still—was he spinning?—and he stumbled to his knees, tripping on one of her legs. She came down with him, catching his arm to soften his fall and half joining him on the floor.

"Ikenna, what in the hells?" she gasped, clearly out of breath from his mindless flailing.

"He's *dead*," Ikenna managed, heaving in deep lungfuls of air, "*Uzoma's dead*."

It was impossible.

He accepted the bowl from Shanaki gratefully, bringing it to his lips and gulping down the fresh water to wet his dry mouth.

It couldn't be true.

Ikenna sat leaned against the central pillar of his den, staring idly into space as Shanaki took the bowl back from him. She set it gently aside and wrapped an arm over his shoulder, rubbing his back briefly and leaning in to ask the question. "What do you mean, Ikenna? How can you know?"

Ikenna shook his head, his shoulders half raised in a shrug. "Remember how I told you we can sense each other? It's that, and it's never stronger than when one of us dies." He looked up at her in disbelief. "Someone finally managed to kill him."

He could tell by her face she wasn't quite sure of the significance of it all. She didn't know enough about the old man for it to mean anything.

Uzoma was untouchable. He was years past his prime,

and he had still been worth three of Baako on his worst days. Ikenna couldn't see how anyone could have done it. Even outnumbered Uzoma always won, he was too clever to get caught out by odds he couldn't match with cunning or skill.

And yet, he had fallen. Joined — as all his kin were — by a sixth spirit, Ikenna *felt* the sudden loss of the old man like a part of his very being had been torn from his core.

Ikenna barked a laugh and N'yewe carried it with a fit of cackling cries. A smile tore across his face as he turned to Shanaki. "He's *dead*." He willed her to understand, to *see* what this meant. He was finally rid of him, the bastard finally got what he deserved.

Shanaki's expression was wistful. She wanted to ask something, he could tell, but she was holding herself back. Ikenna didn't want her to have to do that with him.

"What is it?" he asked, nodding in encouragement.

Shanaki spoke carefully, "What does this mean for us? Won't this change their plans?"

Ikenna could see the apology in her face, the regret for having to bring him down from his joy. He noted, even through his excitement, that it was a purely honest expression. She had left discarded her carefully crafted mask.

Ikenna found it a soothing thought. He recentered himself, smoothing a hand over the back of his head to ease N'yewe's own celebration. Shanaki brushed his hand away and scratched at the hyena's neck herself, her soft scritches almost possessive in their insistence.

Both his selves calmed, Ikenna's thoughts refocused on what Uzoma's death meant beyond his own personal happiness. "There's going to be a power vacuum. The clan needs a new leader." He imagined his kin with someone like Baako or one of his other brothers at their head. His mind answered Shanaki's question in his head — with vivid images of blood and death, and the innocents of Bajok caught in the middle.

Ikenna took Shanaki by the hand and pulled her to her feet. He turned to look her in the eye as he took a burdensome breath.

"We have to go."

SEVENTEEN

SHANAKI

HER HEART RACED, HER MIND AWASH WITH THE EMOTION of the moment. One minute they had been a hair's breadth away from a kiss and the next they were readying for war.

Shanaki was not accustomed to having her inner seas so at storm. She took great pride in her intellect and refused to follow the winds of whim as so many other fools did. She was glad she and Ikenna were finally leaving the cave— finally joining the fight—but she couldn't help but feel something had been lost here just now. In the deep recesses in her mind—very deep—she wanted to stay in the cave with Ikenna, to feel how gentle his lips could be. And she didn't feel such things lightly.

She pulled firmly on the straps of her sandals and watched Ikenna head down the tunnel to their supplies. He was moving with purpose, shoulders back and fists clenched as he vanished into the passage.

Quite the change from the hunched, fidgeting of before, Shanaki mused.

Her thoughts wandered as she waited for him. She could count on one hand how many people in this world that saw her for the woman she was *beneath* her masks. Those that did she had either given glimpses willingly or simply didn't warrant the effort of one in the first place.

Ikenna though... He was worth whatever mask it took to get him under her grasp. She thought she had played the willful, playful card just right, as naturally as she took to any role—and yet he had seen through it. He had seen *her*.

It made him a lot more complex a puzzle than she had expected—if she wanted to make a tool of him and his hyena beast. But the revelation of his insight had her yearning for much more than that, and things were all the simpler for it.

She no longer wanted him. She *wanted* him.

Shanaki had finally found someone she could actually see herself standing beside in the days ahead. Not just through the struggle of this—this glorified *pest* control—but for all the days and nights she would have come to pass.

Ikenna was a man of principle; he had brains, power, and the will to see her own. He was also fun—a wholly underrated quality as far as Shanaki was concerned.

He came back out of the side tunnel, a coil of rope slung over his shoulder.

And the fact that he's a feast for the eyes is purely *secondary*, Shanaki thought as he walked toward her.

"Are you ready?" he asked.

"I am. Are you?"

"Not really, no." Ikenna shook his head, hoisting the rope further up his shoulder. "But I guess we had better go anyway."

She nodded. "You sounded like it was urgent, before."

"It is. With Uzoma gone everything's changed. The clan's free to do whatever it wants until a new head takes over, damn the consequences. And if it ends up being someone like Baako…"

Shanaki shivered at the thought, he'd told her more than enough about his clan for her to fill in the details herself. "Right. Let's go."

———

SHANAKI FOLLOWED BEHIND IKENNA AS HE LED THEM through the tunnels of the den. Excitement and dread were building inside her and her stomach churned. She had never been in a battle before, but she knew from her experience in the healing halls exactly what to expect from them.

Mixed with her fear though was that same nagging feeling inside, the regret for the lost moment between her and Ikenna.

She tried to keep her mind on the task ahead but her eyes kept focusing in on his back. She thought it might be his kishi attraction creeping past her defenses again, but she raised her dampening shroud and the distraction persisted.

Shanaki knew when to listen to her gut, and she decided there and then that she would not go into this battle without first taking what was hers.

She was pulled from her thoughts by muttering. Ikenna was cupping a hand to his mouth and talking quietly into it. It almost looked like he was praying. "Ikenna?" she asked, leaning round his shoulder to better see his face.

He shot a quick glance at her from the corner of his eye, but didn't answer. He just kept talking into his hand.

Shanaki raised an eyebrow. "I thought you said you weren't a follower of the gods?"

He finished whatever he was saying and, as he lowered his hand from his mouth, she caught a glimpse of a small, intricately carved spiral necklace. Its sheen glowed a faint jungle green and there was a sudden smell of melted wax in the air.

Ikenna tucked the bronze into a pocket of his loincloth, explaining, "I'm not. I was just sending a message to Kojo. He gave me the pendant for emergencies only." He patted at a pocket in his loincloth. "I figure if this doesn't count, nothing does."

They pushed on, the tunnel curving slightly to the right in a shallow bend. "That's powerful magic." Shanaki pointed out, surprised Ikenna had such a rare token.

He looked back over his shoulder. "Not really. It can only reach Kojo, and only once or twice. Once the glow dies out, it's just useless bronze."

"Still," Shanaki continued. "It's advanced. Who enchanted it? I didn't think the village had anyone powerful enough."

"It doesn't. It's a ritual spell, woven communally. Bajok has done better than most at keeping the older branches and traditions alive."

Eventually the two of them reached the "stairs" and Shanaki sagged, her back bent low and arms hanging limply in exaggerated despair.

Ikenna chuckled. "Don't worry, Princess. I'll carry you."

Her head shot up, eyes defiant. "You will *not*." She walked to the first ledge and lifted herself up, trying not to strain her injured arm.

TWENTY MINUTES LATER, SHANAKI LOWERED HERSELF carefully down from Ikenna's back with a pout. Her arms ached painfully as she patted the dust of the cave wall from her wrappings. She stared Ikenna straight in the eye, her hand pointing level with his nose.

"We did that for expediency only. And we shall *never* speak of it again."

"Of course, Princess."

Shanaki walked swiftly past Ikenna before his eyes could laugh any more. She promised herself, the first thing she would do when they were out of this mess was get Nya to work her into shape.

They walked toward the boulder that served as doorway to the den. When they reached the tunnel's end, she stepped to the side, making room for Ikenna to pry their exit open.

Ikenna didn't move. Instead, he coughed into his hand with an awkward glance at the ceiling and leaned against the wall beside her.

Shanaki heard a soft rumbling sound as his shoulder pressed against a slight protrusion on the wall—slight enough that she had mistaken it for just another jutting stone. As Ikenna leaned back away, she saw a single, carved sigil in the oval rock and she watched it retreat into the wall.

The grinding of stone filled their ears and sunlight began to steadily fill the tunnel. Ikenna moved an arm over Shanaki's face, giving her time to adjust to the brightness. She thanked him as she rubbed at her eyes, before looking back up and swearing loudly.

"You have got to be kidding me," she said. "I was *so close.*"

Ikenna rubbed the back of his head, smiling out a laugh.

Seeing him there, face lit bright in all senses of the word, Shanaki knew beyond doubt their moment had come. She pushed his arm away from her and reached up to grab the nape of his neck. Pulling him down to her—she kissed him.

Ikenna stiffened in awe. Shanaki pressed her free hand to his waist, refusing to let him run away from her now. When he finally relaxed against her grip, his lips softened, but he left her leading the way. He tasted of sweat and rat and woeful inexperience.

And he was wonderful.

She felt light-headed, all the worries in the world washing from her mind. She was falling into him, her arms wrapping tighter around his body. The hand at his neck rose to scratch beneath N'yewe's maw and the thrill of her dance with the demon only added to the rush pulsing through her. Her blood burned with passion like she had never felt before.

Oh, now I have you, Ikenna. You're mine.

She took a deep breath, practically pulling the air straight from his lungs, and let loose a burst of her power, pushing him firmly away from her.

He fell back against the wall, pure, unadulterated shock written all over his face. She could see him reeling from a rush all his own, no doubt stunned by the sudden smothering of her shroud.

She drew her power back, feeling it wrap around her like a cooling breeze. She was breathing deeply herself, and she could feel a wide smile creasing her face.

She laughed, wiping at her mouth and turning to the sun-lit hills outside the den. She bent a little, arms behind her back, looking back at him. "So… are you coming?"

And she began her walk down through the tight corridors of The Black Rocks.

IKENNA STILL LOOKED MORE THAN A LITTLE DAZED AS the two made their way through the fork in the rocks. Shanaki was thankful for the touch of the open wind; she hadn't realized how much she had missed it.

Ikenna kept his distance as they walked, staying ahead

of her and cautiously poking his head around each bend they took. She caught him shooting nervous glances back her way every now and then, and she knew it wasn't out of nerves for their path. He was thinking about her kiss. She was glad; she was certainly thinking about his.

Eventually, they paused in a small valley littered with bones. Ikenna led them to a rock-face that looked not unlike the entrance to his own den. He pressed his hand to the smooth surface and spoke in a tongue Shanaki only barely recognized from rare religious sermons back home. And then, what was once a smooth surface split in a near perfect line, opening to a wide, empty cavern.

"Something—someone's coming," Ikenna said, and Shanaki heard N'yewe sniffing at the air of the craggy corridor. "No, more. At least three or four. They're moving slowly, though."

He had barely finished speaking when a deep shout echoed at them from the tunnel. "Who goes there?"

Ikenna looked back at Shanaki, eyes wide. He turned his mouth to the cave entrance and shouted back. "Is it true? Is he dead?"

Shanaki saw a shadow move from the side of the tunnel, a figure stepping *just* to the light streaming into the cave. As he stepped from the dark, she recognized him. She could not recall his name, but his face she would never forget. He had been there the first night she had arrived in Bajok.

He was holding something—no, some*one*—tight behind his back, still submerged in the shadow.

The man answered, his tone guarded. "Who's asking?"

Ikenna turned to Shanaki, he seemed to have picked up on her recognition of the man. She gave him an approving nod.

"Ikenna, son of Uzoma," he said. "I'm here with Shanaki, second daughter of Ya-Set."

"Naki!" A voice shot suddenly from the dark and the figure held up by the bearded man shoved him forward. She hobbled to join him in the light, blinking up at Shanaki. Shanaki blinked back.

"Nya?"

EPILOGUE

IKENNA

IKENNA WATCHED SHANAKI FROM HIS DISTANT PERCH outside Bajok. Sat atop the rise of a large crop of boulders —the closest of those scattered around the village but still a good few minutes walk away—Ikenna could see the princess stepping from the village gates. The Ya-Seti were readying for their departure back to their homeland. A great line of wagons and carts stretched out along the village's primary road.

For the last hour, he had seen Shanaki marching the length of the caravan, arms pointing and mouth shouting orderly commands. Her doubled guard trailed frantically behind her, trying to keep up. Ikenna smiled a wan smile, his mood steeped in the bittersweetness of the sight. The princess had been through a lot the past few days and it was good to see her working through the pain. But Ikenna could still see the new weight on her shoulders, the strain in her posture. She was suffering.

The battle with his clan had been hard. His rematch with his brother had taken everything he had to give, and when Yemi—one of his father's rivals and someone Ikenna had thought an ally—revealed his true colors... Well, the battle had been hard fought and hard won. The clan: scattered.

Shanaki had been amazing, negating the other kishi alongside her guard as the Ya-Seti soldiers fought them back. She had been right about what she could do for them with her ability.

Another commanding bellow from Shanaki broke Ikenna from his thoughts. Her duties apparently fulfilled, she started away from the gates and toward his hiding place. The guards at her back followed swiftly, but Ikenna knew she would only tolerate that for so long.

As expected, she left them behind halfway; only Nya accompanied the princess the whole way to the rocks. At a word from Shanaki, she stood guard by the base. Ikenna could see her remaining hand clutched tightly around her spear, ready to spring to her charge's defense even as the stump of her other hung low at her side.

Shanaki began her climb and Ikenna waited in silence as she came to sit beside him. She leaned into him briefly as she swung her legs over the edge of their perch, letting them hang below her. He marveled at how the simple closeness of this could feel so right to him.

She spoke first. "I've arranged to take my place at the back of the convoy."

She meant it then, he thought. *We are really doing this...*

"Your father went for that?" he asked, his tone surprised.

"He did. He wasn't happy about it, but he knows well enough not to test me right now."

Ikenna saw through the cracks of her newest mask. "I'm sorry about—"

She cut him off. "I've told you already, I don't want apologies from you." Her words were sharp and brooked no argument. Ikenna could see the flickering edges of the rage still burning behind her eyes, and he didn't blame her.

When she had heard from Nya what her father had done to her guardsmen—the two Ikenna had taken her from—Ikenna had seen something in Shanaki die. The quiet cool of the ice in her eyes had melted to tears, and in its wake had sparked an inferno of fury that he knew would see the *kor* of Ya-Set burned to ashes.

He waved a hand through the motions of a Mero-Set acknowledgement. "I know, sorry."

She sighed, stress easing from her shoulders with a shrug.

"What does Nya think of your idea?" he asked in gentle jest with a nudge against her arm.

Shanaki's gaze shot sideways down to her friend. "She thinks I'm going to get her into trouble again, so nothing new."

Ikenna chuckled. "And what do you think?" He urged, "Are you sure about this?"

Shanaki turned to look him in the eye. She smiled the first full smile he had seen from her in days and rose to her feet. She stretched her arms above her before lowering her hand to take his.

"Absolutely. Are the two of you ready to see Ya-Set?"

Ikenna heard an answering bark of glee within. He felt the tug of her hand and rose to join her in her stand.

"Let's do it."

Ikenna & Shanaki

A NOTE FROM THE AUTHOR

Thank you for reading my debut novella.
I sincerely hope you enjoyed it.

If not, well, then I sincerely hope you let me know why.
I mean it; post a review. Explain it like I'm five. This is my
first published work —hell, my first written work full stop,
actually —and I'd very much like to learn as much as I can
from the process before I'm back at the writing desk for
round two.

And a thousand thanks to my friend, Antoine, for giving me
this opportunity and encouraging me throughout. It has
been an honour —leave the British spelling damn you! —
and a privilege to write for your world.

May Esowon live in the hearts and minds of the many.

If you enjoyed *Hearts in the Dark*, please leave a review on
your favorite retailer or social media.

DID YOU ENJOY THE ANTHOLOGY?

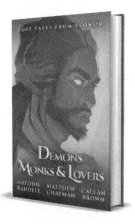

Thank you for reading *Demons, Monks, and Lovers*.

This is the first collection expanding on the world of Esowon outside the primary series.

This anthology was also created by indie authors.

The best way to get independant creators exposure is by providing reviews.

If you enjoyed *Demons, Monks, and Lovers*, please leave a review on your favorite retailer or social media.

MORE TALES FROM ESOWON

A pacifist monk. A threatening darkness. An innocent village hanging in the balance.

Hoping to escape his dark past, Amana travels to the great village of Bajok in search of redemption. The day he arrives, a young woman is slain and the locals point their fingers at the new arrival.

Amana must overcome the village's trepidation. A demon is on the loose and he fears more will die. The solution is obvious—a swift and brutal counterattack.

But his vow of peace is the last virtue that remains in his tattered soul. Is his personal peace more valuable than the lives of the innocent, or will Amana be swallowed by the darkness that has hounded him his entire life?

Delve into an African fantasy inspired by the Angola folklore, where Amana will face mystical villains, ancient secrets, and the demons that smolder within himself.

Visit antoinebandele.com to learn more about this story.

ABOUT THE AUTHOR

Antoine lives in Los Angeles, CA with his girlfriend.
He is a YouTuber, producing work for his own channel and
others, such as JustKiddingFilms, Fanalysis, and more.
Whenever he has the time he's writing
his debut series: *Tales from Esowon*.

antoinebandele.com

ABOUT THE AUTHOR

Truck driver, repairman, amateur artist, and occasional author, Matthew prefers to be called "Matt" because he believes his full name sounds like a sneeze. He lives in Northern California. When he can, he edits and produces videos on his YouTube channel and for the Fanalysis podcast. In his spare time he enjoys cooking, driving, drinking beer and shooting pool with friends.

ABOUT THE AUTHOR

I.T. admin, editor, YouTuber, editor, gamer, and editor again, Callan is a glutton for punishment when it comes to creative work, finally adding the all-stressful experience of the "writer" to his repertoire.

When he is not working — ha — he likes to relax by reading, table-top and video gaming, traveling and hiking. He has the best family and friends in the world and dedicates all works to them.

GLOSSARY

Terms and Locations from Esowon

- **A'bara:** The word for "magic" or "blessing" in the Old Tongue.
- **Aberash:** A small village south of Mount Junga.
- **Ashwagandha:** A mild herb used to aid sleep.
- **Àyá:** The Jo'baran goddess of rivers.
- **Baba:** The word for "father" in many regions of Esowon and its surrounding areas.
- **Bajok:** A farming village once belonging to the Golah Empire.
- **Baobab:** A sturdy tree native to Esowon.
- **Daji:** A forest people northwest of the Kunda jungles.
- **Dawa:** A common root used as an all-purpose healing salve.
- **Dulagi:** The Jo'baran god of illusions, deceptions, and trickery.
- **Fufu:** A dough-like starch eaten by the people of Bajok and the former Golah.

- **Golah:** The former empire which stretched from Bajok in the south to Imtubo in the north.
- **Guela:** A farming village once belonging to the southern reaches of the Golah Empire.
- **Illanga:** The Jo'baran god of dusk and dawn.
- **Illopa:** The Jo'baran goddess of unconditional love.
- **Iwosani:** A strong herb used to remove deep-rooted infection within the body.
- **Ipe:** The great river that runs from Aktah in the north all the way to Jultia in the south.
- **Junga:** A grand mountain in the south of E'Shiya, home to those who are known colloquially as mountain monks.
- **Kijana:** Slang used for male pirates of the Sapphire Isles.
- **Kishi:** A hyena-demon that shares a body with a human male.
- **Kor:** The primary ruler of the Ya-Seti people.
- **Kunda:** A rainforest claimed by ancient mystical creatures in the heart of Esowon.
- **Mbongo:** A spice of a floral aroma used to flavor food.
- **Mero-Set:** The native language of the Ya-Seti people.
- **M'Kahr'ala:** The Jo'bara god of balance, worshipped mostly, and almost exclusively, by the Junga monks.
- **Nyoka:** A river that borders the south of Bajok.
- **Ofé'ala:** The Jo'baran god of magic and free will, worshipped primarily by the Qibasi in Vaaj.
- **Ogó'ala:** The supreme Jo'baran entity who does not have a male or female alignment.
- **Pel'lepe:** Also known as the *forest's fire*. A

common herb used as a rare and dangerous tea by the Junga monks.

- **Ponya:** The Mero-Set term for the strong herb used to remove deep-rooted infection within the body.
- **Shotel:** A sickle blade used by warriors and soldiers mostly in eastern Esowon.
- **Sulan:** A strong herb used mostly to induce deep sleep or unconsciousness. Overuse of the herb can cause coma.
- **Tosi:** A common herb used for numbing.
- **Ugara:** The Jo'baran god of war.
- **Ukuhlu:** Mero-Set term meaning "naïve duckling."
- **Weiya:** A greeting in Mero-Set.
- **Ya-Seti:** One of the Great Nations. Known for their skilled archers and lavish palaces.
- **Yem:** The Jo'baran goddess of oceans.
- **Zyeta:** A river that curls south of the Seven Serpents market, Aberash village, and Mount Junga.

Made in the USA
San Bernardino, CA
28 July 2020